Service Management

AF658592

Service Management

Bholanath Dutta
Asst. Professor
Dept. of Management Studies
CMR Institute of Technology
Bangalore

B. Rose Kavitha
Professor
Dept. of Management Studies
CMR Institute of Technology
Bangalore

TECHSAR™
NEW DELHI

Published and Printed by

Techsar Pvt. Ltd.
4435-36/7, Ansari Road, Daryaganj,
New Delhi 110 002 (India)
E-mail: tech_info@techsarworld.com
Website: www.techsarworld.com

ISBN 978-93-80578-78-1

© 2011 I.K. International Pvt. Ltd.

Reprint 2026

All rights reserved. No part of this book may be reproduced or used in any form, electronic or mechanical, including photocopying, recording, or by any information storage and retrieval system, without written permission from the publisher.

Prof. Bholanath Dutta dedicates this book to his parents
Shri Jatindranath Dutta
Smt. Jharna Dutta
&
his loving wife and best friend
Paramita

Dr. B. Rose Kavitha dedicates this book to her parents
Shri D. Albert and Smt. A. Margarette
&
her loving husband Mr. C. Bharath and
her little angels C. Ishan and C. Ishana
and to her
beloved friend Prof. Bholanath Dutta,
for their emotional support & love.

Preface

This book discusses the basic and fundamental concepts of Services Management in a very simple and lucid manner to create a better understanding on the subject. It covers completely Bangalore University syllabus and also covers syllabus of other Indian Universities for BBM/B.Com courses.

This book provides a comprehensive coverage of various conceptual aspects concerned with services management and application of service marketing concepts in the areas of tourism, travel, hospital, finance and education sector. It includes the following broad features:

- Introduction to Service Management
- Tourism and Travel Services
- Banking and Insurance Services
- Finance and Marketing Services
- Health care and Education Services.

This book will definitely be of great help for the students to grasp the fundamental concepts of services management and further implementation of those.

Every care has been taken to ensure 'zero-effect' in the book. But there is always a scope for improvement. And I would request teaching communities and students to suggest for further improvement of the book.

Please reach to author at: bhola_dutta@yahoo.com

Bholanath Dutta
B. Rose Kavitha

Acknowledgements

While preparing the manuscript, the authors take the help from some foreign books and insert the idea, opinion and data, etc. in order to create attractions to the students and clarify critical concepts. The authors express their heartiest thanks and gratitude as well as indebtedness to the authors and publishers of those books.

In order to get the book ready for the students, all employees of IK International Publishing House have performed such a tremendous job for which no thanks for their contribution will be enough. Our special thanks to Mr. Krishan Makhijani – Managing Director and Mr. Babu, DGM, South India of IK International Publishing House for their all help in bringing out this book.

We feel great pleasure in expressing our profound gratitude to Dr. K.C. Sabita Ramamurthy – President, CMR Jananadhara Trust (CMRJT); Shri K.C. Ramamurthy (IPS Retd.) Chairman– CMRJT; Shri Jayadeep (CEO, CMRJT); Ms. Tristha Ramamurthy (Vice-President, CMRJT); Dr. KVS Anand Babu – Principal, CMRIT; Dr. L Sudarshan Reddy – Vice-Principal, CMRIT; Dr. Col. (Retd.); Mukesh Kumar V – Director (MBA); Prof. K Ravi – Director, Career Guidance & Placement Bureau, CMRIT; Prof. Sundar Raj Vijaynagar; Prof. MB Lobo and all our esteemed colleagues in CMRIT; for their incessant guidance, stimulation and encouragement in our academic endeavour.

Bholanath Dutta
B. Rose Kavitha

Contents

About the Authors

Bholanath Dutta, is an Accredited Management Teacher by All India Management Association, New Delhi, holds an M.Phil (Entrepreneurship), MBA (Marketing), Postgraduate Diploma in Tourism Management, Diploma in Electronics & Telecom Engg., Diploma in Advanced Accountancy, and Couple of courses in specific areas (CRS, Ticketing, Tours & Travels & Airlines Mgmt.) of tourism industry from Indian Institute of Tourism and Travel Management, Ministry of Tourism.

He is currently working as Assistant Professor – Dept. of Management Studies, in CMR Institute of Technology. He has over 20 years of experience as varied as Industry, academic, teaching, administration and research.

He has received two awards: "Best Professor 2009"—a national level event constituted by 24/7—a leading MNC and "Arch of Excellence (Education)" – a national award for his contribution in education. He is an accredited trainer and motivator for developing entrepreneurship in college campus by Visveswarya Technological University.

Dutta is a prolific writer. He has authored 13 books in the area of marketing, entrepreneurship and general management. His more than dozen articles are selected and published in derivative reference books. He has published more than 70 papers till date including articles/research paper/case study in the area of general management, marketing and entrepreneurship in the leading national and international management magazine/journal and still counting. He presented many papers in national and international conferences. He is a Resource Person in Management education and has delivered lectures at other institutes. He is a guest editor to www.mybigeconomy.com and www.mybigstartup.com. He is the Coordinator of "Centre for Research & Publication" and Founder Chief-Editor for a national level Research Journal – "Jnanatapsa". He has chaired many sessions in national and international conferences.

He is a Fellow member of Institute of Marketing Management, member of AIMA, AIMS-International, NEN Network, Indian Society for Training and Development, BMA and life member of Institution of Homoeopathic Practitioners.

B. Rose Kavitha a (Ph.D.) from Karnatak University, Dharwad, is presently associated with CMR Institute of Technology as Professor and Coordinator Soft Skills. She is involved in establishing a Management Training Institute (MTI) to coordinate with all HR Heads from both Academic and Industry. She has graduated in MBA specialized in HR and MSc in (Industrial Psychology) and also continued to acquire Diplomas in Human Resource Development from AIMS and holds a Diploma in Software Management.

She comes with nearly **eleven** years of professional experience in handling subjects like Human Resource Management, Organizational Behaviour, Organizational Culture Change & Development and Learning Organizations & Leadership. ***She has played the role of Student Developer and Counsellor in all the institutions she has worked.***

Her academic and training experience includes her service for various Indian and International Institutions such as:

- Alliance Française, France., and as a Research associate under Dr. N.M. Agrawal at Indian Institute of Management, Bangalore.

As a ***member of NIPM*** she has contributed 24 articles in various magazines and research journals and has co-authored 4 books on Organizational Behaviour and Knowledge Management. ***She has presented research papers and has served as chairperson for both National and International Seminars and have also received 2 best paper awards, from IIM Kozhikode, and Sivasivani Institute of Management, Hyderabad.***

She is a Honorary member of McGraw-Hill Publications–Involving in review of few of their OB related publications. She has conducted **Personality Development Training Programmes** for Officers in **H**industan **A**eronautics **L**imited, **I**ntegrated **P**roperty **M**anagements (Pvt) Ltd., **Airtel** and a few of the other public sectors. Some of the topics handled are Self-awareness, Assertiveness, Attitude and Personality, Negotiating skills, Stress Management, Conflict Handling, etc.

1

Introduction to Service Management

"You can have brilliant ideas, but if you cannot get them across, your ideas will not get you anywhere" – Lee Iacocca

Learning Objectives

At the end of this chapter students will be able to understand

- Meaning of services
- Marketing mix of services
- Classification of service
- Development and importance of service management
- Decision-making process
- Service blueprinting
- GAP model of service quality and different strategies
- Service strategy
- Service recovery and various techniques
- Characteristics of services
- Differences between services and goods
- Segmenting and targeting
- Reason behind growth of service sector
- Service process
- Service quality
- Service measurement
- Service strategy and customer retention

PART–A: ***Introduction to Service Management***—meaning and concepts – characteristics – marketing mix of service–differences between goods and services–reasons for growth of service sector – classification of service – segmenting and targeting – development of service management – importance of service management – decision-making process

PART–B: ***Service Process*** – meaning and concepts – factors in designing service process – service design – service blueprints – steps – importance – role of technology in service process

PART–C: ***Service Quality*** – meaning and concepts – features – customer retention through quality improvement – GAP model – service measurement – quality and satisfaction

PART–D: ***Service Strategy*** – activities – strategies for matching capacity and demand – customer retention – customer switching – loyalty programmes – service recovery strategies

PART–E: ***Service Promotion*** – communication – characteristics – advertising – personal selling – public relations – publicity – direct marketing – words of mouth communication

Part-A: Introduction to Service Management

INTRODUCTION

Service industries are quite varied. The government sector, with its courts, employment services, hospitals, loan agencies, military services, police and fire departments, post office, regulatory agencies, and schools, is in the service business. The private non-profit sector, with its museums, charities, churches, colleges, foundations, and hospitals, is in the service business. A good part of the business sector, with its airlines, banks, computer-service bureaus, hotels, insurance companies, law firms, management-consulting firms, medical practices, motion-picture companies, plumbing-repair companies, and real estate firms, is in the service business. Many workers in the manufacturing sector, such as the computer operators, accountants, and legal staff, are really service providers. In fact, they make up a "service factory" providing services to the "goods factory". Not only are there traditional service businesses, but also new types keep popping up to serve the needs of a changing population.

MEANING AND CONCEPTS

A wide variety of activities labelled as services are practised by both profit-oriented organizations and non-profit oriented organizations. The success of these organizations depends on delivering excellent service quality and creating value to customers. Defining services is therefore not a simplistic task. Over the years service marketing literature has provided readers with an assortment of service definitions.

According to Irons, pure services are intangible but they do usually add value to, or make available, a tangible product. They do not result in transfer of ownership and may leave only memories.

Zeithaml and Bitner claim that in the simplest terms services are deeds, processes, and performances. Their broader definition states that services include all economic activities whose output is not a physical product, is generally consumed at the time it is produced, and provides added value in forms that are essentially intangible concerns of the purchaser.

Kotler (1996) defines service as an activity that one party offers another that is essential intangible and does not result in the ownership of anything. Its production may or may not be tied to a physical product.

Grönroos identifies a service as an activity or series of activities of a more or less intangible nature that normally, but not necessarily, takes place in interaction between the customer and service employees and/or physical resources or goods and/or systems of the service provider, which are provided as solutions to customer problems.

The conclusion derived from the above definition is that

- Services deal with intangible components.
- The purchase of services does not necessarily result in physical transfer or ownership but still creates a bundle of benefits during or after the service interaction or experience.
- Distinguishing between the tangible and intangible components of a service is extremely difficult. Therefore, separating the core service from the augmented service helps to simplify this task. The core service represents the fundamental benefits the service provide to satisfy customers' needs. The augmented service incorporates the core service in addition to the tangible elements and all additional benefits of the service employed to satisfy customers' needs. The core services are mostly intangible because of their lack of physical attributes, while augmented services

provide the customer with the impression of the services' tangibility component, because it can be seen, touched, and transferred to the customer.

- Mostly the result of the service interaction is a product of a tangible nature.
- The bundle of benefits is the customers' expectations from the service. Customers experience positive consequences of service processes as benefits, while negative consequences are experienced as perceived risks.

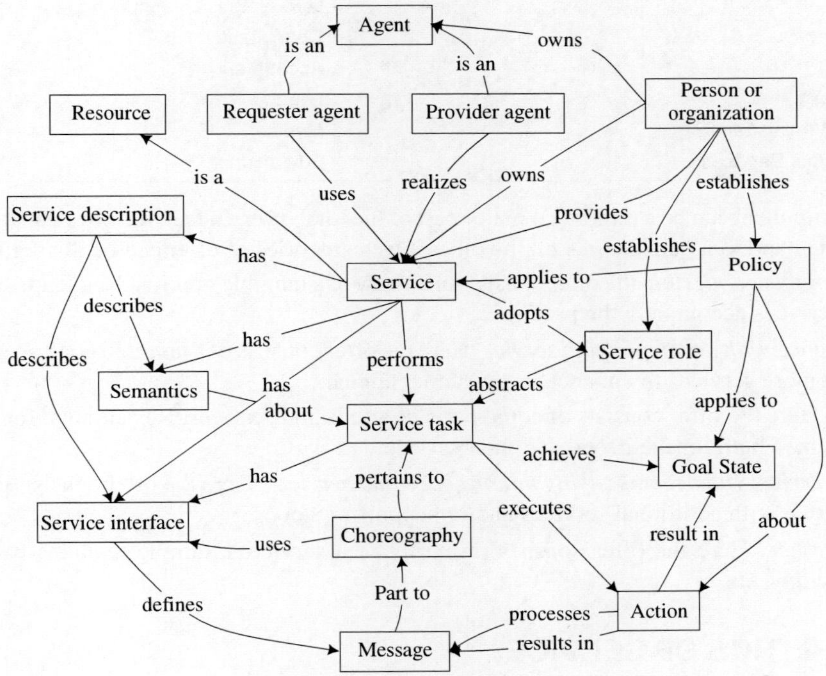

Fig. 1.1 Different aspects of service.

The bundle of benefits and the way the services are delivered is aimed at creating customer satisfaction. In most service processes, consumption and production of services take place at the same time. This procedure requires interaction between the service provider and the customer to complete the service process. The success of the service process is subsequently dependent on the success of the interaction.

From the above discussion Kasper et al., have constructed a broad definition of service in which the relevant topics will be recognized:

Services are originally intangible and activities, which are relatively quickly perishable activities whose purchase takes place in an interaction process aimed at creating customer satisfaction, but this interactive consumption does not always lead to material possession.

Over time, services and the service sector have been defined in many different ways, which add to confusion and disagreement when discussing services and service marketing. For the purpose of this study, the above-mentioned broad definition of services will apply and it will be acknowledged that there are very few pure services, in other words totally intangible offerings.

Table 1.1 Different types of service

Utilities	**Insurance, Banking, Finance**
Electricity	Banks
Water Supply	Share and Stock Brokers
Law Enforcing, Civil,	**Business, Professional and**
Administrative and Defence Services	**Scientific Activities**
Police	Advertising
Army	Marketing Research
Air Force	Consultancy
Navy	Accountancy
Judiciary	Legal
Civil Administration	Medical
Municipal Services	Educational

The service component can be a minor or a major part of the total offer. In fact, the offer can range from a pure good on one hand to a pure service on the other. Five categories of offer can be distinguished:

(i) *A pure tangible good*. Here the offer consists primarily of a tangible good such as soap, toothpaste, etc. No services accompany the product.

(ii) *Tangible good with accompanying service*. Here the offer consists of a tangible good accompanies by one or more services to enhance its consumer appeal.

(iii) *A hybrid*. Here the offer consists of equal parts of goods and services. Restaurants, for example, are patronized both for their food and their service.

(iv) *A major service with accompanying minor goods and services*. Here the offer consists of a major service along with additional services and/or supporting goods.

(v) *A pure service*. Here the offer consists primarily of a service. Example includes babysitting, psychotherapy, etc.

CHARACTERISTICS OF SERVICE

Intangibility Cannot be seen, tasted, felt or smelled before purchasing	**Inseparability** Production and consumption, and from the provider
Variability Service quality depends on who provides and under what conditions	**Perishability** Cannot be stored, for resale or later use

Intangibility

Intangibility is the dominant characteristic of services and is defined as the lack of tangible assets, which can be seen, touched or smelled prior to purchase. However, services vary in the degree to which they are intangible and most services include some kind of tangible element.

The tangibility spectrum places highly tangible offerings at one end of the continuum and intangible services on the opposite end of the continuum. It is clear that very few offerings are totally tangible or intangible. The intangible characteristic of services presents service marketers with several problems. The lack of physical attributes of services makes it difficult to display or communicate services readily and easily to customers. Customers often find it mentally difficult to grasp the service performance or experience without tangible evidence, which makes it difficult to diffuse. Services that rely intensely on customer involvement, present cost calculation difficulties that lead to price setting and inadequacies for service marketers.

Kurtz and Clow, indicate that these problems can, to a certain extent, be successfully resolved by reducing the intangibility of service offerings through stressing the tangibility components of offerings, stimulating word of mouth communication, creating a strong corporate image, encouraging employees to communicate with customers, and using unique attributable cost and perceived value pricing. Service providers must always take into account the fact that customers use the tangible elements, such as the people who provide the service, the environment in which the service encounter takes place, the equipment used, and the price of the offering, to make assumptions about the quality of the service and to compare it to the offerings of other service providers.

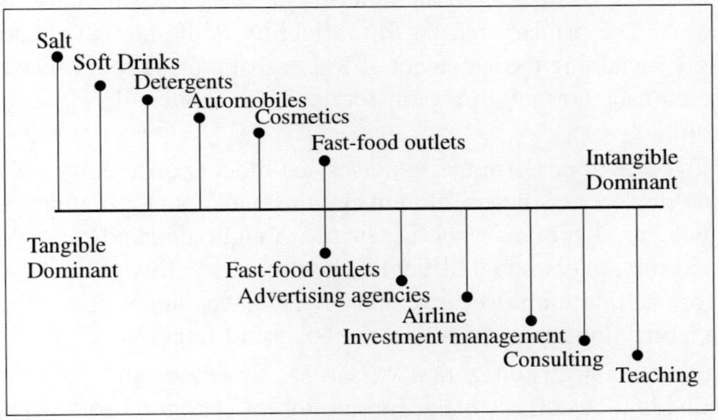

Source: Zeithaml, V.A. and Bitner, M.J. 2000 Services Marketing: integrating customer focus across the firm. 2nd edition. New York: McGraw-Hill, p. 23

Fig. 1.2 Services marketing.

Inseparability

Inseparability refers to the simultaneous production and consumption of a service, thus it is often difficult to separate the service provider from the service performance. Customers are normally present during the service performance and play an active role in the service production process. The quality of the service performance is dependent on the interaction between the service provider and the customer. The customer's involvement in the production process of the service can influence the outcome of the service positively or negatively. Service marketers must recognize that the roles customers play in the service production process influence the service outcome, not only for themselves but also for other customers. The inter-client interaction between customers also plays an integral part in the outcome of service experiences. Service organizations must acknowledge the influential role that service employees play in service processes. The service employees or the service providers are often seen as the service itself.

The inseparability of production and consumption means that very few service offerings can be mass-produced, but almost every service offering can be customized to customers' needs and demands. Customization is to the advantage of service organizations, because customers use the degree of customization of service offerings to measure the quality of services.

Perishability

Perishability is the inability of a service to be inventoried or stored. This characteristic is of major concern to service marketers because it inevitably leads to supply and demand problems. The capacity lost in services can never be regained and to equalize supply and demand is a difficult task. These distinct service problems present service marketers with the challenge of setting up good recovery strategies for service process failures. Research has shown that resolving customer problems effectively has a powerful impact on customer satisfaction and loyalty. The perishability characteristic of services creates the opportunity for the organization to develop creative planning for capacity utilization and management of future demand.

Variability

Variability refers to the unwanted or random variable levels of service quality customers receive when they support an organization. The primary reason for variability is the human element present in the service process, accordingly sustaining the statement of Kotler that the quality of service depends on the service provider. Because humans normally perform services, the chance of two service performances being the same is highly unlikely.

Different service employees will perform the same service process differently and the same service employee will provide a varying service under different circumstances or at different times. Nevertheless, the recipients of the service are also human, with their own unique demands and expectations of the service performance. Service marketers find it difficult to control the quality of the service performances because it is dependent on fallible employees as one of the main inputs. The reliance on people's performances causes standardization service processes to be almost impossible.

The intentional or unintentional customization of service processes and output performances by service employees for individual customers makes promotion of services very difficult. Customers in general perceive the person who delivers the service "as the service". As a result, service providers have the ability to alter the outcome and level of customer satisfaction. Service marketers are confronted with the challenge of controlling service quality because consistent quality service performances play a vital role in the survival of organizations. Service quality is profoundly dependent on the ability of customers to articulate their needs and level of service demands.

Equally, service quality depends on the ability and willingness of the service provider to satisfy customers' needs and demands. Organizations can put into practice service quality control and measurements by recruiting service-orientated employees and training them to provide a service that will meet or exceed customers' expectations.

Ownership

Ownership is the last characteristic of services that distinguish it from goods. Customers receive only the right to a service process when they purchase it. Subsequently it is assumed that payment for services buys only the right of access to a service and not physical transfer of ownership to customers.

Customers view the lack of ownership of a service as a perceived risk. Firstly, they are presented with the uncertainty as to whether the right service has been obtained and secondly with the uncertainty about the consequences of the service purchase. Since services are produced and consumed simultaneously, the option of "returning" a service does not exist. The inability to own a service also has direct implications on the distribution of services. Service customers usually only have use or access to a facility where a service is performed.

Kotler suggests that services call for special marketing solutions. The characteristics of services create problems for service marketers that are not experienced by product marketers. If these problems are not carefully managed, organizations may experience negative influences on service quality that will ultimately reduce customer retention and organization profits. In this regard, Zeithaml and Bitner have proposed a services marketing triangle, which will be discussed in the next section.

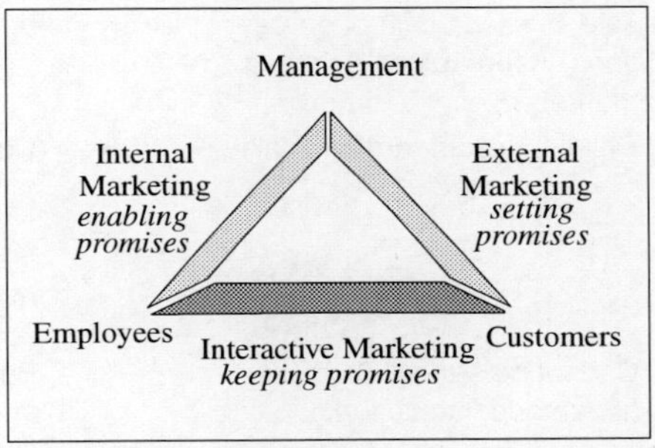

Source: Zeithaml, V.A. and Bitner, M.J. 2000 Services Marketing: Integrating customer focus across the firm. 2nd edition. New York: McGraw-Hill, p. 23.

Fig. 1.3 Integrating customer focus across the firm.

Service marketers face marketing challenges, which revolve around issues such as:

- Understanding customers' needs and expectations of services,
- Making services tangible to customers, and
- Keeping and dealing with promises made to the customers.

The services marketing triangle helps service marketers to address these challenges. The three points of the service triangle represent the organization, the customers, and the employees. Between each of the three points of the triangle different marketing processes such as external marketing, interactive marketing and internal marketing must be successfully carried out for service processes to succeed and to build and maintain relationships with the internal and external customers.

MARKETING MIX FOR SERVICE

The seven Ps in the services marketing mix are:

(i) ***Product:*** It is the most basic marketing mix tool, which stands for the firm's tangible offer to the market, including the product quality, design, features, branding and packaging. A service product refers to an activity or activities that a marketer offers to perform, which results in satisfaction of a need or want of predetermined target customers. The service product consists of core product, which is the primary benefit the customers seek from the service; and the

peripheral services that are the secondary benefits the customers seek. The management often tries to integrate core and peripheral service into a competitive strategy.

Implication of service characteristics and ways of overcoming them

Service characteristics	Implications	Means of overcoming characteristics
1. Intangibility	Sampling difficult. Difficult to judge quality and value in advance. Not possible to patent or have copyright. Relatively difficult to promote.	Focus on benefits. Use brand names. Personalize service. Develop reputation. Increase tangibility (e.g. its physical representation)
2. Inseparability	Requires presence of performer/producer. Direct sale. Limited scale of operations. Geographically limited market.	Learn to work in larger groups. Work faster. Train more service performers.
3. Heterogeneity	Difficult to standardize quality.	Careful selection and training of personnel. Define behaviour norms. Reduce role of human element. Mechanize and automate maximum possible operations.
4. Perishability	Cannot be stored. Problem of demand fluctuation.	Better match between supply and demand by price reduction in low demand season.
5. Ownership	Customer has access to but not ownership of facility or activity.	Stress advantages of non-ownership, such as easier payment scheme.

Source: Cowell, Donald, 'The Marketing of Services'. Heinemann, London.

Fig. 1.4 The marketing of services.

(ii) ***Price:*** It is the only element in the marketing mix that produces revenues, the other elements produce costs. Price should commensurate with the perceived value of the offer or buyers will turn to competitors. The type of organization, the market structure, the life cycle stage of the service, price charged by the competitors and organizational objectives – all have an impact on pricing decisions.

Costs, competition and value to the customer are the three legs of the pricing strategy. The costs to be recovered sets a floor to the price that may be charged; the value of the service product to the customer sets a ceiling; whereas the price charged by competitors for similar substitute products may determine where, within the ceiling-to-floor range the price level should actually be set. In the absence of tangible clues, customers may associate higher prices with the higher levels of performance on service attributes. Companies resolve the pricing issue by selecting a pricing method that includes one or more of the above three considerations. The pricing method will then lead to a specific price.

(iii) ***Promotion:*** It stands for the various activities, the company undertakes to communicate and promote its products to the target market. The basic elements which serve to achieve organizational communications objectives form the promotional mix. This essentially brings

together the various promotional tools used in the marketing programme in a coordinated and controlled way. In consumer services marketing, advertising will be by far the main component (and the most expensive) while in industrial and business-to-business sectors, greater emphasis is placed on personal selling, trade fairs and other promotional tools.

Promotional objectives need to be clearly defined before a strategic promotional programme is designed. The objectives of promotion fall into three main categories: to inform, to remind and to persuade.

(iv) ***Place:*** Distribution or the 'place' element of the marketing mix is concerned chiefly with two main issues – accessibility and availability. The inseparable nature of services means that services must be accessible to potential customers in order for exchanges to take place. Accessibility must be a component of the actual service offering for it to have value. Additionally, the perishable nature of services means it is essential for the service to be available to customers – in the right place at the right time. The services cannot be stored until a later date; it must be available for consumption at the point of production. The simultaneous production and consumption of service indicate that the channel of distribution is generally limited. Location decisions are important in professional services or retail financial services.

(v) ***Process:*** The principles by which service delivery processes can be designed, implemented and monitored are really not different from those mentioned relating to the fields of manufacturing, computing, etc. Service encounter should be a positive one and service quality should be maintained. The following steps should be followed while designing the service process:

- Break down the process into logical steps and sequence
- Identify those steps which have the highest probability of something going wrong because of judgement, choice or chance.
- Set deviations or tolerance standards for these steps thereby providing a performance band for functioning.

(vi) ***People:*** Human element forms an intrinsic part of the service industry not only to service personnel, but also recognizes the role that other people, i.e., the customers play in service delivery. Central to successful service delivery is management of the customer/service provider interface. Employees need to understand their role in the service exchange, and human resources management provides the programmes and strategies to ensure the highest standards of customer care. Development of quality circle, empowerment and a service culture organization all prove the above. In services, marketing is everyone's job. Thus, it is important to have employees with skills, commitment, attitude and ability to use discretion in dealing with customer. This is especially true in those services where there is a high level of contact with customers. By adding value in the way the employees perform and maximizing the impact of their activities, the firm has a competitive edge over the other service companies.

(vii) ***Physical Evidence:*** The important factor influencing consumer satisfaction with a service exchange of any organization is the physical setting within which it occurs. While the physical setting may have an effect upon the exchange of goods as well as services, it is suggested that the setting's symbolic value has greater impact upon the evaluation of a service. This physical evidence can take a number of forms. The building and service environment where the service is delivered are the major evidences of the nature of service. A clean, bright environment used in a service outlet can help to reassure potential customers regarding their purchase decision.

For this reason fast-food and photoprocessing outlets often use red and yellow colour schemes to convey an image of speed service. In case of tourism industry, brochures serve the purpose of evidence.

Physical evidences are of two types:

- ***Peripheral Evidence:*** It can be possessed by the consumer but has little independent value, e.g., bank's chequebook?
- ***Essential Evidence:*** It plays important part in service facilities, which cannot be possessed by the consumer but has independent value, e.g. bank's branch/office.

The service provider must coordinate both types of physical evidences to achieve uniformity in its projected service image.

Product	Price	Place	Promotion	People	Physical evidence	Process
Range Quality Brand name Warranty Post Transaction service	Level discounts, Allowances Commissions Payment terms Consumer's perceived value Quality/ Price relationships	Location Accessibility Distribution channels distribution coverage	Advertising Personal Selling Sales Promotion Publicity Public relation	Training Discretion Commitment Incentives Appearance Inter Personal behaviour Attitudes Other customers Degree of involvement Customer contact	Environment Furnishings Colour, Layout Noise levels Faciliating goods Tangible clues	Polices Procedures Mechanization Employee customer involvement Flow of activities

Source: Booms, B.H. and Bitner, M.J, *Marketing Strategies and Organization Structure for Services Firms,* in Donnelly J and George W.R.(Eds), Marketing of Services, AMA, 1981.

Fig. 1.5 Services mix.

SEGMENTING AND TARGETING SERVICES

(i) ***Identify basis for segmenting the market:*** Different variables are used to segment consumer markets. The variables fall into two broad groups. Some researchers try to form segments by looking at consumer characteristics. They commonly use geographic, demographic and psychographic characteristics. They examine whether these customer segments exhibit different needs or product responses.

Other researchers try to form segments by looking at consumer responses to benefits sought, use, occasions, or brands. Once the segments are formed, the researcher sees whether different consumer characteristics are associated with each consumer response segment. The major segmentation variables are geographic, demographic, and psychographic and behavioural.

(ii) ***Profiling of resulting segments:*** Each cluster is now profiled in terms of its distinguishing attitudes, behaviour, demographics, and psychographics and media consumption habits. At this stage it is important to clearly understand how and whether the segments differ in their profile. If they do not differ, then the benefit that is to be derived from segmentation will not be realized.

(iii) ***Developing measures of segment attractiveness:*** Segments may exist but they may not be of our choice. Segments must be evaluated in terms of their attractiveness. The first question to ask is whether a potential segment has the right size and growth characteristics. Segment growth is normally a desirable characteristic since companies generally want growing sales and profit. A segment might have desirable size and growth but lack profit potential.

(iv) ***Selecting the market segment:*** Having evaluated different segments, the company must now decide which and how many segments to serve. That is the problem of target market selection. The company can either go in for single segment concentration, selective specialization, product specialization, market specialization or full market coverage.

(v) ***Ensure that the target segments are compatible:*** Sometimes the company may choose a target audience with which it is not very compatible. Relationships in business are extremely important. The target market should be full of people with whom the company can relate. This will make life and business a much greater pleasure.

If the groups do not merge well, they may negatively influence each other's experience which may hurt the organization's future business. No matter what product the company has, not everyone is going to buy it. Hence, target demographic should be decided and appropriate media outlets should be used to reach that audience. Trying to appeal to everyone doesn't work.

Keeping aside the ethical and legal matters, some firms do not prefer to have long-term relationship with unprofitable customers, even though they are able to meet their requirements. The reasons may be:

(a) The segment is not big enough to have good marketing approach

(b) The segments cannot afford to pay.

(c) The projected revenue from the segment may not cover the expenses incurred to maintain business.

DECISION-MAKING AND EVALUATION PROCESS IN SERVICES

There are five stages of decision-making and evaluation process in services which are as follows:

(i) ***Need recognition:*** The buying process starts when the buyer recognizes a problem or need; the buyer senses a difference between his/her actual state and the desired state. The need can be triggered by internal or external stimuli. In the former case, one of the persons' normal needs – hunger, thirst, sex – rises to a threshold level and becomes a drive. From previous experiences the person has learned how to cope with this drive and is motivated towards stimulus. For e.g., a person passes a bakery and smells freshly baked cake that stimulates his hunger. These stimuli can trigger a problem or need.

(ii) ***Information search:*** An aroused customer will be inclined to search for more information. We can distinguish between two levels. The milder search state is called heightened attention and the second level is the active information search. How much search a person undertakes depends upon the strength of his drive, the amount of information he already has, the ease of obtaining additional information and the value he placed on additional information and the satisfaction he gets from the search.

In services, the focus is on personal sources. Non-personal sources may not be available because many e-service providers are local and don't have the required finance or knowledge about advertising. 'Word of mouth' influences purchase behaviour of the customers. Because of intangible non-standardized characteristics of service, the customer faces perceived risk.

Services are heterogeneous and so performance may vary across service providers, across employees, some provider and even with the same employee. The extent the customer notices and is willing to accept this variation is called "zone of tolerance". It is the range in which the customer does not particularly notice service performances. When it falls outside the range (either low/high), the service gets the notice of the customer's attention in positive or negative way.

(iii) ***Evaluation of service alternatives:*** There are several decision evaluation processes and most of them are cognitively oriented, i.e., they see the consumer as forming product judgements largely on a conscious and rational basis. In case of services, it is rather difficult to obtain pre-purchase information about services. Thus, the alternatives available for consumer in services are smaller/fewer than those available in case of tangible goods. The customer always demands better quality or service or want personalized attention from the service provider. Thence the service provider do some research and find out what the customer expects.

(iv) ***Purchase decision:*** In the evaluation stage the consumer forms preferences among the service providers in the choice set. He may also form a purchase intention to avail the most preferred service provider's service. However, two factors can intervene between the purchase intention and the purchase decision. The first factor is the attitude of others. The extent to which another person's attitude reduces one's preferred alternative depends upon two things (a) the intensity of the other person's negative attitude towards the consumer's preferred alternative and (b) the consumer's motivation to comply with the other person's wishes. Purchase intention is also influenced by unanticipated situation factors.

(v) ***Post-purchase evaluation:*** After purchasing/availing the product/service, the consumer will experience same level of satisfaction or dissatisfaction. If the product's performance falls short of customer expectations, the customers are disappointed. If it meets the expectations, the customers are satisfied and it if exceeds expectations, the customers are delighted.

Dissonant customers may try to reduce the dissonance by abandoning or returning the product and by seeking information that might confirm its high value. However, this is not possible in case of services because services once availed cannot be returned back.

DIFFERENCES BETWEEN SERVICES AND GOODS

Table 1.2 Differences between services and good

Basis	*Services*	*Goods*
Intangibility	Fully intangible may be physical evidence	Fully tangible
Inseparability of buyer and provider	Both must be present.	Remote transactions easy
Ease of inventory	Cannot store or warehouse the service	Easily inventoried
Sensitivity to time	Needed on demand, or sale is lost	Can usually wait to receive the product.
Difficulty in measuring and controlling quality	Measure and control people and processes instead of products	Measure and control product quality only
High degree of risk/ difficulty of experimen-tation	Cost of failure very high; may not be possible make whole or replace the service	Product can be replaced
Consumption of the offering	Customization likely to enhance customer perception of perceived quality.	Customization increases costs, but unlikely to affect perceived product quality
Personalization of buyer relationship	Relationship can be as important as service	Product is the focus of the transaction

REASONS FOR GROWTH OF SERVICE SECTOR

Manufacturing industries grew because they produced tangible goods which satisfied people's physiological needs of food, shelter and clothing. As the basic need was fulfilled, there was demand for improved satisfaction, and this led to a proliferation of variations of the same product and a number of companies involved in its manufacture. The growth of service industries can be traced to the economic development of society and the socio-culture changes that have accompanied it. Table 1.3 presents the reasons for growth of service industries.

Sometimes, the growth of a specific service industry is the result of a combination of several reasons. Increasing affluence coupled with the desire to utilize leisure time for leisure rather than for doing odd repair jobs in the house had led to the growing tribe of plumbers and electricians. Increasing affluence combined with increasing complexity of life and increasing insecurity has led to the phenomenon of credit cards and travellers cheques which have proved to be almost perfect substitutes for money. These credit cards provide convenience and safety. In fact, convenience is proving to be a key concept in the provision of services.

CLASSIFICATION OF SERVICES

Services may be classified as follows:

(i) ***Based on Service Options:*** First, services vary as to whether they are equipment based (automated car washes, vending machines) or people based (window washing, accounting

Table 1.3 Reasons for growth of service sector.

Reasons	*Types of services required*
Increasing affluence	Greater demand for services (activities which consumers used to perform themselves) such as interior decoration, laundry, care of household products such as carpets, care of garden, etc.
More leisure time	Greater demand for recreation and entertainment facilities, travel resorts, adult education and self-improvement courses.
Higher percentage of women in labour force	Greater demand for crèches, baby sitting, household domestic help

services). People based services vary by whether they are provided by unskilled, skilled, or professional workers.

(ii) ***Based on customer-employee presence:*** Some services require the client's presence. If the client must be present, the service provider has to be considerate of his or her needs. Thus, beauty shop operators will invest in their shops décor, play background music and engage in light conversation with the client. These are interpersonal services. Some services find the presence of customer only. These are known as self-service organizations. For example, ATM service. These are certain services where only the presence of employee is required. These are known as remote services, for example, insurance companies.

(iii) ***Based on ultimate user:*** Services differ as to whether they meet a personal need (personal services) or a business need (business services) or an industrial need (plant maintenance and repair). Physicians will price physical examinations differently for private patients versus company employees on a retainer basis. Service providers typically develop different marketing programmes for personal and business markets.

(iv) ***Based on objectives:*** Service providers differ in their objectives (profit or non-profit) and ownership (private or public). These two characteristics, when crossed, produce four quite different types of service organizations. Clearly, the marketing programmes of a private investor hospital will differ from those of a private charity hospital or a Veterans' Administration hospital.

(v) ***Based on level of tangibility:*** Services can also be classified based on the degree of tangibility of services. There are highly intangible services such as car rentals, vending machines. Then there are highly intangible services such as consultancy, legal service, babysitting, etc. And lastly there are major services linked with minor tangible goods services such as people buying a seat on aircraft are buying transportation service without anything tangible to show for their expenditure.

(vi) ***Based on specialization:*** Services can be classified based on the level of specialization. They are professional services such as the medical, legal, accounting, etc. and there are non-professional services such as babysitting, casual labour, etc.

(vii) ***Based on external and internal services to manufacturers:*** External services are concerned with the normal work done by the company to prepare, price, distribute and promote the service to customers. Internal service covers a wide range of activities undertaken by the company such as training and motivating employees, recruitment, publications, payroll administration, office cleaning, etc.

DEVELOPMENT OF SERVICES MANAGEMENT

Stage 1: In this stage, services management was not properly identified and not distinguished from regular management practices. In this stage, marketers were not differentiating between the marketing or physical goods and of services. The paid service organizations like financial institutions were also thinking that it could be considered a product itself if no physical product was involved. In reality, they were performing the marketing of service. They never considered this as a separate powerful activity which could bring more income and increase the standard of living.

Stage 2: Here, services management was identified as the need for services were recognized. Thinkers such Rathmell, Shostack were the early critics of principles of marketing in relation to services. They argued that the marketing tools used for goods marketing cannot easily be translated to services marketing. Because services were different in many respects from physical products.

Stage 3: In this stage, it was felt that quality service should be provided and every business house needs some type of service which can be made available only by the service sector. Thus, service management is important not only in the services sector but also in every business enterprise – enterprise which is also dealing in physical products and some services being an integral part of business operations. This aspect focuses on the demand side of services which encourages service providers to provide quality service.

IMPORTANCE OF SERVICES MANAGEMENT

(i) ***Creation and expansion of job opportunities***: The development of services sector would open doors; search new vistas for the development of even those sectors which have either remain untapped or have partially been tapped.

(ii) ***Paving avenues for formation of capital:*** The development of services sector will speed up the process of capital formation and the problem of inadequacy of financial resources will be minimized. For accelerating the rate of capital formation, it is essential that we explore opportunities and identify important or the profitable services.

(iii) ***Raising the standard of living:*** For raising the standard of living, it is not only essential that we create enough earning opportunities for the masses but it is also essential that we make efforts to increase public awareness so that they know how to spend, where to spend, what to eat, how much to eat, how to develop our personality, how to keep sound health, and so on. These things contribute immensely to the standard of living.

(iv) ***Environment-friendly technology:*** All the services are technology-driven. The banking services, insurance services, tourism services, hostel services, communication services, education services and by and large almost all services are now technology-driven but environment-friendly. Thus, the technology-driven service generating organizations offer world-class services even without polluting the environment.

Part-B: Service Process

INTRODUCTION

It is sixth element of service marketing mix. The service process refers to how a service is provided or delivered to a customer. Processes involve the procedures, tasks, schedules, mechanisms, activities and routines by which a service is delivered to the customer.

MEANING AND CONCEPTS

It can be defined as the way of understanding the transaction, supplying information and providing services in a way which is acceptable to the consumer and effective to the organization. Process is functional activity that assures service availability and quality.

In a service organization, the system by which you receive delivery of the service constitutes the process. In fast-food outlets the process comprises buying the coupons at one counter and picking up the food against that at another counter.

The process of a delivery function which can be compared with that of operations management implies the conversion of input into the finished product. But in a service organization there is no clear cut input or output. Rather it is the process of adding 'value' or 'utility' to system inputs to create outputs which are useful for the customers. Services can be described on the basis of the types of processes used in the delivery of the services. The three kinds of delivery processes that are applicable in case of service products are line operations, job shop operations and intermittent operations. Self-service restaurants and shops are examples of line operations. The consumer moves through logically arranged operations which are arranged in a sequence. In a self-service departmental store, the consumer starts picking up the items he needs and pays for them near the exit.

This kind of delivery process is relevant when the service you are providing is fairly standard and the consumers' requirement is of a routine nature. When the consumers require a combination of services using different sequences, the job shop type of operation is more useful. Hospitals, restaurants and educational institutions usually have this type of delivery process. In a hospital, some patients need only consultation in the Out Patient Department, some others may need consultation as well as medication or X-ray, and some patients require hospitalization for surgery, medication or investigations. All these categories of consumers require a different combination of dishes. A college may offer courses for full-time students as well as for working people through correspondence.

Intermittent operations are useful when the type of service is rarely repeated. Firms offering consultancy for projects use this kind of delivery system. Advertising agencies also use the intermittent delivery system since each advertising campaign requires a unique set of input factors.

As a manager you are interested in optimizing the efficiency of your organization without sacrificing the qualitative aspect. Some of the critical questions you need to focus upon are:

(a) What are the steps involved in delivering the service to the consumer?

(b) Are they arranged in the most logical sequence?

(c) If not, can some steps be eliminated, combined or rearranged to form a smoother sequence?

(d) What are the steps in which the consumer is involved?

(e) Can the consumers' contact be reduced or totally eliminated?

(f) Can we introduce automation to speed up the delivery process?

OBJECTIVES BEHIND MANAGING THE SERVICE PROCESS

1. To ensure that the service is carried out in the fastest, most efficient, and cost-effective manner.
2. To create and place benchmarks that help monitoring the service delivery for quality and productivity.

3. To facilitate employee learning and allow them to carry out responsibility for individual stages more effectively.
4. To reduce variance through budgeting and workforce planning.

You will appreciate that the importance of process management is that it assures service availability and consistent quality. Without sound process management, balancing service demand with service supply is extremely difficult. Service cannot be inventoried; therefore, it becomes essential to find out ways and means to handle peak load to optimize different customer needs with varied expertise levels within the service organization. In marketing management, operations management has been recognized as an integral function. In manufacturing sector, for example, logistics in distribution are vital to satisfy the customer needs. Similarly, in services sector, where there is no tangible product, the operations management is vital to deliver satisfaction because here the operations management would decide how the process of service delivery would function, or in other words, the interactive experience that would deliver the service benefits to the consumers.

SERVICE DELIVERY SYSTEM

While designing a delivery system, the following three aspects, namely, where to deliver, how to deliver and the time of delivery should be taken into consideration:

(i) ***Place:*** Distribution depends on the nature of service. In case interaction between the service firm and consumer is necessary, then the place factor becomes very important. If the customer goes to the service provider as in case of restaurant, bank, then the location must be convenient to the customer. But when the service provider goes to the place of the customer to deliver the service as in the case of repair and cleaning services, the location will usually be at a place which is cost-effective. And at the same time the service must be made available within a reasonable time.

(ii) ***Cyberspace:*** With the increase in the level of automation, there is a great reduction in the choice of location decisions. The digital revolution has fundamentally altered our concepts of space, time and mass. A company need not occupy much space, it can be virtual and anywhere. Cyberspace has ushered in an age when buying and selling has become more automated and convenient. The telephone was the first electronic medium for obtaining information and placing orders. The arrival of the Internet made it possible to gather information and place orders through the computer. With the imminent emergence of interactive TV, still another electronic medium has become available. Self-servicing machines installed in several convenient localities can work round the clock without any staff around. Once such innovative method is ATM, which has supplemented the personal banking system.

(iii) ***Time and Place:*** Time and place also assume importance. How the activities have to be designed, the interior set-up of service delivery places, whether the service is provided individually or in groups, the duties and responsibilities of the intermediaries are some of the issues concerned and have to be taken into account while designing a service delivery system.

Some service operators such as telephone companies, transportation, BSWWB, BESCOM, hospitals, ambulances, firefighting agencies provide 24 hours service. The traditional business organization such as doctors, lawyers, consultants, etc. may work for 45-50 hours a week. Nowadays, we have both husbands and wives working in offices. This gives them little time to go to banks, etc. Such couples look for extended time of these services to meet their requirement. As time is a critical factor, they prefer all the services available in one place rather than availing the services at different places. Supplementary services such as online information, reservations, etc., are becoming increasingly popular.

SERVICE BLUEPRINTS

A service blueprint is a picture or a map that accurately portrays the service system, so that the different people involved in providing it can understand and deal with it objectively regardless of their role or individual points of view.

- Blueprints are particularly useful at the design and redesign stages of service development.
- A service blueprint visibly displays the service by simultaneously depicting the process of service delivery, points of customer contact, role of customers and employees, and
- The visible elements of service.

SERVICE BLUEPRINTING

A tool for simultaneously depicting the service process, the points of customer contact, and the evidence of service from the customer's point of view.

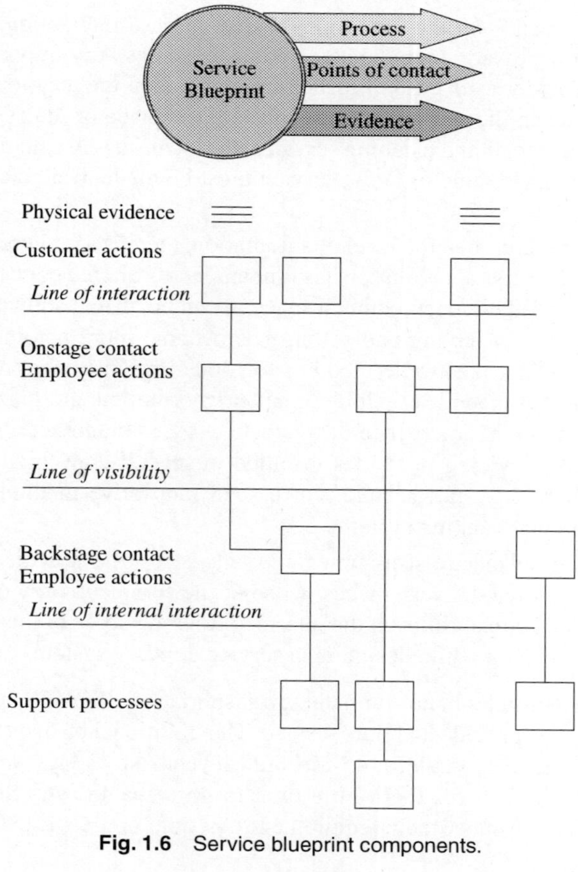

Fig. 1.6 Service blueprint components.

Blueprinting – Key Components

- Customer Action – Line of External Interaction
- "Onstage" Contact Employee Action – Line of Visibility
- "Backstage" Contact Employee Action Line of Internal Interaction
- Support Processes

Steps in Building a Blueprint

1. Identify the service process to be blueprinted
2. Map the service process from the customers point of view
3. Map Contact Employee Actions –
   Onstage – Line of External Interaction
   Backstage – Line of Visibility – what customers should see and which employees are in contact with the customers.
4. Map Internal Support activities – Line of Internal Interaction – clarify interfaces across departmental lines, their interdependencies
5. Add Evidence of Service at each Customer Action Step

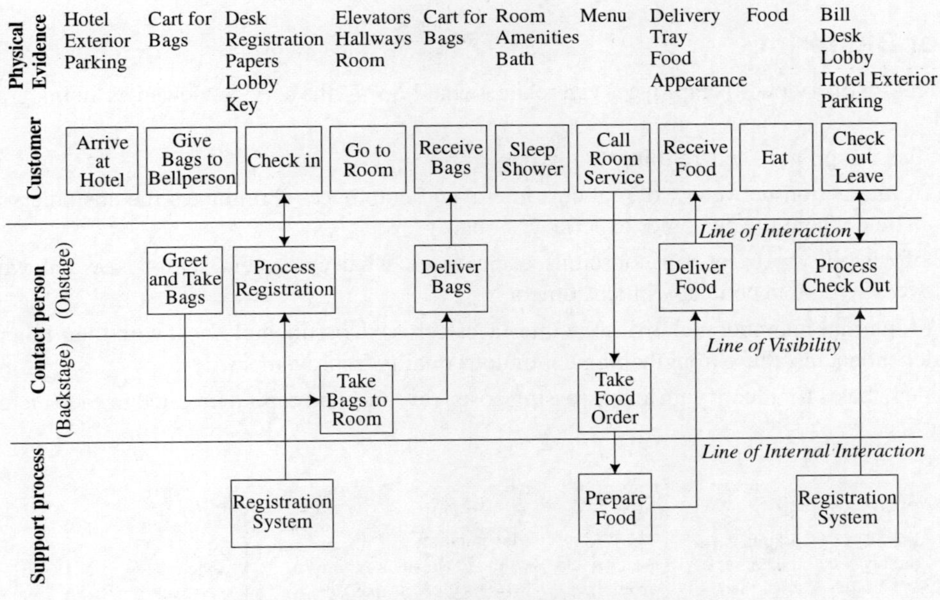

Fig. 1.7 Blueprint for overnight hotel stay service.

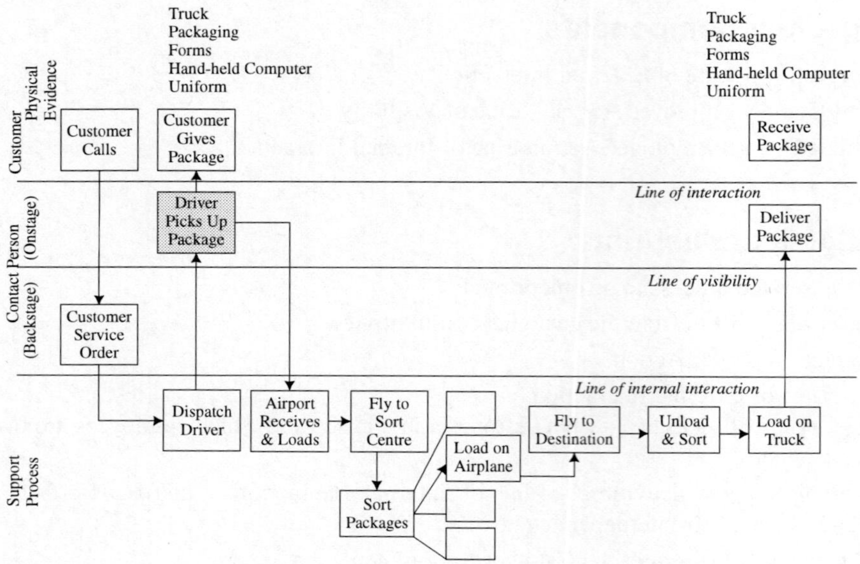

Fig. 1.8 Blueprint for express mail delivery service.

Benefits of Blueprint

1. Provides an overview so employees can relate "what I do" to the service viewed as an integrated whole.
2. Identifies fail points – where things go wrong.
3. Line of interaction between external customer's and employees illuminates the customers and demonstrate where the customer experiences quality.
4. Line of visibility promotes a conscious decision on what customers should see and which employees will be in contact with customers.
5. Line of internal interaction clarifies the interfaces across departmental lines, with their inherent interdependencies, thus strengthening continuous quality improvement.
6. Provides a basis for identifying and assessing costs, revenue, and capital invested in each element of service.

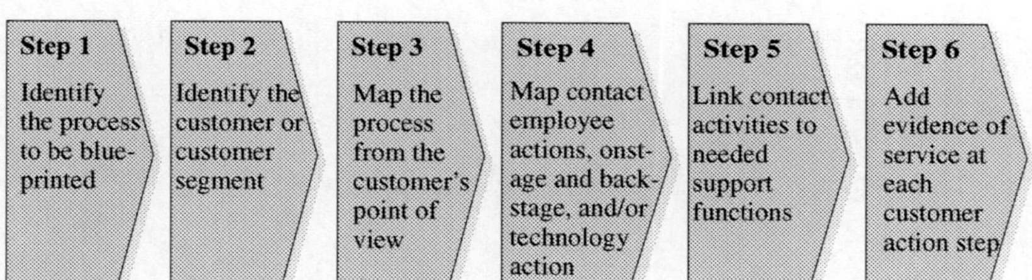

Fig. 1.9 Building a service blueprint.

ROLE OF TECHNOLOGY AND PHYSICAL AIDS IN SERVICE PROCESS

- Cost rationalization
- More effective quality
- Making higher quality possible
- Closer link up with the customer
- Technology as a factor affecting behaviour

Part-C: Service Quality

INTRODUCTION

The subject of service quality has aroused considerable recent interest among business people and academics. Of course, buyers have always been concerned with quality, but the increasing competitive market for many services has led consumers to become more selective in the services they choose. Conceptualizing the quality for services is more complex than for goods. Because of the absence of tangible manifestations, measuring service quality can be difficult but there are possible research approaches. Comprehensive models of service quality and their limitations can be studied. Understanding just what dimensions of quality are of importance to customers is not always easy in their evaluation process. It is not sufficient for companies to set quality standards in accordance with misguided assumptions of customers' expectations. A further problem in defining service quality lies in the importance which customers often attach to the quality if the service provider is distinct from its service offers – the two cannot be separated as readily as in the case of goods. Finally, issues relating to the setting of quality standards and implementation of quality management should be studied.

MEANING AND CONCEPTS

Quality improvement and adherence to accepted norms of quality are central to the modern concept of marketing of services. The quality of service delivery results in customer satisfaction and their retention as it reinforces the perception that the value of the service received is greater that the price paid for it. Some important concepts are:

Modern quality concepts result in better profitability, which is the main goal of all the business.

Quality control has much to do with changing the frame of mind and psychology of the service provider and particularly the front-end and back-end employees actually providing the services. We need to know how this fundamental change in attitude can be brought about.

Traditionally, most service providers have felt that they know all there is to know about the customers and their requirements. This smug or self-satisfied approach needs to be changed. Development of feedback systems is very essential part of the quality improvement. How this can be used to develop better quality standards is an issue of immense importance. Goal setting and adherence to the goals are both essential to ensure continuous improvement in the quality standards.

DEFINITIONS

There are many definitions of quality, and in many senses quality is subjective. The best way to discuss about service quality is to distinguish service quality measurement from customer satisfaction measurement.

To many people, quality implies luxury or excellence; a Rolls Royce rather than a Ford; cordon bleu instead of fast-food. However, quality can also be measured in terms of fitness for purpose, and a Ford Escort is regarded by many owners as a quality family car, while McDonalds provide a quality fast-food service.

FEATURES OF SERVICE QUALITY

- **Customer participation –** Customers are frequently active participants in the service process—they co-produce the service.
- **Intangibility –** Highly intangible services may be based on philosophical or conceptual elements. This abstract nature of some services makes them difficult for the service provider to describe, and for the customer to evaluate.
- **The service encounter –** Services are often comprised of a number of component parts, and it is the sum of these, or the overall experience of the service encounter, which the customer will use to form judgments.
- **Inseparability –** Many specialized services are inseparable—the characteristics of the service provider in terms of expert knowledge or skill, for example, are a constituent part of the service quality.

CUSTOMER RETENTION THROUGH QUALITY IMPROVEMENT

The focus of the modern marketers has shifted away from a one-time sale to making repeated sales to the same customer. Increasing attention is being paid to medium and long-term perspectives, rather than just the short-term perspective. This has been a major revolution in thinking in the field of marketing. Customer retention usually pays dividends by way of:

Lifetime value of the customer: If the customer remains loyal to the company, naturally, the repeated purchases represent a cumulative value which is quite substantial compared to any single transaction.

Reduced costs: It costs much more to acquire a new customer than to retain an old customer. Therefore, the focus of marketing has shifted away from the goal of mere customer acquisition to customer retention in order to substantially reduce marketing costs.

Benefit from wider opportunities to market more products and services to customers who are already loyal to you. The key differentiator between customer retention is customer satisfaction. Satisfaction results when the customer feels that the value of a service received by him is substantially higher than the price he paid for acquiring the service.

Customer satisfaction can be largely attributed to the quality of the service or product. Thus, delivery of high quality service is crucial to the high service value perception. When the major marketing goal of a company is customer retention, the quality of service delivery is, undeniably, the key differentiator.

Service Quality – A Key to Success in the Services Sector

"Service with a smile", "You can count on XXXX for prompt delivery", "With ABC mobile phones you can reach anyone, anywhere, anytime", "ZZZ Airlines—we fly you everywhere" —these are some punchlines of ad campaigns that are currently splashed across media–print, television and hoardings. How many of us can honestly claim to have experienced this service—consistently, day after day, purchase after purchase, transaction after transaction?

Yet, this is the age of the service sector, an era for excelling in quality of service provided. The service sector is growing in spread and depth to encompass all transactions involving buying and selling – be it in the tangible or intangible form. The examples below underscore how the service sector has transgressed all boundaries.

Companies across the country and the world are seeking to outsource many of their cost centres – the resultant surge in service providers like security services, indoor plants and decorative, cleaning and housekeeping and even secretarial services is phenomenal.

Dual-income, nuclear households are getting to be the norm in urban India. In cities like Mumbai, families are experiencing a burning new need – more time. Overstressed with work and travel, they find it impossible to grapple with routine everyday tasks. This has given rise to hitherto unconventional new services.

Housewives now make a cool sum with selling idli/dosa batter and homemade food. Telephonic orders and home delivery are now passed with grocers and vegetable vendors. Supermarkets sell packaged vegetables, which are chopped and cleaned – waiting to be cooked. The makeover is apparent even in traditional services like retailing and banking. These service providers have added peripheral services to reduce transaction time and improve service delivery. Turn to product marketing – tangible products like television sets, air-conditioners, microwave ovens and refrigerators, pagers and mobile phone sets and even cars are being sold on the promise of after sales service. Buyers are not just conscious of the necessity of services after the purchase has been made – they demand it.

Having tasted the joys of greater and enhanced services in all walks of life, urban Indians are clamoring for more. They now want an improvement in the quality of service offered. Service quality therefore is the latest buzzword – in corporate boardrooms, the local bania's siesta conversation with his neighbours and in the king's lair – the urban household.

How then is the service provider to go about the difficult task of analyzing his business operations for chinks in delivery of quality service? What tool would indicate to him that he has misunderstood his customer? Where would he seek a consultant for rectifying this fatal error?

The gaps model of service quality looks into the gaps in service quality. It is a ready reckoned to service providers to analyze their existing service delivery system and rectify matters before the company has lost the attention of the customer.

QUALITY AND PRODUCTIVITY

Mastering quality in services is of utmost importance if a service organization has to survive in today's competitive environment. Same applies to productivity. Productivity is the amount of output produced in relation to the amount of input utilized. Higher productivity can be obtained by reducing resources to achieve the required volume of output.

The productivity and quality in services can be achieved by several methods such as:

- Cost control
- Matching production and demand
- Adopting technology based production
- Avoidance of wasteful expenditure of resources
- Employee training should be undertaken
- Developing systems which allow semi-skilled employees to perform better.

Restructuring backstage and front stage activities can improve the service quality and lead to customer satisfaction. Reduction in cost of production should not be resorted to at the cost of compromising on quality or it can even backfire resulting in counter-production. Designing of 'self-service' system actively involves the customer in production and delivery processes benefitting both the customer and service provider. At times the service provider may delegate some of the functions to a third party for better service productivity.

THE GAPS MODEL OF SERVICE QUALITY

Formal means of gaps in service quality to identify and correct gaps between desired levels and actual levels of performance.

Service quality focuses on the customer's cumulative attitude, which is collected by the consumer from number of successful and unsuccessful service experience.

GAP ONE: NOT KNOWING WHAT CUSTOMERS EXPECT

Not knowing what customers expect is one of the root causes of not delivering to the customer expectations gap 1 is the difference between customer expectations of the service and company understanding of those expectations. Examples abound – foreign banks were right in thinking that customer expectation in terms of ambience was not being met. So they brought in some good ambience and more presentable executives and thought they had bridged the gap. But what they did not understand was that the customer was taking note of the lack of ambience because there was a wait when he was twiddling his thumbs and looking around for a place to sit. In other words, he was really complaining about the lack of speed and ease of operations. Result: Fancy ambience and higher cost attached to the same slow and indifferent service – albeit by better looking personnel in better surrounds.

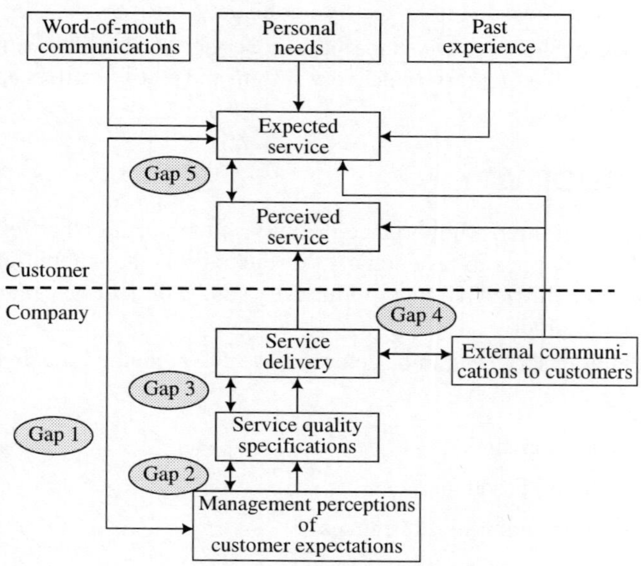

Fig. 1.10 Gaps model of service quality.

Private sector banks understood the problem a mite better but they too slipped up as business grew. They lost out on sustainability of the service promise. Example: A contractor using an electrical subcontractor for the first time may expect the subcontractor to use a certain grade of wire conduit in all of their construction sites, they subcontractor, however, may think the contractor wants to use the lowest grade to keep the cost down. Unless the contractor clearly delineates his expectations, he will probably be dissatisfied because the subcontractor did not do what was expected.

The reverse may also occur. Management can provide a service, they think customers expect without conforming customer expectations. Although on the surface this sounds good because customer expectations will probably be exceeded, there are two dangers. First, if customer expectations are consistently exceeded, in time, these expectations will rise to meet the service being provided.

Example: If customers do not expect their cars to be vacuumed and cleaned inside when the oil is changed at Quik Lube, then at first they will be pleased with this extra touch. But the next time they use Quik Lube, their expectations increase and after a few times of receiving this special touch, it will become a permanent part of their expectations. Failure to vacuum and clean the interior of the car will then result in a negative gap since the vacuuming and the cleaning of the interior becomes something customers expected. The second danger is that the firm may be spending money on providing services that the customers do not expect or perhaps even care about, thus yielding a negative impact on profit.

Causes of Gap One

No direct interactions with customers: When people with the authority and responsibility for setting priorities do not fully understand customers' service expectations, they may trigger a chain of bad decisions and suboptimal resources allocations that result in perceptions of poor service quality. One example of displaced priorities stemming from an inaccurate understanding of customers' expectations is spending far too much money on buildings and appearance of a company's physical facilities when customers may be much more concerned with how convenient, conventional and functional the facilities are. Another example is illustrated by the management of Sears in the early 1990s, when the company failed to understand that the customers had changed there desires and modes of shopping. The company kept its traditional catalogue store long after customers had decided to take their business elsewhere. In the mid-1990s, Sears management rediscovered its customers, now defined primarily as women, and began once again to be profitable and satisfying to customers. The service providers see themselves as indifferent or superior to customers. This typically happens in government-run services such as railways or postal departments where they would not want to know what customer desires.

Unwillingness to ask customers about expectations: Service providers may think that they know what is best for their customers. This is the patronizing attitude towards the customers. In today's changing organizations, the authority to make adjustments in service delivery is delegated to empowered teams and front line people. For example, when AT&T asked its long-distance operators to improve their service to customers, the team identified key customer segments and conducted its own customer research to determine expectations. Gap one was closed without involving management as it is traditionally defined.

Unpreparedness to address the expectations: The service provider may be aware of the shortfalls but may be unprepared to address the issue in the mistaken belief that the customers may be tolerant or that the lapse is unlikely to loss of customer patronage. Another trend related to gap one involves current company strategies to retain customers and strengthen relationships with them. The term relationship marketing is used to describe this approach, which emphasizes strengthening the bonds with existing customers. When customers have strong relationships with their customers, gap 1 is less likely to occur.

Lack of market segmentation to understand the needs are such segment. Market segmentation is the grouping of customers sharing similar requirements, expectations and demographic or psychographic profiles. Segmentation is usually done to understand the needs of customers more elaborately or distinctly. While segmentation has been used by marketers for decades, it may be more critical today than any other time. Customers are no longer satisfied by homogenous products and services for the mass market; now, more than ever before, they seeking and buying services that fit their unique configuration of needs. If the needs are not precisely understood due to lack of segmentation, quality perception is likely to be poor.

Strategies for Reducing Gap One

Service firms have four strategies available to them to reduce the size of gap one. These strategies are: communicating with the customers, conducting marketing research, encouraging upward communication in the organization, and decreasing the number of layers of management. By talking to customers, management will learn what buyers expect in terms of service quality and how they feel about the service they received. Contact and communication between customers and management is common in small business because the owner is often the service operator.

Buyer may not always be honest in their communication with management of service firm. To ensure open, honest communication, service firm can use marketing research, which can either be performed by third parties or, in case of large cooperation, by the marketing department. To be effective, the marketing research much focus on service quality issues and consumer expectations of the service.

For firms where management is separated from the customer contact personnel, upward communication is vital in reducing the size of gap one. Service contact personnel must be encouraged to communicate with management in an open, non-threatening environment. To be effective, upward communication must be requested by top management. Ideas for improvement should not only be sought from service contact personnel, but employees should be rewarded for productive ideas.

As the layers of management increase, the chances of management having a correct understanding of what customer want in terms of service quality became more difficult. Many service firms, therefore, are seeking means to reduce the number of management layers. For much small business, service quality is the major issue in the selection of their telecommunications provider. According to Tony Parella, executive vice-president of Allegiance telecom of Dallas, "People buy from us because they don't necessarily feel appreciated by regional Bell carrier." The goal of Allegiance management is to provide customers with personalized service. To ensure management hears about customer concerns and to ensure Allegiance communicate effectively to customers, Allegiance has instituted a customer Bill of Rights and place a customer service manager in each branch. These actions have been a major step for Allegiance in reducing the size of gap one and ensuring a high level of customer satisfaction.

Formal and informal methods to capture information about customer expectations can be developed through market research. Techniques involving a variety of traditional research approaches must be used to stay close to the customer, among them customer visits, survey research, complaint systems, and customer panels. More innovative techniques such as quality function deployment, structured brainstorming, and service quality gap analysis are often needed.

Many marketers are achieving success with niche marketing – targeting segments of customers and developing services and strategies that fit their needs better than other companies' offerings. Other marketers are embracing the concept of mass customization – creating services for a large group of customers that can be customized or appear to be customized through technological innovations.

Technology affords companies the ability to acquire and integrate vast quantities of data on customers that can be used to build relationships. Frequent flyer travel programmes conducted by airlines, car rental companies, and hotels are among the most familiar programmes of this type. Relationship marketing is distinct from transactional marketing, the term used to describe the more conventional emphasis on acquiring new customer rather than on retaining them. When companies focus too much on attracting new customers, they may fail to understand the changing needs and expectations of their current customers.

GAP TWO: NOT SELECTING THE RIGHT SERVICE DESIGNS STANDARDS

Accurate perceptions of customers' expectations are necessary, but not sufficient, for delivering superior quality service. Another prerequisite is the presence of service designs and performance standards that reflect those accurate perceptions. A recurring theme in service companies is the difficulty executives, managers, and other policy-setters experience in translating their understanding of customers' expectations into service quality specifications.

Gap 2 is the difference between the company understanding of customer expectations and development of customer driven service designs and standards. Customer driven standards are different from the conventional performance standards the most services company establish in that they are based on pivotal customer requirements that are visible to and are measured by customers. They are operation standards set to correspond to customer expectations and priorities rather than to company concerns such as productivity or efficiency.

Example: In the billing division in debit cards, companies charge a hefty interest rate on outstanding amounts. They however fail to check with the department that handles inflow of payments and updating of outstanding amounts. Often, a cheque is sent in on the due date and a statement with the finance charge sent out on the same date. The customer is hopping mad as he has paid up on due date, the debit card company claims that interest starts ticking on due date. Everyone has a valid reason, but the situation is a mess.

In many of these cases, one observes a reluctance to tackle the problem head-on and a lack of commitment to providing quality service. While customer-contact personnel are key to providing quality service, leadership plays a pivotal role in ensuring that quality standards are in place and adhered to.

Causes of Gap Two

Absence of customer-driven standards of service quality: The standards for quality improvement or planning should be clearly those which are desired by the customers rather than those set up by only the service provider. Thus, the involvement of the end user/customer in the goal setting process is crucial to its success.

Absence of formal quality control goals: It is not enough to say that quantification is not possible and, therefore, formal goals cannot be set for services delivery. Even subjective assessment may be vital in setting the standards.

Vague or undefined service design: The service design may have been running traditionally for a number of years without any alterations, or it may have been borrowed from some other concept. Defining the service would go a long way towards determining the standards of customer satisfaction. Poor service design may also be a result of failure to connect service design to service positioning.

Resource constraints: A service firm may understand and even want to deliver services desired by the customers but is unable to because of resource constraints. Example, a local air-conditioner dealer knows that customers want quick repairs. However, demand for both services in springs and early summer will exceed the firm's capacity to provide the service. The number of technician available to repair AC is limited and the number of hours they can work is limited. Because of personnel constraints, these services cannot meet customer expectations for quick service during the peak demand time.

Market conditions: The most competitive market condition impacting this gap is known as competitive parity, a situation where competitors produce almost identical quality goods and services. To prevent a competitor from capturing additional market share, companies often match a competitors offering. In some cases, firms translate customer expectations into matching competitive offerings rather than meeting the wants of their customers. If this is done, there will be a gap between what firms know customer expect and service pacifications, or what the firm actually provides. For example, an airline may know that passengers want more leg room in the airplane but they do not translate this in service specification.

They do not put the seats further apart since other airlines are not doing it and to do so would reduce the potential passengers load. A second market condition affecting gap two is monopoly markets such as cable television services, utilities, and basic telephone services. Each operates with a virtual monopoly with no competitors. These firms may understand certain needs and expectations of their patrons but may not translate them to service specifications unless required to do so by a government agency supervising them.

Their rationale for permitting this situation may be that the cost of meeting customer expectations is higher than the additional revenues that could be generated if the change were made.

Management Indifference: Management may talk about providing high quality service, but in actual practice they may offer only the minimum level of service that will suffice. The goal is not to provide customer satisfaction but to avoid customer dissatisfaction. In the short run, this philosophy may succeed and may even generate greater revenues because more customers can be served. But in the long run, customers will switch to competitors who provide better service. Management complacency is a problem in many corporate owned service facilities because of the pressure to generate short-term profits.

Strategies for Reducing Gap Two

To reduce the size of gap two, service firms must have the commitment of top management. Many mission statements have references to the firm being committed to providing customers with high level of service quality. However, in actual practice, firms often emphasize on cost reduction, gross sales, and net profit rather than a high level of quality. There are two reasons for the discrepancy between mission statements and actual practice.

First is the difficulty of measuring service and the ease of measuring costs, sales and profit. Second the current reward system is often based on non-service criteria. Most managers are promoted and rewarded for generating greater sales, increasing net profits, reducing costs, not for enhancing service quality.

If service firms are going to get serious about providing high quality service, they must start with a commitment by management. Not only must management be committed to providing a high level of service, they must also set an example for their employees. Managers who talk service but fail to deliver an example of good service are not committed.

Reduction of this gap requires setting service quality goals. These goals must be set with the customer, the service contact provider and management in mind. Customer contact employees must understand management's perspective and the need to generate a profit. In exchange, management must understand what is possible and what is not in terms of operations. Service contact personnel can provide their supervisors with valuable input into the best process for achieving service quality goals.

To be effective, the goals must be customer oriented. The service quality standards must be what customers want and desire. Including in the goal setting process is advantageous to both management and service contact personnel. Task standardization will also reduce the size of gap two. Standardization can be achieved through hard technology (substituting machines or computers for people) or soft technology (improving work methods). Both methods are designed to standardize the operation and provide a uniform delivery of the service to customers, reducing the gap between management perception of consumer expectations, and the translation of those expectations into service quality specifications.

Example: Hard technology can be used to completely replace the human provider as in case of ATMs or it could be used to improve the consistency of service, as in the case of the diagnostic computer used by automechanics and the automatic scrubbing machines used by cleaning the service.

Example: The standardized employee training procedure used by McDonalds, the prepackaged tours offered by many travel agencies, and the buffet used by Pizza Hut. By standardizing the training McDonalds strives to ensure that all employees use the same procedure in preparing food for their customers. No matter where one buys a McDonalds hamburger, it will look and taste the same. The same concept applies to prepackaged tours offered by travel agencies and a lunch buffet offered by Pizza Hut.

Closing gap two by demonstrating strong leadership commitment and by setting customers' performance standards—has a powerful positive impact on closing the customer gap. Leadership plays a pivotal role in providing service excellence. Strategic measurement systems are also necessary to close this gap. While company measurement has historically been the bailiwick of finance and accounting, management strategies now call for the addition of key marketing indicators in the overall measurement programme. To achieve competitive superiority in an era when satisfying a customer is a priority, companies need measurement systems that incorporate and align measures of customer perceptions and satisfaction with pivotal operational and performance indicators. Sam Walton of Wal-Mart is hailed as a service leader worldwide. His service philosophy to spur on his people and organization is as follows:

- Realize that customer service is the key.
- Design for comfort and convenience.
- Provide one-stop shopping.
- Customize
- Invert the organizational chart so that the customer is on the top and the management is at the bottom.
- Empower the sales staff.
- Provide servant leadership – Wal-Mart's managers are servants to the needs of their employees and customers.
- Recognize that the customer is always right.

While Sam Walton's philosophy may appear simplistic, it was his adherence to these very principles that led to the soaring growth of Wal-Mart in the 1990s, when others were retrenching and cutting down on costs.

GAP THREE: NOT DELIVERING TO SERVICE STANDARDS

Gap three is the discrepancy between developments of customer driven service standards and actual service performance by company employees. Even when guidelines exist for performing services well and treating customers correctly, high quality service performance is not a certainty. Standards must be backed by appropriate resources (people, systems, technology) and also must be supported to be effective—that is, employees must be measured and compensated on the basis of performance along those standards. Thus, even when standards accurately reflect customers' expectations, if the company fails to provide support for them—if it does not facilitate, encourage, and require their achievement—standards do no good. When the level of service delivery performance falls short of the standards, it falls short of what customers expect as well. Narrowing gap 3, by ensuring that all the resources needed to achieve the standards are in place reduce the gap.

Another problem associated with the bridging of provider gap 3 is that of dealing with franchisees, agents, retailers and brokers. Because quality in service occurs at the moment of truth, i.e., at the point of interaction between the service provider and the customer, control over the service encounter by the company is crucial, yet it is rarely possible.

When one NIIT franchisee falls short of set educational standards, it reflects on the company as a whole. When food at one outlet of Birdy's, McDonalds or Croissants, etc. is below quality standards, the image of the entire chain is tarnished. For this, the firm needs to develop systems to either control or motivate these intermediaries to meet company goals.

Primary causes of this gap are variable and inseparable nature of services. Because most services are performed by people, the quality of service is highly dependent upon well the service provider performs his or her job. If the service contact personnel provide services as specified, customers are usually satisfied and their expectations are met, if employees do not provide the service as specified in the service specifications, customer expectations will not be met and customers will be dissatisfied.

Causes of Gap Three

- Deficiencies in human resources policies.
- Ineffective recruitment: The front-end employees involved in services delivery require certain qualities that enable them to relate to and deal with customers. They require training to achieve this.
- Role ambiguity and role conflict: These include employees who do not clearly understand the role they are to play in the company, employees who feel in conflict between customers and company management, the wrong employees.
- Poor employee-technology job fit
- Inappropriate evaluation and compensation systems
- Lack of empowerment, perceived control, and teamwork.
- These factors all relate to the company's human resource function, involving internal practices such as recruitment, training, feedback, job design, motivation, and organizational structure.
- Failure to match supply and demand: When demand for a particular service exceeds the supply capacity, the general tendency is to shorten the process of the service delivery to speed up the process. Usually, in this case the quality of the service delivered deteriorates.
- Failure to smooth peaks and valleys of demand
- Inappropriate customer mix
- Over reliance on price to smooth demand

- Customers not fulfilling roles: The customer is as much involved in the process of services delivery as the service provider. Therefore, training the customer to receive the service to derive maximum benefit is essentials.
- Customers lacking knowledge of their roles and responsibilities.
- Customers negatively impacting each other
- Lack of training to the franchisee's staff: Whenever service is provided by a franchisee in lieu of the service provider, the front-end employees of the franchisee require elaborate training to be able to cope with the customer demands in a standardized and pre-determined manner. Most service companies face and even more formidable task: attaining service excellence and consistency in the presence of intermediaries who represent them, interact with their customers, and yet are not under their direct control. Among the intermediaries that play a central role in service delivery are retailers, franchisees and dealers.

Strategies for Reducing Gap Three

A common characteristic of successful service companies is teamwork. A feeling of teamwork is created when employees see other employees and management as key members of the team. The lowest-level employee must feel that management; from their immediate supervisor to the CEO of the company, cares about them and that they are a critical part of the firm's success. There must be a spirit of cooperation, not competition, among employees. All of this is achieved when every employee is involved in the company and committed to providing a high level of service to customers, to the company, and to other employees. For instance, Southwest Airlines is often cited as a service provider with excellent teamwork.

If employees are to provide the services according to the job specifications, there must be a fit between employee skills and job requirements. Firms must hire individuals who have the ability to perform the job. Once hired, management must be sure each employee has to do the tasks according the company's procedures. Because of technology, many service firms are using machines, tools, and computers to assist service workers in their job. To perform their job according to company standards, service employees must have the proper equipment. The equipment needs to be in good condition and the employees must have the knowledge and training to properly use the technology to enhance the quality of their work.

To diagnose problems with newer automobiles, computerized diagnostic equipment is essential. The quality of diagnosis is dependent upon the quality and condition of the equipment and the ability of the service technician to operate it. In cleaning carpets in homes and offices, the operator of the equipment can perform a good job only if the shampoo machine is running properly and he or she has the ability to operate it.

An important factor in reducing gap 3 is the concept of perceived employee control. When employees are allowed some flexibility and control in the service process, morale is enhanced, and there is a greater desire to perform the service properly. Flexibility and control also allow service employees to modify the process to meet the particular needs and desires of customers. In addition, by having control of the service encounter, the outcome of the service will become more predictable.

The supervisory control system will have an impact on the size of gap 3. If service employees are encouraged and rewarded for meeting job specifications, the likelihood of employees doing the job according to the specifications increases. However, supervisors often tell employees to follow the correct job specifications but reward or punish employees on other criteria, which is called role conflict. For example, employees may be evaluated by their supervisors on such criteria as a balanced cash register for a bank teller, the number of automobiles repaired by a mechanic, and the amount of time spent cleaning a particular office by a janitor.

When this occurs, employees will shortcut the specifications to improve whatever criteria are used by their supervisors in their evaluations, often neglecting other service specifications. Role conflict is inherent in many service contact positions. How this role conflict is handled will have an impact on how closely the service delivered matches the service specified. The primary conflict faced by service contact personnel is between expectations of customers and expectation of management. This conflict is increased when employees are not given flexibility to meet the needs of customers, when employees have little control over how the service is to be performed, the amount of paper work necessary to carry out the service, and the number of other employees a service provider must contact or use in the process of performing the service.

To reduce role conflict, management should allow service contact personnel adequate flexibility to meet customer needs. Employees need to have some control over the service encounter because the greater the control, the less role conflict experienced. Control and flexibility mean service employees will not have to go to other employees and managers with questions and for permission to modify the service to meet a customers' unique request. It is responsibility of the management to reduce the amount of conflict faced by their service employees. Not only does reducing role conflict aid service employers in meeting the needs of customers but it will increase job satisfaction, job morale and length of employment.

Role ambiguity refers to employees' lack of information or understanding of their job and job requirements. As role ambiguity increases job satisfaction decreases. It also becomes difficult for employees to perform the necessary job specifications if they lack an understanding of what these specifications are.

Management often mistakenly assumes employees understand their job when, in fact, service contact personnel do not have clear understanding of goals and expectations. Although they have been told what to do, they may not have been told how the service is to be performed. To reduce role ambiguity, service firms must do the following:

- Provide frequent and clear downward communication from management on what is expected and how the service is to be performed.
- Provide employees with constructive feedback to help them understand how the service is to be performed and what management expects.
- Provide employees with product and service knowledge so they can perform their jobs better.
- Train and retrain employees in the proper method of performing the service.
- Train service contact personnel to communicate effectively with customers, with supervisors, and with other employees.

GAP FOUR: MISMATCH BETWEEN PROMISES AND PERFORMANCE

Gap four is the difference between the service delivered to customers and the external communications made about the service. Promises are made to consumers by a firm's advertising, sales promotions, and sales staff. These promises may be explicitly stated or they may be implied. If the firm does not provide the service that is promised, there is a gap between what customers expect and the service received.

As consumer expectations for a service increase, the profitability of patronizing the firm will also increase. To increase patronage, firms are tempted to make promises that may be difficult or even impossible to deliver. Communication through these channels tends to raise customer expectations and set certain standards to assess the service in the minds of customers. Any discrepancy between promised and actual service tends to broaden the customer gap. A recent advertisement by a leading pizza chain promised one free pizza with a specified order. On calling in for the offer, one found that the small print indicated that this offer was valid only at the counter and not on home delivery orders. Would the outlet have received so many calls if they had indicated this in bold type? While on the subject of pizzas, one wonders if Domino's manages to keep its promise of delivering anywhere in 30 minutes – especially in Mumbai traffic. If not, they must be making heavy losses on free pizzas.

Causes of Gap Four

Ineffective management of customer expectation: Failure to manage customer expectations through all forms of communication: addition unduly elevating expectations through exaggerated claims, there are other, less obvious ways in which external communications influence customers' service quality assessments. Customers are not always aware of everything done behind the scenes to serve them well. One bank executive indicated that custom were unaware of the bank's behind-the-counter, on-line teller terminals, which would translate into visible effects on customer service. By neglecting to inform customers of such behind-the-scenes efforts, the bank was foregoing an opportunity to favourably influence service perceptions.

Failure to educate customers adequately: In the anxiety to strike a deal or mar the service, sales personnel promise more than what they can ever deliver. Such communication can be either formal or informal. Usually, customers set the service expectations according to such delivery and price quotations.

Overpromising in advertising: During the marketing phase, the sales force may beyond the original script to strike the deal.

Overpromising in personnel selling: While customers may be lost to competition due to under promising, they may be lost due to overpromising as well.

Inadequate horizontal communications: Insufficient communication between sales and operations: If during the person selling phase a commitment was made to strike the deal, it is essential to convey this message to the other people in the organization, especially the production team, failing which, they may not be able to keep up with this additional concede demand.

Pricing of services: In packaged goods many customers possess enough price knowledge before purchase to be able to judge whether a price is fair or in line with competition. With services customers often have no internal reference point for prices before purchase and consumption. Pricing strategies such as discounting, "everyday prices" and couponing obviously need to be different in services in cases where the customers have no sense of the price to start with! Techniques for developing prices for services are more complicated than those for pricing of tangible goods.

Strategies for Reducing Gap Four

To reduce the size of gap four, service firms must address two issues: horizontal communications and propensity to over promise. Service contact personnel should have input in the firm's advertising and promotional to ensure that messages conveyed to the prospective customers can be operationally performed. The reverse is also true; service personnel should be informed prior to an advertising or promotional campaign. In service organizations with field sales representatives, there must be communication between the salespeople and the personnel performing the service. Salespeople will often make promises to prospective customers to gain contacts. If promises are made, the operations department needs to be aware of it so they can ensure the promises will be delivered.

The tendency to over promise increases with pressure to achieve greater profits or to meet competitive claims. In both cases, severe damage to the firm's image can occur since it is unlikely the firm can perform the service as promised. Customers' service perceptions may also be enhanced if the company educates them to be better users of the service. Service companies frequently fail to capitalize on opportunities to improve customers' perceptions. As on bank executive observed, "We don't teach our customers how to use us well and why we do the things we do." Effectively coordinating actual service delivery with external communications therefore narrows provider gap 4 and favourably affects the customer gap as well.

Another function that must be involved in communication is human resources. For employees to deliver excellent customer service, firms must serve the employees through training, motivation, compensation and recognition to have a powerful impact on the quality of service the employees deliver.

External communications–whether from advertising, pricing or the tangibles associated with the service – can create a larger customer gap by raising expectations about service delivery. In addition to improving service delivery, companies must also manage all communications to customers so that inflated promises do not lead to higher expectations.

CASE: TAJ MAHAL

"Archetypal Drives" of a customer who visits Taj Mahal: The study was of the visitors including spouse, family, and group of friends or relatives. The primary drives of the tourist to this place are the beauty of the place and historical significance. The facilities sought in the vicinity of the Taj Mahal and basic amenities like safe drinking water, clean toilets, small grocers, cafeterias and milk. The sample interviewed was of the opinion that the Taj Mahal bedecked in moonlight was a picture of delight, and should not be missed. However, for those who could not make it on that crucial night of the month, similar creations could be made through a light and sound show. On the full moon night some cultural events could also be planned and offered. Since the main charm in visiting the city of Agra was the Taj Mahal, the tourists were keen on knowing the timings and approach to the spot and any rules that govern visiting this wonder of the world.

External Communication Content on Taj Mahal: The information provided on the government websites on Taj Mahal is not indicative of the facilities sought by the tourists. On fundamental information, the prevailing basic amenities in the vicinity of Taj Mahal are not listed, once in Agra how to reach Taj Mahal is not known. The visiting hours and weekly offs, if any are not notified. Also people travelling with families must be provided with information on basic amenities in and around the Taj Mahal.

For the bespoke customer, the historical significance, this is a selling point for Taj Mahal is not adequately flaunted. There is neither imagery nor mystic incorporated in the communication content. Taj Mahal bedecked in moonlight, a much sought after experience is also not adequately represented. Though there is a mention of the Taj's beauty on a full moon night but there is no mention of when the full moon is expected in the next few months. Tourist could be provided with calendar data of full moon nights along with associated special events. There could be plans for special shows on full moon night to make experience more memorable. There is no mention of any light and sound show on any day. Taj Mahal is one of the wonders of the world, hence providing conservation guidelines for tourists in the communication content is an expectation.

MEASURING SERVICE QUALITY

When evaluating service quality, consumers examine five dimensions: tangibles, reliability, responsiveness, assurance and empathy.

Using SERVQUAL to Measure Service Quality

The SERVQUAL instrument was based on the premise that service quality is the difference between customers' expectations and their evaluation of the service they received. The first part of the questionnaire asks customers to indicate the level of service they would expect from a firm in a particular industry. The second part of the questionnaire asks customers to evaluate the service performed by a specific service firm. Gap theory is the method for calculating service quality that involves subtracting a customer's perceived level of service received from what was expected.

SERVQUAL uses 21 questions to measure the five dimensions of tangibles, reliability, responsiveness, assurance and empathy. Through SERVQUAL, firms can measure customers' evaluations of their service performance. For example, if customers consistently give firm low scores for one dimension, such as reliability, then the firm's management can take steps to improve that particular dimension of their service offering.

Problems with SERVQUAL

Although SERVQUAL is an excellent instrument for measuring service quality, managers must be aware of potential problems with the instrument, as well as with the gap theory methodology on which it is based. An understanding of these problems may prevent service companies from misinterpreting the results and developing inappropriate marketing plans.

The SERVQUAL instrument has three potential problems. First, SERVQUAL measures customers' expectations of the ideal firm in a particular service industry. This may or may not be relevant to the capabilities of a particular service firm or the set of service firms available to a consumer. For example, consumers may indicate that physicians should provide their services at the time they promised. Seldom do patients see the doctor at the scheduled time. No one likes waiting after their appointment time, yet, because of excess demand, patients will continue to wait.

The second problem with SERVQUAL is its generic nature. Since it's not industry specific, it does not measure variables that may be important for a particular industry. For example, in the airline business, on-time arrival is a very important dimension to travellers, but SERVQUAL does not measure travellers' perceptions of this variable.

The third problem with problem with SERVQUAL deals with the gap theory methodology used for measuring the level of service quality. Measuring consumer expectations after a service has been provided will bias consumers' responses. If customers had a positive experience at Blockbuster, they will tend to report lower scores for their expectations, so there is a measurable gap between what they expected and the actual service they received.

Apart from conducting customer surveys like the one using SERVQUAL as described above, some of the other methods which service organizations use to obtain information about their service quality are briefly explained below:

(a) ***Transaction Surveys:*** This type of research involves tracking the information about one or all of the key service encounters with the customer. These surveys are also called 'trailer calls' or 'post transaction surveys'. This is usually done with the help of a small questionnaire immediately

after a service transaction has taken place, e.g., survey of airlines passengers while disembarking or that of a hotel guest while checking out. These surveys also provide the management a tool for monitoring the performance of individual service contact personnel.

(b) ***Complaint Solicitation and Analysis:*** Customers tend to voice their dissatisfaction through complaints. An analysis of the complaints can help in identifying quality failure points. We will discuss the issue of complaint management in detail in the last unit of this block.

(c) ***Mystery Shopping:*** In this method outside research companies are used by the service organization that sends people posing as customers in order to judge the service quality. The mystery shopper is unknown to the service provider. This is a popular method in the retail sector. Mystery shopping, also termed as Ghost Shopping, can be a very effective way of reinforcing service quality standards.

(d) ***Asking Customers:*** This involves asking customers directly what they would like to be done to increase the quality of service and their satisfaction. This can be very effective in business-to-business situation.

This primarily concerns with the expectation aspect. A slight variation of this, which includes perceptions about the service quality as well, is to form customer panels, i.e., ongoing groups of customers who are assembled to provide perceptions about a service over a period of time.

(e) ***Intermediary Research:*** This form of research is useful in services where intermediaries form an important part of the service delivery process and have a major direct contact with customers. In such situation intermediaries can provide valuable feedback to the service firm regarding quality of service as perceived by the customers.

Correct Use of Gap Theory

Managers can use the gap theory methodology for measuring service quality performance if precautions are taken to reduce the problems just discussed. If SERVQUAL is used, the instrument should be modified to apply to the specific industry for which it is being used. Additional variables should be added that are relevant and important to customers. When interpreting the results, managers must remember that respondents are comparing their firm with the ideal firm in the industry. To prevent biases from interfering with the gap scores, consumer expectations should be measured prior to the service and service perceptions after the service. Because consumers are affected by advertising and word-of-mouth communications, the time between measuring expectations and measuring the quality of service received should be relatively close.

QUALITY AND SATISFACTION

A review of the literature will reveal that the terms 'quality' and 'satisfaction' are quite often used interchangeably. While both concepts are related and appear to be merging, there are still gaps in the understanding of the two constructs, their relationship to each other and their antecedents and consequences. A distinction has often been made between the two constructs. According to Cronin and Taylor, 'this distinction is important to both managers and researches alike, because service providers need to know whether their objective should be to have consumers who are satisfied with their performance or to deliver the maximum level of perceived service quality.' Oliver takes the view that satisfaction is 'the emotional reaction following a disconfirmation experience'. Getty and Thompson defined satisfaction as a 'summary psychological state experienced by the consumer when confirmed or disconfirmed expectations exist with respect to a specific service transaction or experience'. Rust and Oliver suggested that customer satisfaction or dissatisfaction – a 'cognitive or affective reaction' – emerges as a response to a single or prolonged set of service encounters.

Satisfaction is a 'post consumption' experience which compares perceived quality with expected quality, whereas service quality refers to a global evaluation of a firm's service delivery system. Perceived quality, on the other hand, may be viewed as a global attitudinal judgment associated with the superiority of the service experience over time. Not surprisingly there has been considerable debate concerning the nature of the relationship between the constructs of satisfaction and quality. While the majority of research suggests that service quality is a vital antecedent to customer satisfaction there is now strong evidence to suggest that satisfaction must be a vital antecedent of service quality. Regardless of which view is taken, the relationship between satisfaction and service quality is strong when examined from either direction.

Satisfaction affects assessments of service quality and assessment of service quality affects satisfaction. In turn, both are vital in helping buyers develop their future purchase intention.

So, conclusion is that the key difference between the two constructs is that quality relates to managerial delivery of the service, while satisfaction reflects customers' experiences with that service. They argued that quality improvements that are not based on customer needs will not lead to improved customer satisfaction.

WHY WAL-MART IS SUCCESSFUL?

- Wal-Mart is committed to improving operations, lowering costs and improving customer service. But the key to retailer Wal-Mart's success is its ability to drive costs out of its supply chain and manage it efficiently.
- The Wal-Mart business model would fail instantly without its advanced technology (Wal-Mart has the largest IT systems of any private company in the world) and supply chain (Wal-Mart has made significant investments in supply chain management).

Customer Relation

- Wal-Mart's suppliers both large and small either break even or make profit supplying at Wal-Mart's stores. But the real winners are Wal-Mart's customers who save thousands of dollars buying at low prices.
- Nearly two million employees at Wal-Mart focus on cost, customers and continuous improvement on a daily basis.

JIT Distribution Approach

- Every Wal-Mart store operates like a small company. Store managers are trained to manage one store at a time, one department at a time, and one customer at a time.
- Wal-Mart has implemented advanced logistics solutions like **RFID (radio frequency identification)** RFID solutions help maintain lower costs, identify out-of-stocks and increase sales.

Part-D: Service Strategy

ACTIVITIES OF SERVICE STRATEGY

- Identify market and define your target area: Decide what services you want to offer and who can be the potential customers.
- Develop your service offerings: Build on/improve your services.
- Develop strategic assets: Develop new services.
- Help clarify the relationships between different services, processes, strategies, etc.

STRATEGIES FOR MATCHING CAPACITY AND DEMAND

Managers can use a wide variety of strategies for matching capacity and demand. This requires a clear understanding of demand patterns as well as the organization's capacity constraints. The strategies to be adopted can be broadly divided into two categories:

(1) Changing demand to fit supply (capacity) – marketing mix strategies

(2) Changing supply (capacity) to fit demand – input scheduling strategies

Let us discuss the above two strategies in detail.

(1) Strategies for Managing Demand

The organization should determine the optimum level of demand for its given capacity. Once this has been determined, it can vary its marketing mix elements of product, price, place and promotion to change demand in line with the capacity.

(a) Product: As a service provider you can alter the service offering to even the demand. The changes in service offering may be seasonal or based on days of the week or time of the day depending on the nature of demand fluctuations. A hotel, for example, may focus on weekend family entertainment and recreation package to cope up with low demand from business executives during weekends. A management institute may offer more management development programmes during the vacation period of its regular management programme students. However, as marketers you must ensure that by offering different types of services the image or positioning of the service firm is not diluted or confused. Increasing demand during slack period doesn't mean that you should take business from any segment that is available.

(b) Pricing: The demand curve suggests that quantity of product demanded varies with the price. Many service marketers reduce price during the periods of low demand to increase the demand. Airlines offer low fares during odd hours like late night flights, movie theatres offer a lower price ticket for the morning show, hotels offer large discounts during off seasons and also higher than normal prices during say Christmas or New year, restaurants and many retail outlets offer happy hours wherein discounts are offered. Using price as an effective tool for managing demand would require a proper understanding of the demand curve – its shape, slope, etc.

Also, you should appreciate the existence of different demand curves for different segments during the same time period. As marketers you may also face an additional challenge when multiple segments are served at the same time and these segments have paid different prices. This requires putting in certain usage conditions (for example, for availing low priced fares in airlines customers have to book in advance and there are higher cancellation charges) and/or providing value enhancement to higher paying customers.

(c) Place (Distribution): Many service firms modify their time and place of delivery as a strategy to match demand and capacity. Bank may change its timings on specific days or during specific period, finance companies use mobile vans for distribution and collection of forms, hospitals like Apollo have created satellite clinics to deal with routine consultations, tests and medical services.

(d) Promotion: You can also shift the demand by properly communicating with your customers. The customers should be made aware of the peak timings of the demand and also the benefits they can get in availing the service during non-peak timings. They should also be properly informed about changes in product, pricing and distribution. This can be done by putting signages at the service outlets (like banks) or advertising. Service firms can also use sales promotion to manage demand. Many airlines offer free ticket for companion in the business class, some business hotels offer free stay for spouse during the weekend stay. Proper promotional strategy can help the service organization in shifting demand from high to low period as well as stimulating demand during low periods.

(2) Strategies for Managing Capacity

Managing capacity involves changes in different components of the resources of a_firm like people, facilities, equipment, time, etc. By making changes in these components, you can achieve a better match between demand and capacity.

(a) Using Part-time Employees: During periods of peak demand, service firm may hire additional part-time employees. This helps in increasing capacity as well as reducing costs. However, issues like attitude of part time employees, training concerns, higher turnover, etc. have to be properly addressed.

(b) Employees Working Overtime: Some of the concerns raised above regarding part time employees can be eliminated by having employees work over time. However, working for longer hours may have adverse impact on service quality and also involves higher costs as overtime charges are generally at higher rates.

(c) Cross Training Employees: Cross training of employees results in a flexible capacity, wherein employees can perform several different jobs. Southwest Airlines strongly believes in this philosophy. The same employee may move from ticketing to gate counters. This helps in avoiding underutilization of resources and also increasing the efficiency of the employees.

(d) Scheduling: During peak demand periods people, facilities, and equipment are used at full capacity. However, facilities and equipments also require proper maintenance. This can be scheduled during periods of low demand. Similarly, for human resources, off-peak periods can be used for training purposes as well as for granting vacations.

In addition to the above, service firms can also meaningfully manage its capacity by increasing customer participation (customers can be used as productive resources e.g. self-service in restaurants), outsourcing, modifying the capacity (e.g., reconfiguring hotel rooms), renting facilities or equipments, and taking a subcontract work.

The strategies discussed above for managing demand and capacity have been summarized in Table 1.4 on the next page.

Table 1.4 Managing demand and supply.

	High Demand/Slack Supply	*Slack Demand/Over Supply*
Managing Demand (Changing demand to fit capacity)	• Educate customers to curtain usage during peak periods (through signages or advertising) • Offer incentives for usage during non-peak periods • Change full price–no discounts or premium pricing • Take care of regular customers first	• Modify service offerings • Offer discounts, sales promotion schemes • Modify hours of operations • Bring service to the customers
Managing Capacity (Changing capacity to match demand)	• Hire part-time employees • Keep employees overtime • Cross train employees • Outsource, rent facilities/equipment	• Schedule training of employees • Maintenance,repairs, renovations • Schedule employee vacations • Take on subcontract work

CUSTOMER RETENTION

Services marketers understand that having customers, not merely acquiring customers is crucial for service companies. There is a direct link between customer retention over a period of time and profitability and growth. Further, customer retention to a great extent depends on service quality and customer satisfaction. It also depends on the ability of the firms to encourage customers to complain and then recover when things go wrong. Complaints are a natural part of any service activity as mistakes are an unavoidable feature of all human endeavour and thus also of service delivery. Service recovery is the process of putting things right after something goes wrong in service delivery.

Service marketing literature also suggests that offering well-designed service guarantees help in attracting and retaining customers. This unit begins with a discussion on the importance of retaining customers for service firms. The unit further explains the details of a complaint management system and service recovery process. The last part of the unit deals with service guarantees.

Importance of Customer Retention

The importance of retaining customers should be properly understood by the services marketers. It is the cornerstone of a successful service. Generally, the longer a customer stays with a company the more that customer is worth. It influences employee and supplier loyalty as well, as people like to work for companies where customers are loyal. It also produces profits that influence shareholder loyalty. In fact, this all results in a positive spiral. Employee retention and loyalty results in high quality of services which leads to customer satisfaction and delight which makes the customer stay with the organization and increases its profitability which in turn brings employee loyalty. This sequence is shown diagrammatically in the Figure 1.11.

Why are customers more profitable for service firms over period of time? There are a number of reasons for this. To begin with, to acquire a customer a company incurs promotional costs like advertising, sales promotion, personal selling, etc. It is said that it costs five times more to attract a new customer then retaining one. The operating costs decrease when a customer stays.

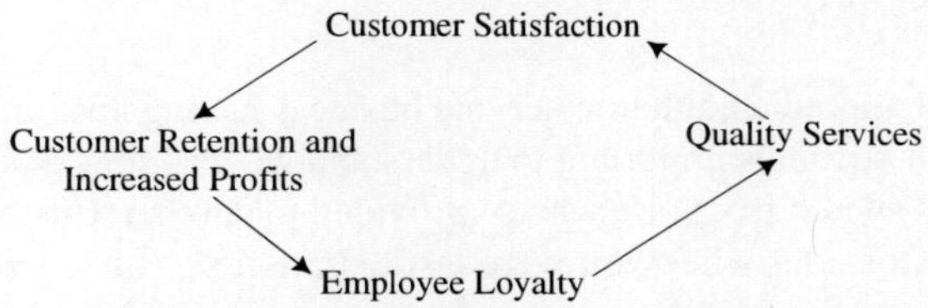

Fig. 1.11 Customer retention and service quality.
Source: Zeithaml and Bitner, Services Marketing, Tata McGraw-Hill, 2nd edn. 2000, p. 143

Services being rich in experience and credence qualities, it takes some time for customers to get accustomed to it and once they are used to the service and are satisfied with a service provider, they tend to purchase more over a period of time. As they remain satisfied with a service provider they will spread a positive word of mouth, which is extremely effective in case of services for attracting new customers. Longer the customer stays with an organization, more the organization knows about him, which enables it to offer customized services which make it difficult for the customer to defect. This may even provide opportunities to the organization to charge price premium by offering individualized services which may be difficult for the competitors to offer.

Indian service companies are increasingly recognizing the importance of retaining existing customers. "We believe that if we are able to satisfy existing customers; it will enable us to gain new customers through word-of-mouth", says ICICI Bank General Manager (Business World, 4 Nov. 2002). Considering the importance of retaining customers in service business, Reichheld & Sasser coined a term 'Zero defection'. They highlighted that companies can boost profits by almost 100% by retaining just 5% more of their customers. In their path breaking article "Zero Deflections: Quality comes to services" (Harvard Business Review, Sept. – Oct., 1990) they conclude that "Just as the quality revolution in manufacturing had a profound impact on the competitiveness of companies, the quality revolution in services will create a new set of winners and losers. The winners will be those who lead the way in managing towards zero defection". You should appreciate as services marketers that when you lose a single customer you do not lose a single order but a lifetime opportunity of profitability with that individual. You must therefore understand the lifetime value of a customer. Consider a simple example of a telephone company. For example, if on an average customer pays Rs. 500 a month and stays with the company for 20 years, his average lifetime value for the company will be Rs. 500 × 12 × 20 = Rs. 1,20,000. Further, if by a positive word-of-mouth, he brings just one more customer to the organization his value to the organization doubles. Therefore, it is important for all the employees within an organization to understand the lifetime value of their customers. Once they understand it, they will treat the customer accordingly and will focus on building relationship with the very people who keep them in business.

The following is an interesting case of retaining customers:

Southwest Airlines is amongst the most profitable US airlines and has made profits all through its existence. It is well known in the industry for its service quality and customer focus. As part of its effort to keep employees informed, Southwest Airlines communicates the importance of every single customer by educating employees about how many customers the company actually need to make a profit. By demonstrating to employees how just a few people can make the critical difference, the company encourages them to think about how their individual behaviours influence customer service.

CUSTOMER SWITCHING

By now, you will have well appreciated that in service business having customers, not merely acquiring them is crucial. Therefore, it becomes important to understand what actions of service companies or their employees make customers switch from one service provided to another. Customers leave a provider for a wide variety of reasons. Consider when you were last dissatisfied with a service provider or changed a service provider. What were the specific reasons for your reaction? Was it because of perception of poor quality or failure of a service encounter? Susan Keavenly identified following reasons for customer switching in service industries.

(a) Pricing (high price, price increase, unfair pricing, deceptive pricing)
(b) Inconvenience (location/hours, wait for appointment, wait for service)
(c) Core service failure (service mistakes, billing errors)
(d) Service encounters failures (uncaring, impolite, unresponsive, and unknowledgeable)
(e) Response to service failures (negative response, no response, reluctant response)
(f) Competition (found better service)
(g) Ethical problem (cheating, unsafe)
(h) Involuntary switching (customer moved, provider closed)

An important aspect of the above to be understood by you is that six of the eight service switching factors are controllable from a service organization's point of view. Some of the aspects to be examined and action be taken to stop customer switching would include philosophy to deliver a technically correct service every time. However, in case something goes wrong there should be strategies in place for effective service recovery. We will discuss this aspect in detail in subsequent section. In order to reduce inconvenience the organization should have effective queue management, waiting line strategies and strategies for management of demand and capacity.

Customer defection caused by unsatisfactory service encounters – employee customer interactions can be reduced by proper training of employees, listening to customers and keeping the customers informed.

LOYALTY PROGRAMMES

Loyalty programmes are often used in service industries like cellular companies, airlines, hotels, credit card companies, retail outlets, etc. in order to build customer loyalty. They aim at locking on the consumer by rewarding him for patronizing a particular service for a period of time. In fact, number of similar terms like relationship marketing programme, frequency programme, continuity programme, points programme and loyalty programme are often used interchangeably. One of the most visible forms of loyalty programmes is the frequent flyer schemes offered by airlines which reward customers with a free flight on accumulating a certain number of points. Similarly, hotels award regular customers with points, which can be redeemed for free meals or stay.

While loyalty programmes are primarily aimed at ensuring that a customer stays loyal and buys more, they can also be used as a marketing tool to attract new customers and maximize their use of the particular service. The First Citizen club (of retailer Shopper's Stop), Jet Privilege programme (of Jet Airways), Taj's Inner Circle are all examples of programmes which offer incentives for customer loyalty.

COMPLAINING AND SERVICE RECOVERY

When an error or service failure occurs the customer may or may not complain. A customer who doesn't complain is less likely to come back to the service provider. Therefore, service provider has to make specific efforts to encourage customers to voice their concerns. Complaints provide feedback on how the service provider is performing in the marketplace. When customers complain, two potentially positive things happen for a service provider.

(1) The provider gets the chance to fix the problem and retain the customer (service recovery)

(2) Complaints can point to areas of the business that need improvement.

A good complaint culture and good complaint process may well lead a service provider to improved financial performance. Researchers have shown that excellent complaint management service recovery can significantly influence customer satisfaction and loyalty. The service provider in order to improve solicitation of complaints should make it easy for the customers to get in touch.

This can be done by providing multiple means of contact like toll free numbers, website, and customer contact point with service personnel. Further, these should be published on a continuous basis and the customers should be made to feel that their feedback is invaluable and their opinions are wanted. The company should treat a complaint as a gift and the one who complains as a friend.

SERVICE RECOVERY STRATEGIES

The above discussion gives you a fair idea of need for complaint management, its components and the importance of service recovery. Let us now focus on strategies for service recovery. Consider the following incident regarding airlines (British Airways). "An aircraft door was left open in a rainstorm before takeoff and a passenger near the door unfortunately got showered".

Now imagine that you were a part of the airlines. What steps you would have taken in such a situation? Now let us see what was actually done by the service provider. "The flight attendant not only did everything that was routine – offered to have the customer's garments cleaned or replaced and made sure that a customer relations representative contacted the customer later to demonstrate that we genuinely cared – but also made special gesture by offering the passenger a complimentary choice of certain tax-free goods". (Source: "Competiting on Customer Service: An Interview with British Airways' Sir Colin Marshall, Harvard Business Review, Nov-Dec 1995).

Hart, Heskett and Sasser suggest that service companies must become gymnasts, able to regain their balance instantly after a slipup and continue their routine. According to them companies that want to build the capability of recovering from service problems should do the following things:

(1) Measure the costs of effective service recovery

(2) Break customer silence and listen closely for complaints

(3) Anticipate needs for recovery

(4) Act fast

(5) Train and empower employees

(6) Close the customer feedback loop

Let us briefly discuss the above strategies.

Measure the Costs: As services marketers you should not underestimate the profits lost when a customer departs unhappily. This has been highlighted in the earlier part of this unit as well. Once this is appreciated, it will get due attention as it is said that what gets measured is truly what gets managed. The company should also keep in mind the costs the customer has to incur when service failure occurs. Excellent service companies will go that extra mile to cover the costs a failure incurs, or if the inconvenience is so great that the company cannot completely compensate the customer, the tone of the response must signal the company regret.

Break the Silence: This refers to soliciting and encouraging complaints from the customers. In the preceding pages, we have discussed this issue in detail. Anticipate Needs for Recovery: Service providers can look for the weak links or the areas which tend to be problem prone and address them in their service recovery strategies.

Act Fast: Customers who complain want quick responses. The urgent resumption of service and an apology are often sufficient to make amends (but not always). Empathize with customers. Statements like "I can appreciate how you feel," "You're right", "It shouldn't have happened that way," all convey empathy for the customer. Also, symbolic atonements should be made. It can be money, flowers, a 'sorry' note, free dessert by a restaurant, free upgrade in airlines etc. The speedy response to complaints/service failures requires appropriate system and procedures as well as trained and empowered employees.

Train and Empower Employees: The organization must train the frontline people and empower them. Simulated real life situations can be an effective way to develop recovery skills among employees. The company should empower the frontline employees to act and should give them the authority, responsibility and incentives to follow with customer.

Close the Loop: If a customer complaint leads to corrective measure, the company should tell the customer about the improvement. Even if something can't be fixed, the company should explain it to the customer. Effective way of closing the loop includes making timely telephone calls and letting the customer know that his suggestions might be implemented.

Part-E: Service Promotion

Communicating information between the seller and potential buyer to influence the attitude and behaviour of the potential buyer. Promotion is any form of communication a business or organization uses to inform, persuade or remind people about its service and improve its public image.

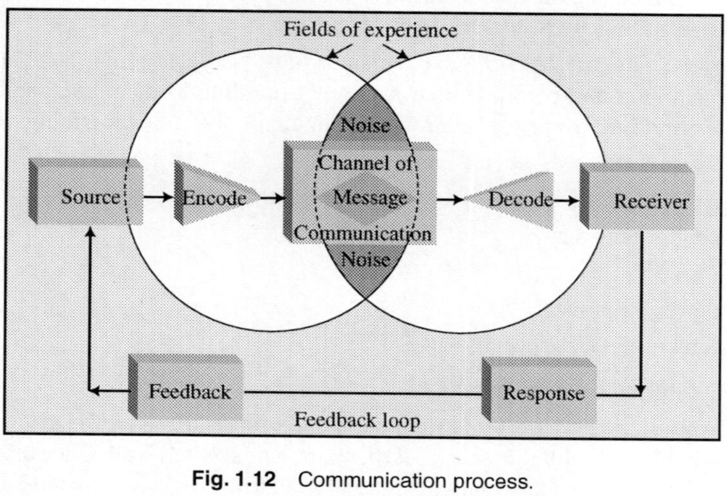

Fig. 1.12 Communication process.

PROMOTION MIX FOR SERVICES

- Advertising.
- Public relation/Publicity.
- Sale promotion.
- Personal selling.
- Direct marketing.
- Word of mouth.

ADVERTISING

Advertising is any paid form of the non-personal presentation and promotion of ideas, goods and services by an identified sponsor. Examples – advertisements in magazines, newspapers, radio, and TV.

Advantages

- Mass communication.
- Cost-effective.
- Supports other elements of the marketing mix.
- Can be highly effective in creating strong brand image and appeal.

Disadvantages

- High development costs.
- Rising cost of media space and airtime.
- Lack of immediate feedback.
- Low attention focus of audience.

SALES PROMOTION

Sales promotion consists of variety of incentive tools mostly short-term designed to stimulate quicker and/or greater purchase of particular services by consumer or the trade. Example: Coupons, Free samples, Rebates.

The following are the different sales promotional tools used in service marketing:

- Aimed at consumers include coupons, samples, price off, future discounts, prize promotion.
- Aimed at trade include buying allowances, free service, allowances, dealer sales contests.
- Aimed at sales force include bonuses, contests, sales rallies.

PERSONAL SELLING

Personal selling is defined as personally persuading or aiding a prospective customer in purchasing a product or service.

Personal selling includes:

- Face-to-face interaction with the customer
- Greater flexibility in the sales presentation.
- The opportunity to persuade or bring about attitude formation or change.

PUBLIC RELATION/PUBLICITY

Public relation: It is defined by the British Institute of public relations as "the planned and sustained effort to establish and maintain goodwill between an organization and its publics. These publics include group of people and organization which have interest in the company.

Publicity: Refers to communication about organizations, product or services which is not paid for or sponsored by the organization in question. Often it takes the form of news reports and announcement.

Listed below are few characteristics of services promotion through publicity:

- Low cost.
- Audience specificity.
- Believability.
- Difficult to control.

Promotion tools in public relation

- Publicity through media/press release/press conferences.
- Involvement in social and community initiatives.
- Sponsorship of events.
- Corporate brochure, in house journals and other publicity material.

DIRECT MARKETING

Direct communication with consumers to generate a response in the form of an order, a request for information, or a visit to a retail outlet. Examples – direct mail, catalogues, telemarketing, online marketing

WORD OF MOUTH COMMUNICATION

Personal recommendations by the current users of the service. It constitutes the favourable references made to others by satisfied customers of the service.

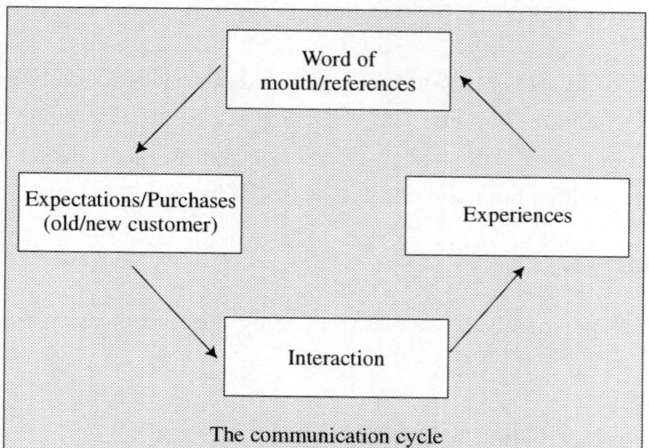

Fig. 1.13 The communication style.

Guidelines for Managing Service Promotion

- Promising what is possible.
- Communicating continuity.
- Make the service understood.
- Provide tangible clues.

Let us Sum Up

Kotler (1996) defines service as an activity that one party offers another that is essential intangible and does not result in the ownership of anything. Its production may or may not be tied to a physical product. The four essential characteristics of service are: intangibility, inseparability, perishability and variability. The three extended Ps in services marketing are: people, process and physical evidence. Service can be classified based on service options, customer-employee presence, ultimate users, objectives, and level of tangibility, specialization, external and internal services.

The service process refers to how a service is provided or delivered to a customer. Processes involve the procedures, tasks, schedules, mechanisms, activities and routines by which a service is delivered to the customer.

A service blueprint is a picture or a map that accurately portrays the service system, so that the different people involved in providing it can understand and deal with it objectively regardless of their role or individual points of view.

Quality improvement and adherence to accepted norms of quality are central to the modern concept of marketing of services. The quality of service delivery results in customer satisfaction and their retention as it reinforces the perception that the value of the service received is greater that the price paid for it.

Managers can use a wide variety of strategies for matching capacity and demand. This requires a clear understanding of demand patterns as well as the organization's capacity constraints. The strategies to be adopted can be broadly divided into two categories:

(1) Changing demand to fit supply (capacity) – marketing mix strategies

(2) Changing supply (capacity) to fit demand – input scheduling strategies

Communicating information between the seller and potential buyer to influence the attitude and behaviour of the potential buyer. Promotion is any form of communication a business or organization uses to inform, persuade or remind people about its service and improve its public image.

Promotion mix for services:

- *Advertising.*
- *Public relation/Publicity.*
- *Sale promotion.*
- *Personal selling.*
- *Direct marketing.*
- *Word of mouth.*

Questions for Discussion

1. Explain the meaning of service marketing with examples.
2. List out the features of service marketing and explain each with examples.
3. Explain the concept of extended marketing mix of service.
4. Mention the types of services. What are the components of service?
5. State the classification of service.
6. Write short notes on: (i) Intangibility (ii) Inseparability (iii) Perishability (iv) Variability.
7. Explain the role of services in economy.
8. Distinguish between goods and services.
9. Explain the concept of service and service management.
10. Explain the development of service management and its importance.
11. What are the potential tools used in services? Explain briefly.
12. Explain different methods of classification of service.
13. What are the challenges faced by service managers in marketing of services?
14. What are the seven Ps in the services marketing mix?
15. What are the stages of decision-making and evaluation process in services?
16. Explain the steps involved in segmenting and targeting services.
17. Define service process and service design.
18. Explain the concept of service blueprinting with diagrammatic representation.
19. List out the importance of service blueprinting. Explain the process of service blueprinting.
20. Explain the meaning of service quality. Briefly explain the features of service quality.
21. How customers can be retained by providing quality service? Explain.
22. Draw the diagram of service quality gap and explain each gap and strategies for reducing the gap.
23. Write a short note on ***SERVQUAL.***
24. Explain the strategies for matching capacity and demand.
25. Write short notes on: (i) Customer retention (ii) Customer switching (iii) Customer loyalty programmes (iv) Customer recovery.
26. Explain the process of customer recovery.
27. Explain the decision-making and evaluation process in case of service.
28. Explain the segmenting and targeting strategy of services.
29. Explain briefly service promotion strategies.

2

Tourism and Travel Services

"I would like to spend my whole life travelling, if I could borrow another life to spend at home." – William Hazlitt (1778-1830) British essayist

Learning Objectives

At the end of this chapter, students will be able to understand

- Meaning and concepts of tourism and travel industry
- Meaning of tourism
- Growth of tourism
- Marketing strategies of tourism product
- Demand and seasonality of tourism product
- Different types of hotels
- Hotel pricing and distribution
- Impact of aviation industry on tourism
- Understand travel agents and its functions

Tourism industry *– meaning – tourist – features – classification – growth of tourism – basic components and elements of tourism – barriers to travel – promoting Indian tourism – tourism marketing mix – characteristics of tourism marketing – importance – implications of marketing concept – price elasticity of demand – seasonality – segmentation – product mix – price mix – promotion mix.*

Hotel market *– early history – types of hotel accommodation – supplementary accommodation – Indian hospitality industry – demand of hotel facilities – hotel product – hotel pricing and distribution.*

Airline connection *– history – influence of aviation on tourism – low cost carrier – future of tourism and aviation – Indian aviation industry.*

Travel Agency *– functions – Travel Agents Association of India*

INTRODUCTION

Tourism is considered a smokeless industry; it is more environment-friendly than other industries. Tourism brings immense benefits to a country. Foreign exchange earnings, tax earning for government, employment opportunities, development of the local economy of tourism centre, perpetuation of cultural heritage, creation of social assets like tourism attractions, preservation of arts and handicrafts, broad based investment in transport, hostel and restaurant industries, international understanding, etc. are some of the salient benefits derived from tourism. Lured by these, every country vies with each other to woo more tourists.

Tourism industry involves the movement of people, in contrast with other industries where the products are transshipped. Movement of people is conditioned by certain factors that influence movement of people are discretionary income, discretionary time, discretionary mobility and desire and drive.

People have been travelling from one place to another since the primitive age when they were living in a small group and did hunting and gathering for their daily life. The movement of people has become clearer when nation-states emerged. They were moving within or across borders for various purposes such as travel, trade, migration, spread of cultural, and dissemination of knowledge and understanding (Amartya Sen); hence, contributing to the development of human civilization.

As for recreation purpose, a lot of wealthy middle class people in Roman era were visiting Pompeii and Herculaneum, seaside resorts, to escape from hot summer in Rome (William, 1998). Thus, tourism is not the recent phenomenon.

In this 21st century, tourism is growing very fast and plays an important role in the world economy. According to Tourism Highlight 2006 edition, published by World Tourism Organization, international tourist arrivals and receipts worldwide in 2005 was approximately 800 million and $680 billion respectively despite terrorism in US and Europe, tsunami in some parts of Asia, SAR in China and South-East Asia, and rising of oil price.

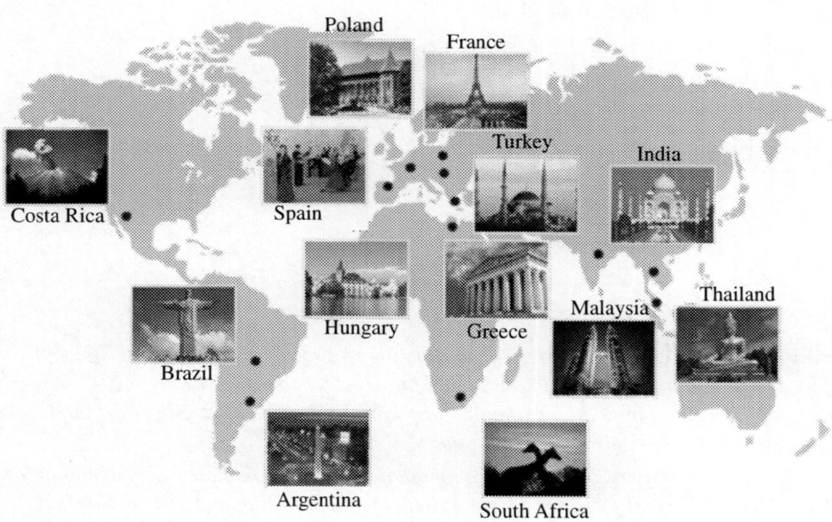

Fig. 2.1 Major tourist attractions of few countries.

DEFINITION

Since tourism has been developing very rapidly from time to time and particularly in the 21st century, it is better to search for more definitions to reflect the current situation and to understand its present characteristics. The characteristics of tourism in the 18th century are, of course, different from what it is now in the 21st century. According to World Tourism Organization (2002), 'Tourism' is defined as "the activities of persons travelling to and staying in places outside their usual environment for not more than one consecutive year for leisure, business and other purposes not related to the exercise of an activity remunerated from within the place visited." This definition identifies clearly the activities and length of stay in the destination outside the usual environment where people use to be.

To sum up, tourism has been changing progressively according to the development of technology and the development of industry sector. Thus, its definition also has been upgrading to reflect the real situation. It is not just as simple as the movement of people and their length of stay in the destination away from their environment. In developing country like Cambodia, tourism means more than travelling. Tourism is the engine of economic growth and employment creation for the people.

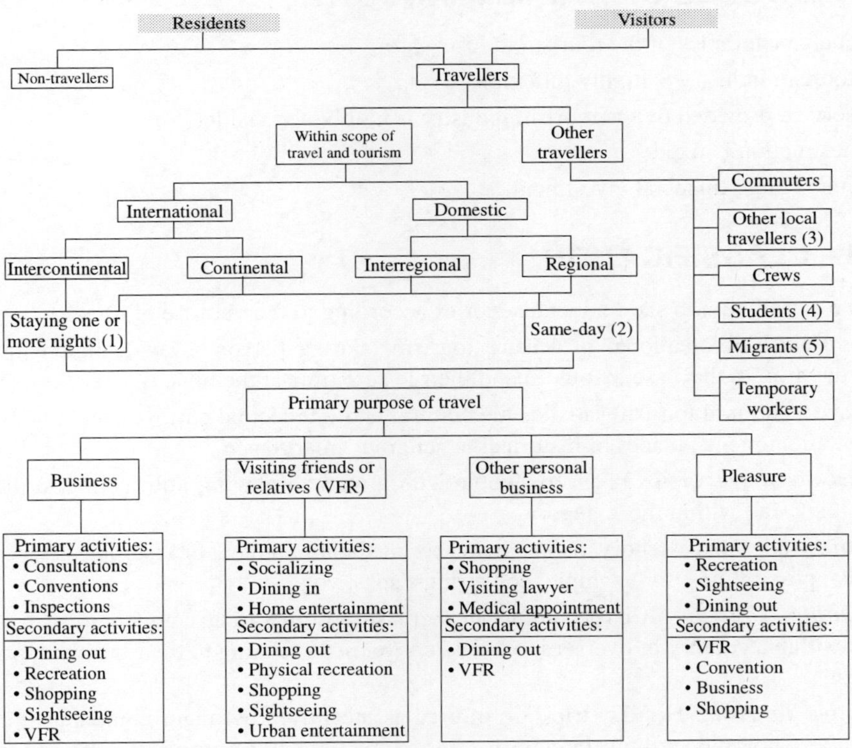

(1) Business international technical definitions.
(2) Excursionists in international technical definitions.
(3) Travellers whose trips are shorter than those that quality for travel and tourism: e.g., under 50 miles (80 km) from home.
(4) Students travelling between home and school only—other travel of students is within scope of travel and tourism.
(5) All persons moving to a new place of residence, including all one-way travellers, such as emigrants, immigrants, refugees, domestic migrants, and nomads.

Fig. 2.2 Different types of travellers.

TOURIST

World Tourism Organization has defined tourist as a temporary visitor staying for at least twenty-four hours in a country visited when the purpose of journey can be classified under one of the following headings:

(a) ***Leisure:*** Recreation, holidays, health, study religion and sports; or

(b) ***Business:*** Family, mission, meetings.

Travellers, straying for less than twenty-four hours according to WTO are "Excursionists".

This definition adds an array of travellers to those travelling for fund, that is, person travelling for business family mission or meeting purposes. Today, the term tourist has several connotations – some of them not very favourable. For instance, when we say 'tourists' class accommodation, we mean inexpensive or cheap accommodation. In United States tourists are known as 'guests' in hotels and 'patrons' in restaurants. In most other countries, they are called 'visitors'.

SALIENT FEATURES OF TOURISM INDUSTRY

The four main characteristics of the tourism industry are:

(i) The tourism industry is highly inflexible.

(ii) The service provided by the tourism industry is highly perishable.

(iii) The destination is fixed.

(iv) It requires large financial investment.

TOURISM – CLASSIFICATION

Tourism can be classified into six distinct categories according to the purpose of travel:

(i) ***Recreational:*** Recreational or leisure tourism takes a person away from the humdrum of everyday life. In this case, people spend their leisure time at the hills, sea beaches, etc.

(ii) ***Cultural:*** Cultural tourism satisfies the cultural and intellectual curiosity and involves visits to ancient monuments, places of historical or religious importance.

(iii) ***Sports/Adventure:*** Trips taken by people with a view to playing golf, skiing in the mountain and hiking, fall within this category.

(iv) ***Health:*** Under this category, people travel for medical treatment or visit places where there are curative possibilities, for example, hot springs, spas, yoga, etc.

(v) ***Convention Tourism:*** It is becoming an increasingly important component of travel. People travel within a country or overseas to attend conventions relating to their business, profession or interest.

(vi) ***Incentive Tourism:*** Holiday trips are offered as incentives by major companies to dealer and salesmen who achieve high targets in sales. Similar to it being offered by government and corporate enterprises in the form of LTC in our country.

GROWTH OF TOURISM

The phenomenal growth in tourism during the last thirty-five years has been due to several economic and technological factors:

(i) ***Increased Leisure:*** Increasing intervention of ILO and other Labour organization in fixing holidays per year increased the leisure for many.

(ii) ***Industrial development and urbanization:*** Large-scale industrial development coupled with pollution and overcrowding in the cities has led to the people's search for sun, sand and the pure fresh mountain air during annual holidays.

(iii) ***Revolution in transport:*** The development of air transportation leading to the evolution of Jumbo jets has resulted in unbelievable low air fares. This has democratized the holiday market.

(iv) ***Rising standards of living:*** The rapid economic development has raised the standard of living in developed countries with sizeable disposable income. A part of this income is now spent on travel for fun.

(v) ***Publicity and promotion – Government Interest:*** Most governments are actively promoting tourism like any other product. This has resulted in the current travel boom.

BASIC COMPONENTS AND ELEMENTS OF TOURISM

Tourism does not exist in isolation. It consists of certain components, three of which may be considered as basic. These three basic components of tourism are:

(i) Transport

(ii) Location

(iii) Accommodation

Peters has drawn up an inventory of the various attractions which are of significance in tourism. His five categories are given here:

(i) ***Cultural:*** Sites and areas of archaeological interest, historical buildings and monuments, places of historical significance, museum, modern culture, political and educational institutions, and religious institutions.

(ii) ***Traditions:*** National festivals, arts and handicrafts, music, folklore, native life and customs.

(iii) ***Science:*** National parks, wildlife, flora and fauna, beach resorts, mountain resorts.

(iv) ***Entertainment:*** Participation and viewing sports, amusement and recreation parks, zoos and occeanariums, cinemas, and theatres, night life, cuisine.

(v) ***Other attractions:*** Climate, health resorts or spas, unique attractions not available elsewhere.

BARRIERS TO TRAVEL

In spite of numerous factors listed above favouring the development of tourism, there are some that act as barriers to travel. They fall into the following categories:

(i) ***Cost:*** People are subject to monetary restraints and cannot afford the expense of travel.

(ii) ***Time:*** This is characteristic of those who are not in a position to leave their business or profession to take time off from work.

(iii) ***Health:*** Many persons, especially old people cannot travel due to poor health and physical limitations.

(iv) ***Family:*** Parents having small children are not in a position to travel due to family responsibilities and convenience of travel.

(v) Lack of ignorance and lack of information about interest of other places and people can be a major barrier to travel.

PROMOTING INDIAN TOURISM: INITIATIVE

(i) Improvement in the immigration system at the airports to facilitate easier and less time consuming custom checks, etc. for tourists.

(ii) Simplification of the visa system.

(iii) More foreign currency changing facilities in both hotels and other accommodation.

(iv) Investments in facilities existing at Airports and bring them up to excellent international standards.

(v) Air-conditioned coaches of the most modern type for foreign tourists. Hence, there is a proposal that the department of tourism may be allowed the facility of importing such coaches to strengthen their existing fleet and coach standards.

(vi) Introduction of the Air Taxi Service with a wide coverage. The import of Aircraft for this purpose is to be considered.

(vii) Since the Palace on Wheels has shown considerable success, it is proposed that similar trains in the Southern, Eastern and Western Region may be introduced.

(viii) Relaxation of visiting restrictions in Northern and Eastern region of the country, so the tourists can visit Gangtok, Meghalaya, Assam and Manipur more easily.

(ix) Incentives for new hotels to be given to interested parties for setting up hotels in rural areas, hilly areas, place of pilgrimage and new areas identified as suitable for tourism. Emphasis is placed on opening budget hotels.

(x) The year 1991 is Visit India Year. For this, a lot of incentives to hoteliers are proposed to be given by the government.

(xi) Paying guest accommodation is proposed to be developed to supplement the hotel accommodation which caters to low budget economy tourists.

TOURISM MARKETING MIX

The tourism marketing mix comprises:

(i) ***Product:*** Includes accommodation, restaurants, attraction, recreation, shopping, transportation.

(ii) ***Price:*** Transport charges, accommodation charges, communication charges and other allied charges.

(iii) ***Place:*** Includes information and communication, transportation, accommodation and food, amusement shopping, etc.

(iv) ***Promotion:*** Advertising, sales promotion, word of mouth communication, personal selling.

(v) ***People:*** Marketing personnel. Sales personnel, airline and transportation crew, hotel staff and the tourist guide.

(vi) ***Process:*** Travel information, preparation of itineraries, liaison with providers of services, planning and costing tours, ticketing, provision of foreign currency and insurance.

(vii) ***Physical evidence:*** Comfortable seats while travelling, ambience, layout, design of the resort, etc.

TOURISM MARKETING

Tourism marketing is defined in a number of ways. It could be defined as the 'systematic and coordinated efforts exerted by the National Tourist Organizations and/or the tourist enterprises at international, national and local levels to optimize the satisfaction of tourists, groups and individuals, in view of the sustained tourism growth'.

Accommodation sector
Hotels/motels
Guest houses/bed and breakfast
Farmhouses
Apartments/villas/flats/cottages
Condominiums/time share resorts
Vacation villages/holiday centres
Conference/exhibition centres
Static and touring caravan/camping sites
Marinas

Attraction sector
Theme parks
Museums and galleries
National parks
Wildlife parks
Gardens
Heritage sites and centres
Sports/activity centres
Themed retail/leisure/entertainment centres
Festivals and events

Transport sector
Airlines
Shipping lines/ferries
Railways
Bus/coach operators
Car rental operators

Travel organizer's sector
Tour operators
Tour wholesalers/brokers
Retail travel agents
Conference organizers
Booking agencies (e.g., accommodation)
Incentive travel organizers

Destination organization sector
National tourist offices (NTOs)
Destination marketing organizations (DMOs)
Regional/state tourist offices
Local tourist offices
Tourist associatons

Fig. 2.3 The five main components of travel and tourism industry.

According to Krippendorf, J., Marketing in tourism means 'systematic and coordinated execution of business policy by tourist undertaking and coordinated execution of business policy by tourist undertaking whether private or state owned at local, regional, national or international level to achieve the optimal satisfaction of the needs to identifiable consumer groups, and in doing so to achieve an appropriate return'.

Comparing marketing in travel and tourism to other forms of marketing students of travel and tourism often find it difficult to be clear about the way marketing in travel and tourism differs from other forms of consumer marketing practice. Standard texts on marketing principles are not much help. Generally speaking, however, it is common ground that the principles of the body of knowledge about marketing and its main theoretical elements hold good for all types of product. In other words, the basic or core principles of marketing are relevant to all products, whether they are based on services or manufactured goods. Marketing managers at senior levels of responsibility can, and frequently do, switch between industries with little difficulty. This is only possible because of the integrity of the body of knowledge. In travel and tourism in particular, many marketing managers have been brought in from manufacturing and other service industries to bring their expertise to bear as firms grow faster than the level of expertise available from within their own sector of business.

Against this evidence of common ground, however, experience convinces many in the industry, including the authors of this book, that there are some special characteristics of travel and tourism services that are so dominant in their implications that standard marketing principles must be considerably adapted to ensure success in an operational context.

This is clearly a very important consideration and it is based on the belief that marketing in travel and tourism reflects five aspects of demand and supply in the industry, which individually and combined give marketing practice its special approach and style.

- The characteristics of demand
- The characteristics of supply
- Products and prices, which match the supply to the demand
- Characteristics of promotion used to influence demand
- Characteristics of distribution used to facilitate purchase

Characteristics of Tourism Marketing

(1) ***Tourism is an Intangible, Non-Material Product:*** No tangible product is bought or sold. Services, facilities, installations are given for a specified time in exchange for money. A room in a hotel, a houseboat, skiing services, sightseeing tours is carried out to customer or advice or information offered to him by the local tourist authorities.

(2) ***Production and Consumption are Interrelated:*** Production can only take place when the customer is really present. Most services can only be personal and to no other person can it be exchanged or transferred. The tourist service can be very unreliable and risky as the customer cannot see, inspect, compare or try out tourist services before deciding to use them.

(3) ***A Wide Range of Services Constitute the Tourism Marketing Product:*** This cannot be provided by a single enterprise. Each component of the tourist service requires a high degree of excellence, perfection and specialization and its total is a part of the final product. Naturally the need for cooperation and coordination is of paramount importance in tourism marketing.

(4) ***Highly Unstable Nature of the Tourism Demand:*** Different factors–seasonal, economic, political, etc. influence tourist demand. Seasonally places strain on the transport system and hotel divisions. So not only is employment affected but also return from investments. In these days of escalating violence, political unrest cause fluctuation in tourism growth and even damages it for longer period.

(5) ***Dominant role of Intermediaries:*** As in most industries where manufacturers control distribution, promotion and pricing, in tourism the manufacturers are sales intermediaries like tour operators, travel agents, airline operators, hotel brokers who play the most important role and enjoy superior marketing strength. Different pricing to suit different levels of tourists for different services, package deals pricing policies and promotion strategies to be adopted by tourist enterprises is decided primarily by travel sales intermediaries.

(6) ***Diverse Motivation:*** Prompt people to take diverse destinations and there is simply no concrete reason for certain decisions. The subjective and objective reasons, expectations and desires influence tourist's choice for holiday destination, type of an accommodation and vacation activities which are heterogeneous.

Importance of Tourism Marketing

(1) Marketing helps to create new customers by offering to satisfy their needs and aims primarily at customer satisfaction. His second task is to motivate potential customers to purchase their services. Their crucial role is in promoting distinct destination prints citing cultural, social scenically important, historical and entertainment-oriented places. Tourism marketing begins by a detailed assessment of the actual and potential demand and on this assessment developing facilities and services.

(2) Customer needs in tourism are more than particular products: What the traveller needs on his travel is a hygienic and a good place to sleep, safe, clean place to eat moderately priced good food and a comfortable mode of travel be it by train, bus or plane. Such basic needs can be a effectively give by a guests. Hospitality should become a way of life and personal prejudices as sexist, religious and racist should be effectively controlled.

(3) Merchandising becomes more effective under tourism marketing management because management view their tasks as that of supplying want satisfaction rather than creating demand for its products among the customers. The physical product is only a part of the satisfaction rather than creating demand for its products among the customers. The physical product is only a part of the satisfactions sought by the buyer because he wants in addition convenience, service and certain other symbolic values.

(4) he managements are able to create more harmony between their own interests and those of the society because the market orientation under this concept means that the management build, their future products from satisfying human needs better.

Marketing in tourism duet to the various factors mentioned above needs a somewhat different approach unlike the normal consumer product or service.

Implications of Marketing Concept in Tourism

Before we can consider how marketing policy and strategy might be incorporated in a destination's overall tourism development approach, we need to consider those basic characteristics of tourism that have implications for the marketing function.

Fragmentation of supply

The tourist product is a composite one, a combination of attractions, transport, accommodation, entertainment and other services. In most countries, there are many separate suppliers of these various components – airlines, hotel companies, tour excursion organizers, etc. It is an important feature of tourism that, though an individual supplier of tourist services may serve more than one market, rarely, if ever, does a single supplier provide the entire range of products/services required by a tourist on a visit to a destination. Whether sold as a package or assembled by the tourist himself or by a travel agent, the tourist product is in practice a composite one. It is apparent, then, that given the fragmented nature of supply on one hand, and the demand for a combined set of products on the other, a fundamental challenge for a destination is to achieve coordination and integration of all components across all sub-sectors of the tourism industry, that is, of supply.

Interdependence and complementarity of tourist services

It follows from the fact that tourism demand is for a composite product that the various tourist products and services are interdependent and complementary. The supply of one (for example, international air transport to/from a destination) depends on the supply of another (such as hotel accommodation) and they complement each other. A destination's reputation can be set by the weakest link in the tourist product chain. This leads to the marketing policies and actions of one enterprise directly influencing other enterprises. A country with a liberal charter policy and/or an airline with an aggressive pricing policy may result in the attraction of low budget tourists, something that could damage the high quality image central to the marketing of a five-star hotel chain in the destination. There is again then the need for coordination and cooperation in order to enhance the effectiveness of individual marketing and promotional efforts of the various tourism suppliers.

Rigidity of supply

Much tourism demand cannot be easily and quickly be adjusted in the short term to variation in demand. A hotel, for example, cannot add or remove rooms in line with demand. This relative lack of flexibility has obvious operational and economic implications. When demand falls below capacity, waste of resources occurs; when it exceeds capacity, the tourism industry fails to maximize its revenue. This "short term" can extend to years if the rigidity is caused by lack of airport or hotel capacity, given the extensive lead-time to construct a new airport or hotel.

Fixed in time and space

The composite tourism product cannot be stored – it is perishable – so a hotel room on a particular night or a seat on a given flight is available only once, and if not utilized, the sales opportunity is lost. Similarly, it cannot be transported. The need is to bring the consumer to the tourist product. The importance of ensuring, through marketing, as high a level of utilisation as possible is particularly marked because of the high fixed costs of many tourist operations. A hotel has to meet its fixed costs whether it has 5 guests or 200. The non-transportability of tourism products means there is no physical distribution in the strict sense in tourism marketing. Similarly, there are limited opportunities for merchandising activities, in consequence of the fact that the tourist product, unlike consumer goods, cannot be displayed at points of sale other than via proxy representations.

Intangible – "expectation – experience – memory"

Tourist products, except items like souvenirs, are services rather than goods. As such they are intangible. The tourism product is subjectively perceived – each destination or individual tourist operation is a mental concept for each individual prospective tourist encompassing both physical characteristics and other abstract attributes. The subjective nature of perception involves an emotional and also an irrational element. In consequence, the tourist has to be offered psychological benefits. Clearly, this has important implications for advertising and promotion in tourism and generally on how a tourist product is presented to consumer groups.

In consequence of the intangibility of tourist products, when a supplier of a tourist services considers the potential market, the essential thought process should be: expectations – experiences – memories. This is the same whether the supplier is a destination promotion authority seeking to attract tourists to a specific country or location within that country, or the operator of a fixed-site facility like a hotel, restaurant or attraction, or a provider of tour excursion.

Each tourist is a set of expectations. The tourism product cannot be test driven or known about with certainty in advance of being consumed. The tourist, therefore, builds mental images of the destination and of the facilities and other components of the tourism product of that destination. He/she has a set of expectations about the place to be visited.

Experiences because the intangibility of tourism products means that the tourist engages in a series of activities – typically, for example, riding on transport, visiting attractions, staying in some form of accommodation, eating, drinking, recreating, interacting with other people – none of which produce a final physical product to take home. Each tourist trip, therefore, is a combination of various experiences.

At the end of the trip the tourist is left with nothing more than memories – the derivation of the word souvenirs and proxies of the trip – such as photos or videos.

The key for the marketer is that the expectations created achieve the fine balance between attracting the tourist while not promising more than can be delivered. The experiences are assessed by the tourist against his/her pre-trip expectations. A major determinant of success is how well the experiences match or exceed these expectations. This assessment has relative as well-absolute dimensions. A destination may have a perception in the marketplace of being expensive or offering poor service, something which will limit its drawing power. If the tourist finds it is not so costly or that service is better than expected, his/her level of satisfaction will be higher. Of course, the reverse can also be the case with more damaging consequences for the destination.

The intangibility of the tourist product and the consequent need for the marketer to address the potential market's perceptions of the tourist product has two dimensions: first, the need to offer psychological benefits to the prospective tourist; and, second, to recognize that the perception is the reality – with each tourist having sovereign power over his/her destination decision-making – and that marketing activities should be designed to alter the market's prevailing images in line with the marketer's desired position.

Price elasticity of demand

Most forms of tourism demand involve the use of what economists call personal discretionary disposable income and free time. Holidaymakers or vacation travellers need both money and time to engage in tourism. They have freedom of choice as to how to use their money and time for tourism purposes, affecting decisions such as how much to spend, how long to go for, where to go, when to go, etc. As a result, tourists are highly sensitive to price, and generally their demand for tourist services exhibits a significant degree of price elasticity.

The marketing implication of these demand characteristics is that the travelling public is susceptible to price inducements and to other marketing efforts in respect of choices relating to destination, place and type of accommodation, and timing of the trip. The price elasticity factor is growing in significance because of two interlinked factors, namely increased pressure on free time and greater ease of international travel, i.e., more frequent services to more destinations at fares rising below prevailing rates of inflation. This will increasingly lead to a pattern of shorter but more frequent holidays.

Seasonality

It is a characteristic of most tourism markets that demand fluctuates over the course of the year. The principal determinant is climatic – either in the destination or the tourist generating markets. Residents of northern parts of the European and North American continents tend mostly to take domestic or intra-regional holidays in the summer months of June–September whereas they take long haul, inter-regional holidays more in the winter when the climate at home is generally cold and wet. As a result, tourist operators have periods when demand is near capacity and others when the level of utilization can be 30 per cent or even less, with the remaining months – the shoulder season – falling in between these two extremes.

These demand variations are all the more acute because of the fact that any tourism product cannot be stored – the perishability factor – and the concern of marketers is to generate as much demand in the trough periods as possible since the fixed cost element of any tourism operation do not change between seasons. The marketing response to seasonality can range from the reduction of prices in order to induce people to travel in periods other than would be their normal preference to targeting geographic markets with different seasonal patterns of travel so that the demand for the destination from one group complements that of the other group.

Other tourists as part of the tourism product

It follows from the fact that the production and consumption of tourism products and services are simultaneous – and that they cannot be made in advance and stored – that the producers/distributors of such products and services are part of the tourist experience – hence the importance of vocational training programmes. It is also the fact that other tourists in the vicinity of the tourist when he/she is receiving tourist products/services constitute part of the experience. In tourism the customer is part of the product. This applies not only to hotels and restaurants, and tourist attractions or excursions, but to the whole destination. The type, quality, volume and other characteristics of restaurant customers, hotel guests or visitors to a destination influence the overall perception of that restaurant, hotel or destination by other potential customers, guests or visitors – that is, the market. Therefore, in marketing it is vitally important to identify and target the most appropriate market mix and ensure compatibility of the different target market segments. It would be unwise for a hotel to accept block bookings from two tour operators that specialize in older generation tourists and young tourists because the interests of these two groups are likely to be quite different and the behaviour of one an irritant to the other.

Importance of intermediaries

A distinguishing characteristic of tourism is the relatively dominant role played by travel intermediaries. Tour operators or wholesalers and travel agents are all traditionally important in product design, pricing, distribution and promotion. In international tourism marketing the influence of travel intermediaries has its origin both in historical factors and in the physical distance between the generating tourist source markets and the destinations (or tourist receiving countries). This latter factor leads to the necessity for a special distribution channel.

At the same time, the fragmentation of supply creates the need for the coordinating and facilitating role of the travel intermediary. Further, the relative lack of marketing expertise and capital resources on the part of individual destination-based suppliers of tourism products or services makes them dependent on travel intermediaries for the distribution and sale of their individual offerings. This often gives rise to the need for destination tourism operators to promote and supply at two levels through tour operators and travel agents (intermediaries) and direct to the ultimate consumer/tourist. The advent of sophisticated electronic technology has changed the balance of power, making it easier for destination operators – even relatively small ones – to communicate direct and at low cost with consumer. Nonetheless, the travel intermediary remains a major player in tourism distribution.

The Marketing Response

The distinctive characteristics of all service industries – identified by Middleton and Clarke (2001) as inseparability and intangibility, perishability based on fixed capacity in the short run and inability to create stocks, seasonality, high fixed costs and interdependence – coupled with those other aspects detailed above specifically related to travel and tourism strongly influence the attitudes and decisions of management in all sectors of the travel and tourism industry as they seek to respond to, and influence, prospective customers' demand for their products and services – the marketing response.

The role of marketing in the travel and tourism industry is to manage or manipulate sales – customer purchasing behaviour – on an orderly, continuous, regular basis, in order to utilize the maximum level of available, inseparable capacity, and to generate extra or marginal sales that contributes revenue at minimal additional cost.

While the principles of the body of knowledge about marketing, and its main theoretical elements, can be applied in all industries, the special characteristics of travel and tourism are so dominant in their implications, that standard marketing principles must be considerably adapted to be successfully utilization in travel and tourism applications.

Middleton and Clarke (2001) identify three propositions about marketing in travel and tourism that are relevant to all the forms it takes:

- In the context of opportunities and constraints arising from the business environment of a major global market, products in tourism are designed, adapted and promoted to meet the long-run needs, expectations and interests of prospective customers. This is the common ground with all forms of consumer marketing, and the cornerstone of all marketing theory;
- Service products generally have particular characteristics of inseparability and perishability, which call for a different application of the traditional marketing mix variables. This is the common ground with the developing theory of services marketing as distinct from marketing goods; and
- Marketing in travel and tourism is shaped and determined by the nature of the demand for tourism and the operating characteristics of supplying industries. The forms of promotion and distribution used for travel and tourism products have their own particular characteristics, which distinguish their use in comparison with other industries. These characteristics form the common ground on which marketing for travel and tourism is based.

Users of Tourism Services

The users of tourism services can be categorized in a number of ways. One such way of classifying the users is by dividing them into categories such as General, Sex, Region, Education, etc.

1. General: Domestic, Foreign Kids, Teens, Youths, Seniors, Students, Executives, Artists, Politicians, Movie stars
2. Sex: Men, Women
3. Region: Rural, Urban
4. Education: Literate, Illiterate
5. Status: Rich, Poor
6. Profession: Executives, Academics, Sportsmen, Artists
7. Occupation: White collar, Blue collar

Another method of classifying users of tourism services is on the basis of the frequency of usage of services.

1. Non-users: They lack the willingness, desire and ability (income and leisure time).
2. Potential Users: They have the willingness but the marketing resources have not been used optimally to influence their impulse.
3. Actual Users: They are already using the services generated by the tourist organizations.
4. Occasional Users: They have not formed the habit of travelling.
5. Habitual Travellers: They have formed a habit and avail of the services regularly.

Need for Segmentation

Consumer behaviour can be defined in psychological terms as the whole range of the generation of wants and their transformation into buying or using decisions. Users have values, perceptions, preferences and expectations which are the result of environmental influences. There are a number of factors that influence the behavioural profile of consumers.

In recent years, the users have become more discriminating in their using habits and therefore their needs for different services, products and brands change constantly. This makes it essential that the marketers analyze their behavioural profile and undertake segmentation so that they know the level of expectations.

In a nutshell, tourist organizations need to undertake segmentation in order to simplify their task of creating and stimulating demand. In this way, they can identify the potential tourists, transform them into actual tourists and further into habitual tourists.

Segmentation

Though there are a number of bases for segmentation of tourists, one of the most important is lifestyle. Travelling decisions are fantastically influenced by changing lifestyles. They are also affected by other factors such as level of income, availability of leisure time, etc.

Such segmentation is useful when deciding the offerings to target a particular segment. For example:

- The mass market consists of vacationists that travel in large groups and prefer all-inclusive tours. They are generally conservative.
- The popular market consists of smaller groups going on inclusive or semi-inclusive tours. This group includes pensioners and retired people.
- The individual market consists of chairmen, senior executives, etc.
- As the lifestyle changes, consumption of services might change. For example, a newly married couple might prefer romantic holidays, but once they have children they would prefer family vacations where there are plenty of activities to entertain kids.
- Teens and youth might prefer adventure holidays whereas senior citizens would probably prefer more relaxing vacations.

PRODUCT MIX

The tourism product is essentially an intangible thing. Also, because tourism is a multi-segment industry, the task of formulating a product mix becomes more difficult and challenging.

Selling a holiday is 'selling dreams'. The way to win the customer's heart is through the peripheral services provided along with the core product. Thus, a tourism product is quite a complex one, including the destination, airline seat, hotel room, occasional tangible products such as souvenirs, a free bag or bottle of whisky, etc.

Innovation in the tourism industry helps to raise the sensitivity in this regard. There is nothing fixed or fundamental about the tourism product. The content factor is within the jurisdiction of the government that undertakes the maintenance, development and conservation of tourist attractions such as parks, museums, beaches, historical treasures, etc. Unless these factors are developed in the right fashion, the marketing professionals would never be successful in making the marketing resources productive.

Base of segmentation	**Categories**
Holiday	Mass market
	Popular market
	Individual market
Demand	Primary
	Secondary
	Opportunity
Geography	International
	On the basis of regions, cities, etc.
Psychography	Lifestyle
	Personality motive
	Knowledge
Demography	Age
	Sex
	Religion
Socio-economic	Rich, poor
	Rural, Urban
	Literate, Illiterate
Purpose	Business Travel
	Cultural Tourism
	Common Interest Convention
Age	Teens
	Youth
	Seniors

Fig. 2.4 Bases for tourism market segmentation.

Thus, the direct or indirect patronage of the government is essential to get a positive response. The government and private tourist organizations work together to undertake activities such as developing infrastructural facilities such as transportation, water, banking, medicare facilities, etc., and also developing and maintain hotels, cottages, havelis, lodges, etc.

Accommodation: 5 star, 4 star, 3 star, 2 star, 1 star, cottages, havelis, tents, ecotels	Recreation: Theatres, pubs, music meetings
Restaurants: Western, Chinese, Indian, etc.	Shopping: Artistic, Handicraft, garments, jewellery, books, handloom.
Transportation: Airways, Railways, Roadways, Local transportation.	Attractions: Lakes, parks, museums, heritages, etc.

Fig. 2.5 Product mix.

PRICE MIX

In pricing decisions, the product or the service mix of the tourist organization is important. They have to set prices in line with the quality of services to be made available to the customers. Pricing decisions are influenced by internal and external factors. The tourism professionals are supposed to watch the emerging trends in both the markets. They are required to think in favour of discounting price.

These may include discounts for cash payments, seasonal discounts, trade discounts, etc. But while offering the discounts, it is not to be forgotten that it may also create image problem since some of the value sensitive tourists may doubt the quality.

PROMOTION MIX

Creation of awareness has a far reaching impact. The tourist organizations bear the responsibility of informing, persuading and sensing the potential tourists in a right fashion. The marketers need to use the various components of promotion optimally so that they succeed in increasing the number of habitual users. Promotion helps in maximizing the duration of stay, frequency of visit by offering new tourist products in the same country to areas which hitherto have remained untapped or partially tapped. The various dimensions of tourism promotion are as follows:

Advertising: Advertisement helps in furnishing important information to the actual and potential tourists. Its coverage is wide. Advertising is aimed at the public to create awareness of the travel offers available on a resort and its attractions to influence their business decisions.

Intangibility can be compensated with the help of visual exposure of scenes and events. We can project hotel bedrooms, well-arranged restaurants and cafeterias, swimming pools, etc.

Publicity: It focuses attention on strengthening the public relations measures by developing a rapport with media people and getting their personalized support in publicizing the business. It helps in projecting the positive image of tourists organizations since the prospects trust on the news items publicized by the media people. E.g. Kumarakom in Kerala after Prime Minister A B Vajpayee's visit. The publicity programme includes regular publicity stories and photographs to the newspapers, travel editors, contact with magazines on stories, etc.

There are different groups in publicity, such as advertising publicity, projected publicity, structural publicity and personal publicity.

Sales promotions: Sales promotion measures are the short-term activities seeking to boost sales at peak demand periods to ensure that the firms obtain its market share and are used to help launch a new product or support an ailing or modified one. The tool of sales promotions is designed to appeal particularly to those customers who are price-sensitive. There are a number of techniques to promote sale and the tourist professional need to use them in the face of their requirements vis-à-vis the emerging trends in the business. Example in the tourism industry, a travel company offers give-aways to their clients, such as flight bags, wallets for tickets and forex and covers of passport.

The hotels offer a number of facilities like shoe shine clothes, first aid sewing kits, shower caps and shampoo. Further, the VIP clients also get fruits and flowers in their rooms.

Thomas Cook offered 3-tier sales promotion based on price and one more novel technique as detailed below:

- Cook agreed to match the price of any holiday they sold which was known as price promise.
- Money back guarantee to the clients who purchase the product or any tour operator known as trading charter.
- Matching of customers need with a particular holiday known as formal guarantee.
- A business travel challenge in which the details of expenditure on staff business travel booked through other agents over a 3 months period were submitted by companies to cook, specially to calculate expected savings, provided the bookings are made through them.

Word-of-mouth Promotion: Most communication about tourism takes place by word-of-mouth information which in a true sense is word-of-recommendation. In the tourism industry it is found that the word-of-mouth promoters play the role of a hidden sales-force, who instrumentalize the process of selling. The high magnitude of effectiveness of this tool of promotion is due to high credibility of the channel, specially in the eyes of the potential tourists. The sensitivity of this tool makes it clear that tourist organizations need to concentrate on the quality of services they promise and offer. The marketers or the tourist organizations need to keep their eyes open, identify the vocal persons or the opinion leaders and take a special care of them so that they keep on moving the process of stimulating and creating demand.

Personal Selling: Personal selling is based on the personal skill of an individual. The oral representation in conversation bears the efficacy of transforming the motivation into persuasion. The travel and hotel business depend considerably on the personal selling. The development of travel and tourism has been possible due to well-educated and trained sales personnel. The development of tourism business has been influenced by the services rendered by the travel agents and travel guides since they work as information carriers.

Personal selling is the personal presentation of a tangible product or intangible services or ideas to the personal customers. It is important to mention that in the tourism industry, the personnel who attend tourists form an essential ingredient of the product, such as sales personnel are found responsible for dealing with customers behind the counter, the resort representatives cater to the need of tourists when they reach the destination, etc. all of them play a vital role in ensuring that the tourism products satisfy the tourists. The phrase– the customer is always right applies specifically to the tourism industry. No reduction in price would compensate for impolite and indecent travel guide, a solvent waiter and a surly or a haughty coach driver. These facts are testimony to the proposition that the travel business is linked with the performance and behaviour of sales personnel or travel staff.

Telemarketing: It is a method of selling in which a professionally sound telemarketer expands the business. The quality of technology and the communicative ability of the telemarketers determine the magnitude of success of this component. In tourism, the travel agents, offices of airways, receptionist, secretaries can't work efficiently if the telephonic services are not up to the mark. This makes a strong advocacy in favour of recruiting a person considered to be professionally sound, personally-committed sales personnel having an in-built creativity, innovation and imagination.

PLACE

Place or distribution management is concerned with two things – availability and accessibility. Researchers in tourism must determine how and where potential customers prefer to buy tourism products and services.

Most tour operators sell their services through travel agents, however, some deal directly with the consumers and eliminate middlemen. Other companies may also utilize more than one method of distribution. Airlines, for example, sell tickets through travel agents, and sell seats on flights to tour operators, and also offer travellers to book seats themselves through their own booking offices.

There exist, however, a number of intermediaries in the tourism marketing channel. It depends largely on the channel type. The intangibility feature in the service sector prevents intermediaries from taking possession or ownership of goods. Tourism, however, proves an exception where cuisine and souvenirs are goods and ownership is possible for the intermediaries.

Transport also plays a major role in the tourism industry. It makes the destinations accessible to people from around the world. Also, in the case of tangible products in tourism such as souvenirs and cuisine, transportation becomes a major logistical component.

PEOPLE

We can't deny the fact that sophisticated technologies have been successful in accelerating the pace of development. We also agree with this view that new generation of information technologies have simplified the task of decision-makers. At the same time we also have to accept the fact that the sophisticated technologies can't deliver goods to the development process if the employees operating and maintaining these technologies are not of world class. Technologies need due support of human resources who invent, innovate and develop technologies.

Like other industries, the tourism industry depends substantially on management of human resources. The tourism industry is an amalgam of the services of a lot of people and hence this industry cannot work efficiently if the travel agents, tour operators and travel guides lack world-class professional excellence. Of course the offices of travel agents depend on the new technology but after all employees and the other staff contribute significantly to the process. The travel guides need professional excellence since the projection of a positive image regarding a destination in particular requires their due cooperation, failing which even the world-class services offered by the travel agents are found meaningless. The tour operators also need to manage human resources efficiently.

In the management of people, the related organizations are required to think in favour of developing an ongoing training programme so that we find a close relation between the development of technologies and the quality of personnel who are supposed to operate and maintain the same. They need a lot of credentials to fulfil the expectations of the customers. The organization has to make the environmental conditions conducive and focus has to be laid on the incentives to the employees for energizing the process of performance orientation. Employee orientation requires due weightage to efficiency generation, value-orientation and perfection.

In the tourism industry the travel agents and the travel guides are the two most important people who speak a lot about the industry. Hence, it is imperative that they have to be at their best at all times. Travel guides especially, are expected to have a lot of patience, good sense of humour, tact to transform the occasional tourists into habitual ones, thorough knowledge of the places, linguistic skills, etc.

Hotel Market

INTRODUCTION

Accommodation constitutes a vital and fundamental part of tourism. An adequate supply of accommodation suitably tailored to the requirements of the tourist market is one of the basic conditions of tourism development. The provision of accommodation facilities and their growth is regarded in a broader context as it contributes to the economy as a whole. In the promotion of tourism, of all the constituents of the tourist industry, accommodation sector constitutes the most important segment and it has to play a distinctive role in the development of this expanding industry. This lesson will help you to understand the emergence and development of hotel and aviation industry and its impact on tourism industry.

EARLY HISTORY

The traveller, who leaves his home, requires accommodation at his destination and for journeys which cannot be completed in a single day. For this, he needed overnight accommodation, perhaps inns may be such accommodation units. It is understood through history, in ancient time and during Roman Empire many inns found providing food, during and also entertainment to travellers. During fifteenth century, the travel to religious pilgrimage purposes in several countries of Europe made the Church to take major responsibility for accommodation. The facilities being provided by inns were expanded. The English Common Law declared the 'Inn' to be a public house and imposed social responsibility of the inn-keeper for the well-being of the traveller. In United States of America another type of accommodation unit called 'tavern' become popular.

In India, the concept of shelter for traveller is not new. The historical records are replete with mention/ references of vihars, dharamsalas, saris, mosafirkhanas, etc. These establishments provided a home to all travellers. Hence, the demand for some kind of accommodation away from home is an important function of travel.

TYPES OF HOTEL ACCOMMODATION

Over the years the concept and the format of hotels have changed a great deal. There are various types of hotels catering to the increasing demands of tourists. The size, the façade, architectural features and the facilities and amenities provided differ from one establishment to another. The following are the main types of hotels:

(i) ***International Hotels:*** These hotels are placed in various star categories. These hotels provide in addition to accommodation all the other facilities which make the stay a very comfortable and interesting experience, various facilities provided include well-appointed reception and information counters, banquet halls, conference facilities, etc. There are also a number of shops, travel agency, money changing and safe deposit facilities. Restaurant facilities, bars and banqueting are an integral part of the business of a hotel. These hotels also provide entertainment for the guests in the form of various dance and music programmes, sports and games.

(ii) ***Resort Hotels:*** These cater to the needs of the holiday maker, the tourist and those who by reason of health desire a change of atmosphere. Resort hotels are located near the sea, mountain and other areas abounding in natural beauty. Rest, relaxation and entertainment are the key factors around which resorts are built. The primary motive of a person visiting resort hotels is rest and relaxation which he is looking far away from his routine busy work life. The type of services and amenities located in resort property include recreation facilities such as swimming pool, golf course, tennis courts, skiing, boating surf-riding and other various indoor sports. Other important amenities include coffee shops, restaurants, conference rooms, lounge, shopping arcade and entertainment.

Resorts can be of various types and can be classified on the basis of climate and also topography. Broadly they fall in the categories of (i) Summer resorts (ii) Winter resorts (ii) Hill resorts (iv) All season resorts and (v) Health resorts.

(iii) ***Commercial Hotels:*** The hotels direct their appeal primarily to the individual traveller as compared to international or resort hotel where the focus is on the group travel. As these hotels cater primarily to people who are visiting a place for commerce or business, these are located in important commercial and industrial centres of large towns and cities.

(iv) ***Residential Hotels:*** These hotels can be described as apartment house complete with hotel service. These are often referred to as apartment hotels. The tariff of rooms in these hotels is charged on monthly, half yearly or yearly basis and is charged for either furnished or unfurnished accommodation. These hotels which are located mostly in big cities operate exclusively under the European plan where no meals are provided to the guests.

(v) ***Floating Hotels:*** These hotels are located on the surface of water. It may be on sea or water, river water or on a lake. All the facilities and services of a hotel are provided in these hotels. In many countries old luxury ships have been converted into floating hotels and are proving very popular among tourists. The atmosphere they provide is exclusive and exotic. In India, floating hotels in the form of houseboats are very popular with tourists in Kashmir valley.

SUPPLEMENTARY ACCOMMODATION

Supplementary accommodation consists of various types of accommodation other than the conventional hotel type. It may be described as premises which offer accommodation but not the services of a hotel. The supplementary accommodation as compared to the conventional type of accommodation is moderately priced. The following are some of the principal forms of supplementary accommodation:

(i) ***Motel:*** Primarily designed to serve the needs of motorists, motels almost exclusively meet the demand or transit accommodation. They serve the function of a transit hotel except that they are geared to accommodate motor travelling guests for overnight stay. The important services provided by motels include parking, garage facilities, accommodation restaurant facilities, public catering and recreational facilities.

(ii) ***Youth Hostels:*** Youth hostel can be defined as a building which offers clean, moderate and inexpensive shelter to young people exploring their own country or other countries and travelling independently or in groups on holiday or for educational purposes. In most of the countries, youth hostels are developed and managed by non-commercial organizations whose main aim is the development of youth tourism. The services provided include accommodation, means and also recreation.

(iii) ***Caravan and Camping Sites:*** These are also known as open air hostels, tourist camps or camping grounds. Camping originally practised by hikers on foot is increasingly giving way to car camping. The sites are usually located within the large cities in open spaces. Equipped to received mobile accommodation in the form of caravans, the camping sites provide facilities for parking, tent-pitching, water, electricity, toilet, etc. the other services include restaurants, recreational rooms.

(iv) ***Pension:*** This accommodation is very popular in certain European countries. Pension is also described as a private hotel/a guesthouse or a boarding house. Catering facilities are optional and are usually restricted to the residents. Mostly managed by a family, pension accommodation is much cheaper than hotel accommodation.

(v) ***Bed and Breakfast Establishment:*** These establishments provide only accommodation and breakfast and not the principal meals. These are usually located in large towns and cities along commercial and holiday routes and also resort areas and are used by en route travellers. Some of these establishments are very popular with holiday-makers.

(vi) ***Tourist Holiday Villages:*** Tourist villages were established in some European countries after World War II. These villages are situated at warm sea sides and in the regions which offer certain facilities for the tourists. The village complex is a centre of accommodation providing extensive sports and recreation facilities, riding, swimming, tennis, mini-golf and yoga.

INDIAN HOSPITALITY INDUSTRY

The Indian hotel industry derives around 65% of its revenues from premium segments which has a share of just 25.82% in terms of number of rooms. Due to the huge inflow of tourists and outsourcing boom the occupancy rates, average room rates and revenue per available room across major cities in India are increasing. As a result of this, the demand-supply mismatch is getting closer.

The companies operating in Indian hotel industry are moving up the value chain to management contracts and branding as a part of their de-risking model. Indian hotel industry is fast adopting the technologies such as wireless, online reservation system and customer relationship management (CRM) like in the west. In order to mitigate risk due to its seasonality nature and to boost revenues the companies operating in the industry are entering into new emerging areas such as service apartments and spas.

Few major Indian hoteliers are: ITDC, Indian Hotels Company Limited, Taj Luxury Hotels, Taj Business Hotels, Taj Leisure Hotels, The Oberoi Group of Hotels, Welcome Group of Hotels, Hotel Leela Venture Limited, etc.

DEMAND FOR HOTEL FACILITIES

The total hotel market, which consists of the total demand for hotel facilities, may be divided into various segments. These segments are determined as per the needs of the people and the means they possess to pay for their satisfaction. The market for the hotel will be served according to what is provided, how it is provided, and for how much. At a managerial level, it is relevant to conceptualize the demand for the hotel sector at both the primary and secondary levels, to be able to assess the requirements on the supply side.

Table 2.1 Primary and secondary level of demands

Primary level	(i) Basic demand which exists for hotel facilities but not being served at present. (ii) Displacement demand arising from the clientele for other hotels where the customers' needs are not fully met by the market package offered.
Secondary level	(i) Created demand which does not exist so far, and arising from people who do not normally use hotel facilities, or from people who do not use the hotel facilities in particular area. (ii) Futuristic demand which may occur at sometime in the future, due to certain socio-economic or socio-psychological factors or both, e.g., rise in the standard of living and per capita income ('green revolution' areas, new industrial complexes), increase in population, changing social systems and habits, etc.

A new hotel introduced in a particular segment of the hotel market may eventually be able to exploit all these levels of demand. It is essential that there should be substantial basic demand which can be tapped by a new hotel. Displacement and created levels of demand require a period of time and sustained sales effort to realize their potential, whereas, the assessment of future demand relates to the continuing long-term prosperity of the hotel. If the basic demand is absent but if the displacement, created and future levels of demand promise well for an investment appraised on '10 to 15 year basis', the decision to start a new hotel under such circumstances has perforce to be a long-gestation decision.

For accommodation, each segment of the market, together with its primary and secondary divisions, contains some or all of the potential buyers of hotel accommodation, as shown in Table 2.2, which may sometimes overlap. There may well be more types according to the geographical, economic, industrial, and social characteristics of the location of each hotel. Similarly, for food and beverages, each segment of the hotel market contains varied categories of potential buyers of catering services which may also sometimes overlap.

Table 2.2 Potential buyers for accommodation and catering services

Accommodation	• Transit tourists, passing through the particular location. • Terminal tourists, for whom the location represents end of a journey. • Travelling businessmen. • Visiting personnel, i.e., business or industrial employees for whom travel is an occasional part of their job. • Organized tours. • Conventions, conference, workshops, meetings, where the location is pre-fixed by the organizers. • Social visitors, i.e., guests to weddings or other social functions.
Catering	• Occupant customers staying in the hotel. • Transit or change customers — people other than local residents of the areas patronizing the hotel either by impulse of intentionally planned for meals, refreshments, etc. • Organization and societies consisting of members acting in unison. • Local business customers who patronize the hotel due to local industrial or commercial activity. • Meetings and conferences organized by agencies from outside areas. • People on tour who step into the hotel for meals, refreshments, etc.

HOTEL PRODUCT

The hotel product has a number of components like accommodation, food and beverage, recreation and health, shops, car rental service, apart from others. But of all these, the accommodation and food and beverage components are the primary ones. Philip Kolter has identified 5 levels of a hotel product. These levels are:

Table 2.3 Different levels of a hotel product

1. Core benefit	The fundamental benefit the customer is buying (hotel: rest/sleep)
2. Basic product	Basic, functional attributes (Room; Bed, Bath...)
3. Expected product	Set of attributes/conditions the buyer normally expects (clean room, large towel, quieter location)
4. Augmented product	That meets the customers' desires beyond expectations (prompt room service, music, check in/out, aroma)
5. Potential product	The possible evolution to distinguish the offer (all-suite hotel)

From the above table it is quite clear that at the "Core" level all hotels are alike and the differentiation starts as you start moving up. The accommodation component of the hotel product requires a clear identification of the type of clientele the hotel wishes to attract and serve. Regardless of 'star' categorization, as customers tend to graduate from one 'star' category to another, accommodation can be either of the luxury type almost regardless of the price, or the economy type providing the essentials of shelter frugally. Between these two there are a variety of accommodation facilities catering to customers whose accommodation is paid for; leisure customers who pay for their accommodation; customers who are part of groups either on business or on pleasure. However, once the hotel property has been constructed to serve identified and specific customer segments, the possibility of variation is severely restricted. Admittedly, the economy type property cannot be moved up into a luxury one without considerable expense and time although a reversal from the luxury to the economy class is more feasible and less problematic.

To tide over the above difficulties, hotel architects, the world over, are now designing properties with as much flexibility as possible to make multipurpose adjustable public rooms feasible. In the case of a hotel where such flexibility does not exist, the hotel product decision for accommodation will depend entirely on the accuracy of selling rooms to the right type of customer. On the other hand, the food and beverage component of the basic hotel product offers greater scope for flexibility. Qualitative differentials can be very wide and would range from high class a la carte high-price menu restaurants with complete table service to the medium or low-priced menu dining rooms.

Capital expenditure is relatively lower– decor, furnishings and fittings can be changed more easily to transform the image of a restaurant or dining room in either way. Availability of room service from either the hotel's own kitchens or from outside is another area of flexibility. It is obvious, however, that resident guests in a hotel know what exactly they are buying in room occupancy and in food and beverage sales. Hence, their experience of the hotel product will condition their future relationship with the hotel and the patronage afforded.

Table 2.4 below gives the various ways in which accommodation and food service products can be augmented.

Table 2.4 Hospitality product augmentation

Accommodation	*Food and Beverage*
Reservation system convenience	Speed of food service
Reservation system simplicity	Ordering convenience
Acknowledgement of reservations	Telephone
Lift attendants	Advance orders
Room service	Order-taking table staff
Standard of housekeeping	Complaints procedures
Courtesy	Advance reservations
Procedures for handling overbooking	Reliability of food/beverages quality
Information service	Customer advice on wines
Customer recognition	Provision of special foods
Credit provision	Cooking to order
Baggage handling	Acceptance of credit cards
Pet/child care	Variations in portions
Provision for disabled	Home deliveries
Group accommodation	Extent of non-available menu items
Discounts on club referrals, etc.	Fibre/calorie information
Cleaning/laundry	Provision of doggy-bags
Courtesy care	Function-catering facilities
Willingness to bill later	Quality of table appointments
	Entertainment
	Privacy/discretions

Source: Francis and Buttle, Hotel and Food Service Marketing

HOTEL PRICING AND DISTRIBUTION

Pricing

It is difficult for a hotel to exercise differential pricing except for certain specific purpose. These may typically be differentials in tariffs and prices during the peak and lean seasons; group rates; contract rates for airline crew; special conference rates or special concessions to attract customers, etc. However, by and large, hotel pricing tends to follow or conform to pricing standards applicable to the particular city area or resort, to competitive hotels, to the amount of traffic being generated in the hotel location, tourist location, international or national conference venue, and so on. Nevertheless, hotel pricing also suffers from a degree of lack of flexibility, although to a lesser extent than that of the hotel product. The depreciated valuation of the hotel property, its financial management efficiencies, credit policies and other factors, specially cost of empty room-nights, fixed overheads, also have a bearing on tariffs and menu prices.

Distribution

Hotel distribution relies on interdependence with other industries serving travellers and tourists such as the transportation industry (airlines, railways, roadways, shipping lines), travel agents and tour operators, national and state tourism organizations, shopping and entertainment providers. In sum, those services which provide certain other facilities to the traveller or the tourists which are bought when accommodation and food are assured.

Some interesting features of hotel distribution need critical examination. The first is cooperative distribution which operates in passing on traffic overflow from one hotel to its neighbour, on a reciprocal basis, without affecting regular business with the main intermediaries in the distribution system such as travel agents; tour operators; airlines and special business clientele. The second is the increasing development of franchising. Franchising may take various forms but it basically involves making available to the franchisee (the beneficiary) of a service, system that is designed and controlled for quality standards by the franchiser. The franchisee gets the advantage of being part of a reservation and sales system which ensures a certain level of business which may not be available otherwise. The franchisee also benefits from the image of the franchiser, professional advice and training provided by the franchiser. In the process, he improves his own operational image and efficiency. The franchiser also benefits as his investment is not required in the franchisee's properties. At the same time, the franchiser's distribution system is expanded and the franchisee is well motivated to succeed in his own business. Hotel distribution is, thus, an important element of the marketing mix.

Table 2.5 Different types of strategies used by hotel

To increase sales

- Induce potential guest/customers to visit the hotel
- Obtain enquiries through mail/telephone on a priority basis
- Promptly announcing special offers or any other attraction
- Secure enquiries from travel agents/tour operators/wholesalers
- Stimulate impulse action (e.g., book a table for dinner)
- Induce conference buyers to contact hotel
- Publicize unique selling points of the hotel – location, atrium or special architectural features and any other specific feature – which would attract attention
- Support regular travel/tour agent in selling the hotel

To create awareness or interest in 'Facilities/services available'.

- Individual facilities (rooms, suites, pool, bar, health club, etc.)
- Group of facilities, e.g., speciality restaurants, etc.
- Special facilities/services, e.g., CCTV, audio-visual equipped conference hall, full office-cum-secretarial services with Internet, STD telephone, fax, etc.

To create awareness or interest in 'Benefits to be gained by patronizing hotel':

- Specific, e.g., tangible, psychological, aesthetic
- Financial e.g., prices, discounts, credit, etc.
- Quantitative, e.g., portions, size of guest rooms, private balconies, etc.
- Qualitative, e.g., guest room climate control, wide range of items on menu

To create awareness or interest in 'Versatile advantage of hotel'.

- Qualitative, e.g., guest room climate control, wide range of items on menu
- Mini- Frigidaire in guest room "do-it-yourself" tea/coffee/breakfast kit in guest room
- Multipurpose meeting room-cum-wedding hall
- Collapsible bed-cum-divan/room convertible into meeting and private dining room
- "Wake-up call"-cum-"appointment reminder" device in guest room

Table 2.5 Contd..

Table 2.5 Contd..

To create awareness or interest in 'Resources behind the hotel'.

- Stand-by generator for uninterrupted power supply
- Water purification system: "Drink from bathroom tap"
- "Take a tour of our kitchen": latest equipment
- "Meet our managers": quality of service-oriented staff

Table 2.6 Promotional tools used by hotel industry

Type of Promotions	*Example*
1. Price-off Promotions	Special terms for specific clients at specific time; e.g., off-peak discounts: discounts for specific departure/hotel stay dates or times, etc.
2. Premium Offers	Special package deals, e.g., three weeks stay for the price of two; family plans; children free if accompanied by parents; special introductory prices, etc.
3. Couponing	Coupons entitling the holder to special terms, e.g., discounts at shopping centres, discounts for petrol, free excursions and sightseeing tours, free use of hotel recreation facilities, etc.
4. Contests (consumer)	Prizes awarded to consumers winning special contests, e.g., free holidays/stays.
5. Contests (trade)	Prizes awarded to travel trade winning special contests, e.g., free holidays/stays, or other articles, usually products of the destination country concerned.
6. Loyalty Schemes	"X" sum of money off next booking if done within a certain period of time; "Give away" to loyal customers.
7. Trade Incentives/Discounts	Offered to retailers/wholesalers for achieving specified sales volumes, e.g., bonuses, override commissions, quantity or volume discounts, etc.
8. Guarantees	Money-back guarantees in case of cancellation of flights; tours failures, bad weather, etc.
9. Credit Schemes	Purchase of tours on instalment payment basis, normally extended by travel trade organizations with bank affiliations–"Travel now, Pay later schemes", etc. Acceptance of payment by credit card.
10. Cooperative Advertising	Allowance or financial assistance given to a tour operator or travel retailer advertising specified hotel/product.
11. Training Schemes	Free familiarization tours for travel agents/tour operators; training seminars and briefings for sales personnel, etc.
12. Merchandising Support	Free display material and other selling aids offered to retailer/wholesaler as a part of the special campaign.
13. Quiet Weekend	There is a particular pattern in all the commercial hotels around the world, namely, a quiet weekend, because business people go home. How a hotel should go about for generating additional business, because anything extra that one gets is really worthwhile. The hotel or hotel organization can contact the people to organize fairs, exhibitions, fashion shows, cultural sessions, etc., during these days. And one can contact them either personally or through direct mailing.
14. Welcome-cocktail	To generate more demand for "Food and Beverage", hotels offer the first drink free as part of sales promotional efforts because after one drink the guest may well ask for more and thus give additional business to the hotel.

Table 2.6 Contd..

Table 2.6 Contd..

15. Honeymooners Return Trip	Some hotels give special coupons to honeymooners to come and celebrate their first or subsequent wedding anniversary. This gives an aura and finesse to the hotel. It also ensures permanent customer and future business.
16. Discount for Agents and Airlines' crew	Travel sales promotional efforts help in developing good relations with the travel trade and may help in getting favourable publicity.
17. Free Ticket for Sound-n-Light Show	Some of the hotels give free tickets to their guest for sound and light shows conducted in their hotels. This promotional effort helps in developing and cementing good guest relations.
18. Sun-n-shine Guarantees	Some of the beach resort hotels whose business depends on sunshine can give such type of guarantees to their guests during the off-season. If there is no sunshine the money paid is returned to the guest. If the hotel has some credible system of good weather forecast, one can get good business.
19. Consumer Contests	Some hotels in collaboration with consumer goods organisations, organize contests for joint promotion.

AIRLINE CONNECTION

History

An airline provides air transport services for passengers or freight, generally with a recognized operating certificate or licence. Airlines lease or own their aircraft with which to supply these services and may form partnerships or alliances with other airlines for mutual benefit.

Airlines vary from those with a single airplane carrying mail or cargo, through full-service international airlines operating many hundreds of airplanes. Airline services can be categorized as being intercontinental, or domestic and may be operated as scheduled services or charters.

Flight museums such as the Virginia Aviation Museum remind us what a short history the airplane has, photo by Cyane Lowdon, Courtesy of the Science Museum of Virginia.

DELAG, Deutsche Luftschiffahrts-Aktiengesellschaft (German: acronym for "German Airship Transport Corporation") was the world's first airline. It was founded on November 16, 1909 with government assistance, and operated airships manufactured by Zeppelin Corporation. Its headquarters were in Frankfurt. (Note: Americans, such as Rufus Porter and Frederick Marriott, attempted to start airlines in the mid-19th century, focusing on the New York-California route. Those attempts foundered due to such mishaps as the aircraft catching fire and the aircraft being ripped apart by spectators.) The five oldest non-dirigible airlines that still exist are Australia's Qantas, Netherland's KLM, Colombia's Avianca, Czech Republic's Czech Airlines and Mexico's Mexicana. KLM first flew in May 1920 while Qantas (for the Queensland and Northern Territory Aerial Services Limited) was founded in Queensland, Australia in late 1920.

Influence of Aviation on Tourism Industry

Tourism and Air Transport industry are complement to each other. Tourism depends on transportation to bring visitors, while the transportation industry depends on tourism to generate demand for its services. The growth in tourism industry directly reflects onto the air transportation. Over the last 25 years, the number of international tourists has more than doubled. The expansion of international tourism has a large impact on the discipline of transport geography.

Transport is the cause and the effect of the growth of tourism. To start with, the improved facilities have stimulated tourism, and the expansion of tourism has stimulated transport. Accessibility is the main function behind the basics of tourism transport. In order to access the areas that are mainly aimed, tourists will use any transportation mode. However, air transport is the main mode for international tourism. Air transport plays a dominant role in inter-regional movements of tourists, which normally entails travel over long-distance. Growth rates of international air traffic are pegged with growth rates of international tourism. Attractive package tours, competitive airfare attract more and more tourist day by days, therefore, both the industry is expanding rapidly.

Transport policies and decisions of governments can make a big difference in the destinations available to tourists, for instance the Suvarnabhumi Airport Bangkok, Thailand. Air transport is far advance than the transport mode. Air transport has revolutionized the geographical aspect of distances; the most remote areas can now be attained, any journey around the world can be measured in terms of hours of travelling. With jet that, can reach up to 1950 km/hrs, international tourism is no longer an on going adventure.

About 6.7 million jobs worldwide are in tourism industry directly supported by the spending of foreign visitors arriving by air. Taking into account both the overseas visors and workforce employed it can be said that the industry is giant in shape "The world's largest industry of Travel and Tourism". How big the airline industry and its market share are an example will give you a clear image – in a statistics it shown that, American Airlines saves US$ 40,000 in a year by eliminating one olive from each salad served in first class only.

Importance

In intercontinental or long-distance travel, air transport has been responsible for the 'Explosion' in world tourism and in certain areas where the terrain and other conditions prevent normal development of other forms of transport, air travel is the only means of tourism. Historically, it is established that the improvements in travel facilities, especially reduced time and increased comfort, have encouraged and influenced travel movement and created an upsurge in the volume of traffic.

Air transport is essentially international, large and above al a dynamic and developing industry. Its extensive network spans all continents, serves nearly all countries. Air transport has become the largest single item in international trade (barring oil) and its importance to tourism cannot be overemphasized. Only air transport has brought tourism on a large industrial scale to many tourist centres, not least to developing countries, thereby contributing in an unprecedented way to their social and economic amelioration. Jets in particular have revolutionized travel and Jumbos have dramatically accelerated the revolutionary charge. By their achievements in speed, safety, comfort and economy, they have attracted great number of travellers.

The considerable increase in international tourism world is mainly due to air transport, which has facilitated long-distance travel, particularly for passengers with higher incomes from the developed countries. The UN Conference on International Travel and Tourism held in 1963 at Rome recognized the paramount importance of Public and Private Transport as an element in the growth of tourism.

Low-Cost Carrier

A low-cost carrier (LCC) or low-cost airlines — also known as a no-frills, discount, or budget airline — is an airline that offers generally low fares by eliminating many traditional passenger services. This concept, experienced first in the United States with Pacific Southwest Airlines in the early 1950s, gave birth to one of the biggest success stories of the last twenty years in the air travel industry. Southwest Airlines, which began service in 1971, is LCC' s biggest U.S. success story. They have been a model that other low-cost carriers have emulated. The LCCs now represent over 30 per cent of total air travel in the United States and 25 per cent in Europe, and are making gains in Asia.

Some typical business practices of LCCs are:

- One passenger class
- One type of airplane to reduce fleet maintenance costs
- Using secondary airports
- Quick airport turnarounds
- Point-to-point service
- Unreserved seating
- Employees working in multiple roles
- Internet booking
- No frills, just low fares

Low-cost carriers are growing, threatening the major carriers and making major carrier profitability a more difficult task. Brand names like Southwest, JetBlue, Ryan Air, West Jet, and Easy Jet are growing and gaining ground against their larger competitors. They are also making a profit. They are being joined by new low-cost carriers in all parts of the world.

The bright spot in the global air industry is Asia and the Pacific. The dynamic economy of the region is making its own airlines profitable and helping carriers from outside the region with extensive Asia/ Pacific operations. At present, the Orient is the world's number – one growth centre for air travel.

The world's economy and the tourism industry need a healthy air transportation system. Without airline passengers, rental cars go unrented, hotel beds go unsold, and attractions go unvisited. The airlines have revolutionized long-haul travel and the range and speed of jet travel have greatly expanded what tourists or business travellers could once accomplish with the equivalent time and funds at their disposal. Today, for example, it is possible to fly around the globe in less time than it takes to drive across the United States. The system is also incredibly efficient. You need to make only one call to an airline or a travel agent or get on the Internet to purchase a ticket to your desired destination; then all you have to do is go to the airport and check your bags through to the final destination. The logistics that make it happen are complex, but the system works well. For example, United Airlines (including United Express and Ted) offers over 3600 flights a day to 210 domestic and international destinations. Other airlines have similar structures and combine to make a total system that blankets the world.

Although the major advantage of air travel is speed, which results in more time for other activities, there are negative aspects for those who wish to travel by air. These include some people's fear of flying and a lack of geographic accessibility, since many communities in the country are not served by air transportation. An additional not getting to and from the airport. Frequently, this time exceeds that spent en route.

In the United States, air carriers are classified as major if they record over $1 billion in revenue annually. There are twenty: ABX, AirTran Airways, Alaska Airlines, American Airlines, American Eagle, ATA, Atlas/Polar, Comair, Continental Airlines, Delta Air Lines, ExpressJet, FedEx, JetBlue, Mesa, Northwest Airlines, SkyWest, Southwest Airlines, United Airlines, UPS Airlines, and US Airways. National carriers are those recording annual revenues of $100 million to $1 billion and include Air Transport International, Air Wisconsin Airlines, Allegiant, Aloha Airlines, Amerijet International, ASTAR Air Cargo, Atlantic Southeast, Champion Air, Continental Micronesia, Evergreen International Airlines, Executive Airlines, Florida West, Frontier Airlines, Gemini Air Cargo, Hawaiian Airlines, Horizon Air, Independence Air, Kalitta Air, Mesaba Airlines, Miami Air International, Midwest Airlines, North American Airlines, Omni Air International, Pinnacle Airlines dba Northwest Airlink, PSA Airlines, Ryan International Airlines, Spirit Airlines, Sun Country Airlines, Trans States Airlines, Transmeridian, USA 3000 Airlines, USA Jet, and World Airways. There are about thirty-one regional airlines with annual revenues under $100 million. In addition, there are fifty-five small certified commuter airlines.

Future of Tourism and Aviation

The travel and tourism industry employs 72 million people worldwide. Global tourism expenditure is estimated to be nearly US$ 3 trillion. Tourism accounts directly for 3.8% of worlds GDP. Tourism is expected to maintain its growth by 2014, the World Travel and Tourism Council expects the torsion industry to employ more than 84 million people globally.

Tourism as an upcoming industry. The World Tourism Organization (UNWTO) forecasts that international tourism will continue growing at the average annual rate of 4%. By 2020 Europe will remain the most popular destination, but its share will drop from 60% in 1995 to 46%. Long haul will grow slightly faster than intraregional travel and by 2020 its share will increase from 18% in 1995 to 24%.

With the advent of e-commerce, tourism products have become one of the most traded items on the Internet. Tourism products and services have been made available through intermediaries, although tourism providers (hotels, airlines, etc.) can sell their services directly. This has put pressure on intermediaries from both on-line and traditional shops. It has been suggested there is a strong correlation between tourism expenditure per capita and the degree to which countries play in the global context. Not only as a result of the important economic contribution of the tourism industry, but also as an indicator of the degree of confidence with which global citizens leverage the resources of the globe for the benefit of their local economies.

Space tourism is expected to "take off" in the first quarter of the 21st century, although compared with traditional destinations the number of tourists in orbit will remain low until technologies such as a space elevator make space travel cheap.

Technological improvement is likely to make possible air-ship hotels, based either on solar-powered airplanes or large dirigibles. Underwater hotels, such as Hydropolis, expected to open in Dubai in 2009. On the ocean tourists will be welcomed by ever larger cruise ships and perhaps floating cities.

Some futurists expect that movable hotel 'pods' will be created that could be temporarily erected anywhere on the planet, where building a permanent resort would be unacceptable politically, economically or environmentally.

INDIAN AVIATION INDUSTRY

The aviation industry in India began with the birth of Tata Airlines, through the business relationship between Mr. Nevill Vintcent, a Royal Air Force pilot and Mr. JRD Tata, the first Indian to get an A-licence. Tata Airlines became Air India in August 1946. In 1953, the Air Corporation Act nationalized all existing airline assets and established the Indian Airline Corporation and Air India International for domestic and international air services respectively.

These two companies enjoyed monopoly power in the industry until 1991, when private airlines were given permission to operate charter and non-scheduled services under the 'Air Taxi' scheme to boost tourism. These carriers were not allowed at the time, to fly scheduled flights or issue air tickets to passengers. As a result, a number of private players including Jet Airways, Air Sahara, Modiluft, Damania Airways, NEPC airlines and East West Airlines commenced domestic operations. In 1994, following the repeal of the Air Corporation Act, private players were permitted to operate scheduled services. Ultimately the carriers with more efficient operations and strategies survived and by 1997, only Jet Airways and Air Sahara made the cut from the original group.

The next big change in the industry came in late 2003 with the emergence of India's first no-frill airlines, Air Deccan. It revolutionized the industry, offering fares as low as INR 500 (USD 10 roughly), compared with Full Service fares offered by the incumbents, averaging about INR 3000 or more. Since then, Spice Jet (restructured Royal Airways and Modiluft), Go Airways and Kingfisher Air have also entered the industry. Paramount Airways is another player, though it is positioned on the other end of the spectrum, as an 'all business class' airline. With the further advent of online ticket sales through companies such as makemytrip.com, prices have crashed and tickets are available for as little as INR 0.99. In fact, now many airline tickets can be bought for a price comparable to an upper class railway ticket for the same route.

In December 2004, Indian scheduled carriers with a minimum of 5 years of continuous operations and a minimum fleet size of 20 aircraft, were permitted to operate scheduled services to internationals destinations. On January 11, 2005 the government designated four scheduled Indian carriers (Air India, Indian Airlines, Jet Airways and Air Sahara) to operate international services to and from Singapore, Malaysia, Thailand, Hong Kong, the UK and the USA.

TRAVEL AGENCY

Travel agency is the species of the genus tourism management. In the organization of tourism, the role of private sector is conspicuously crucial. In most countries which are in any many manners concerned with the tourist industry, the private sector plays a very important role. The private sector's role is not linked merely in selling the tourism product but often also in producing it as many individuals, companies and corporations are involved in promoting, developing and financing tourism. Travel agency is one such organization in the private sector which plays a key and crucial role in the entire process of developing and promoting tourism. It is the travel agent's job which packages and processes all the various attractions of the country and presents them to the tourists.

Functions of Travel Agency

(i) Provision of travel information
(ii) Preparation of itineraries
(iii) Liaison with providers of services
(iv) Planning and costing tours
(v) Ticketing
(vi) Provision of foreign currencies
(vii) Insurance

Travel Agents Association of India (TAAI)

The travel agents decided to form an Association on All India basis as early as in the year 1952 when an All India Travel Agents Association was established. The main objective of the Association is to safeguard and protect the interests of its members by way to having a constant dialogue with the concerned government agencies.

The vital role played by the travel agents in the growth and development of tourism in the country and its promotion is recognized by all segments of the travel industry. The government works in close collaboration with them not only in India but abroad as well, encouraging them to plan and organize package tours for various destinations in India. In suitable cases, the Department of Tourism recommends the release of foreign exchange to travel agents to enable them to open their branch offices abroad.

Let us Sum Up

According to World Tourism Organization (2002), 'Tourism' is defined as "the activities of persons travelling to and staying in places outside their usual environment for not more than one consecutive year for leisure, business and other purposes not related to the exercise of an activity remunerated from within the place visited." This definition identifies clearly the activities and length of stay in the destination outside the usual environment where people use to be.

Tourism marketing is defined in a number of ways. It could be defined as the 'systematic and coordinated efforts exerted by the National Tourist Organizations and/or the tourist enterprises at international, national and local levels to optimize the satisfaction of tourists, groups and individuals, in view of the sustained tourism growth'.

The tourist product is a composite one, a combination of attractions, transport, accommodation, entertainment and other services. In most countries, there are many separate suppliers of these various components – airlines, hotel companies, tour excursion organizers, etc. It is an important feature of tourism that, though an individual supplier of tourist services may serve more than one market, rarely, if ever, does a single supplier provide the entire range of products/services required by a tourist on a visit to a destination. Whether sold as a package or assembled by the tourist himself or by a travel agent, the tourist product is in practice a composite one. It is apparent, then, that given the fragmented nature of supply on one hand, and the demand for a combined set of products on the other, a fundamental challenge for a destination is to achieve coordination and integration of all components across all sub-sectors of the tourism industry, that is, of supply.

The tourism product is essentially an intangible thing. Also, because tourism is a multi-segment industry, the task of formulating a product mix becomes more difficult and challenging.

Selling a holiday is 'selling dreams'. The way to win the customer's heart is through the peripheral services provided along with the core product. Thus, a tourism product is quite a complex one, including the destination, airline seat, hotel room, occasional tangible products such as souvenirs, a free bag or bottle of whisky, etc.

Creation of awareness has a far-reaching impact. The tourist organizations bear the responsibility of informing, persuading and sensing the potential tourists in a right fashion. The marketers need to use the various components of promotion optimally so that they succeed in increasing the number of habitual users. Promotion helps in maximizing the duration of stay, frequency of visit by offering new tourist products in the same country to areas which hitherto have remained untapped or partially tapped.

Accommodation constitutes a vital and fundamental part of tourism. An adequate supply of accommodation suitably tailored to the requirements of the tourist market is one of the basic conditions of tourism development. The provision of accommodation facilities and their growth is regarded in a broader context as it contributes to the economy as a whole. In the promotion of tourism, of all the constituents of the tourist industry, accommodation sector constitute the most important segment and it has to play a distinctive role in the development of this expanding industry. This lesson will help you to understand the emergence and development of hotel and aviation industry and its impact on tourism industry.

Tourism and Air Transport industry are complement to each other. Tourism depends on transportation to bring visitors, while the transportation industry depends on tourism to generate demand for its services. The growth in tourism industry directly reflects onto the air transportation. Over the last 25 years, the number of international tourists has more than doubled. The expansion of international tourism has a large impact on the discipline of transport geography.

Transport is the cause and the effect of the growth of tourism. To start with, the improved facilities have stimulated tourism, and the expansion of tourism has stimulated transport. Accessibility is the main function behind the basics of tourism transport. In order to access the areas that are mainly aimed, tourists will use any transportation mode. However, air transport is the main mode for international tourism. Air transport plays a dominant role in inter-regional movements of tourists, which normally entails travel over long-distance. Growth rates of international air traffic are pegged with growth rates of international tourism. Attractive package tours, competitive airfare attract more and more tourists day by days, therefore, both the industries are expanding rapidly.

The travel agents decided to form an Association on All India basis as early as in the year 1952 when an All India Travel Agents Association was established. The main objective of the Association is to safeguard and protect the interests of its members by way to having a constant dialogue with the concerned government agencies.

Questions for Discussion

1. Define tourism and tourist. Explain the importance of tourism industry.
2. Historically trace out of the developments of modern travel.
3. Bring out the dynamic relationship between travel and tourism.
4. Bring out the importance of various modes of travel for successful tourism management.
5. Bring out the importance of accommodation for better tourism management in India.
6. What are the different types of accommodation available for tourists in India?
7. Explain the following: (i) Motel (ii) Resort hotels (iii) Youth hostel (iv) Floating hotels.
8. What are the different types of traveller?
9. Explain challenges in tourism marketing.
10. Explain characteristics of tourism marketing.
11. Discuss the importance of tourism marketing.
12. Explain the various users of tourism product.
13. Explain various bases for segmenting tourism market.
14. Discuss the product mix in tourism.
15. Explain the promotion mix of tourism industry.
16. Explain the importance of hotel in tourism.
17. Briefly explain different levels of tourist product.
18. Explain pricing and distribution in hotel industry.
19. What are the different promotional tools are used in promoting hotels?
20. Explain importance of aviation in tourism.
21. Explain the concept of travel agent and its functions.

3

Banking and Insurance Services

"It is a wise man who lives with money in the bank, it is a fool who dies that way" – French proverb

Learning Objectives

At the end of this chapter students will be able to understand

- Meaning and concept of banking
- Types of bank
- Trends in banking service
- Reserve Bank of India
- Concept of insurable risk and insurable interest
- Life insurance
- LIC
- IRDA
- Various services rendered by bank
- Banking activities
- IT and banking
- Meaning and concept of insurance
- Types of insurance
- Non-life insurance
- GIC

PART–A: ***Banking*** *– introduction – meaning and concepts – traditional services – modern services – recent trends in banking services – types of bank – IT and banking – Reserve Bank of India.*

PART–B: ***Insurance*** *– introduction – meaning and definition of insurance – types of insurance – life insurance – products of life insurance – general insurance – types of general insurance – LIC – GIC – IRDA*

Part-A: Banking

INTRODUCTION

A bank is defined as a commercial institution licensed as a receiver of deposits and giver of loans – both short and long term. Section 5(1)(b) of the Banking Regulation Act, 1949 defines banking as, "the accepting for the purpose of lending or investment, of deposits from the public, repayable on demand or otherwise, and withdrawal by cheque, draft, order or otherwise."

Section 5(1) (c) defines a banking company as, "any company which transacts the business of banking in India."

Banking involves therefore:

- The borrowing, raising or taking up of money;
- The lending or advancing of money either with or without security;
- The drawing, making, accepting, discounting buying, selling, collecting and dealing in bills of exchange, hundis, promissory notes, coupons, drafts, bills of lading, railway receipts, warrants, debentures, certificates, scrip and other instruments and securities whether transferable or negotiable or not;
- The granting and issuing of letters of credit, travellers' cheques and circulars notes;
- The buying and selling of foreign exchange including bank notes;
- The buying and selling of bullion and specie;
- The acquiring, holding, issuing on commission, underwriting and dealing in stocks, funds, shares, debentures, bonds, obligations, securities and investments of all kinds;
- The purchasing and selling of bonds, scrip or other forms of securities on behalf of constituents or others, the negotiating of loans and advances;
- The receiving of all kinds of bonds or valuables on deposit or for safe custody or otherwise;
- The providing of safe deposit vaults;
- The collecting and transmitting of money and securities;
- Carrying on and transacting every kind of guarantee and indemnity business;
- Managing, selling and realizing any property which may form the security or part of the security for any loans or advances or which may be connected with any such security;
- Acting as agents for any government or local authority or any other person or persons;
- Contracting for public or private loans and negotiating and issuing the same;
- The effecting, insuring, guaranteeing, underwriting, participating in managing and carrying out of any issue, public or private, municipal or other loans or of shares, stock, debentures or debenture stock of any company, corporation or association and the lending of money for the purpose of any such issue;
- Undertaking and executing trusts;
- Undertaking the administration of estates as executor, trustee or otherwise;
- Establishing, supporting and aiding institutions funds, trusts, etc. for the benefit of its present employees and granting money for charitable purposes;
- Acquiring, constructing and maintaining any building for its own purpose;

- Selling, improving, managing, developing, exchanging, leasing, mortgaging or disposing its property;
- Doing all such things that are incidental or conducive to the promotion or advancement of its business;
- Doing all other business specified by the Central Government as the lawful business of a banking company. Leasing and factoring has been specified as permissible for banks by the Central Government.

PROHIBITED ACTIVITIES

There are some activities banks are not allowed to do. The Banking Regulation Act prohibits banks from:

- Engaging directly or indirectly in trading activities and undertaking trading risks.
- Buying or selling or bartering of goods directly or indirectly. However, a bank can realize securities given to it or held by it for a loan, if need arises for the realization of the amount lent.
- Any activity that may be in direct conflict with their other work. This includes acting as brokers on the stock exchange or in the money market or in trading goods.
- Engaging on its own account alone or with others in wholesale or retail trade including import or export trade.
- Acquiring or purchasing any immovable property or any interest except as necessary for the purpose of conducting its business or of housing or providing amenities for its staff or for its own use. Otherwise it should not be held for more than seven years. This period may be extended by the Reserve Bank by another five years if it is satisfied that this extension is in the interest of the depositors.
- Acquiring or holding any part of the share capital of, or otherwise have a direct interest in any financial, commercial, agricultural or other undertaking.
- Engaging in any trade or buying, selling or bartering of goods for others except in connection with undertaking the administration of estates as executor, trustee or otherwise.
- Holding shares in any company whether as pledgee or mortgagee or absolute owner of an amount exceeding 30 per cent of the paid-up capital of that company or 30 per cent of its own share capital and reserves whichever is less.
- Investing in a subsidiary company, financial services company, financial institution, stock or other exchange where the investment exceeds 10 per cent of the bank's paid-up capital and reserves. Investment in all such companies should not exceed 20 per cent of the bank's paid-up capital and reserves.
- Participating in equity of financial services ventures including stock exchanges without obtaining the prior approval of RBI.

SUBSIDIARY

Banking companies may form a subsidiary company, after obtaining the prior approval of the RBI for:

- Undertaking of any business permitted for a banking company.
- Carrying on the business of banking exclusively outside India

- Undertaking of such businesses which, in the opinion of the Reserve Bank, would be conducive to the spread of banking in India
- Transacting leasing business and or investing in shares of equipment leasing companies

Services Rendered by Banks

- Acceptance of deposits;
- Provision of credit;
- Collection of cheques, demand drafts, bills of exchange, promissory notes, hundis and foreign documentary and clean bills;
- Purchase of local and foreign currency documentary/clean bills, negotiation of bills under inland and foreign letters of credit, advising of inland and foreign letters of credit established by branches and correspondents;
- Carrying out standing instructions for payments;
- Issuance of performance and financial guarantees;
- Keeping in safe custody deeds and securities;
- Purchase and sale of securities;
- Remittance of funds;
- Collection of interest on securities, dividend on shares and collection of bills;
- Credit transfers;
- Issue of travellers' cheques and gift cheques;
- Acting as executors and trustees;
- Issuance of credit cards;
- Underwriting, acting as bankers to new issues and as bankers for refunds.

SCHEDULED AND NON-SCHEDULED BANKS

Those listed in the Schedule II of Reserve Bank of India Act, 1934 and satisfy the following conditions:

(a) Paid-up Capital and Reserves of Rs. 5 lacs

(b) Business not conducted in detrimental way

Maintain reserve with RBI and enjoy privileges like financial accommodation and remittance facilities from RBI at concession. Every other bank is non-scheduled bank.

PUBLIC AND PRIVATE SECTOR BANKS

Public sector banks include:

- State Bank Group (subsidiaries of SBI)
- Nationalized Banks
- Regional Rural Banks–Generally majority stake is held by government.

STATE BANK GROUP

State Bank of Bikaner and Jaipur, Hyderabad, Indore, Mysore, Patiala, Saurashtra, Travancore.

NATIONALIZED BANKS

The banks acquired by government–BOI, PNB, BOB, Central Bank, Canara Bank, Syndicate Bank, Indian Bank, IOB.

REGIONAL RURAL BANKS

Established to cater the rural areas where the commercial banks failed to reach.

- Governed by Regional Rural Bank Act, 1976
- One or more districts – as area of operation
- 100 branches are expected
- This number is already exceeded in practice

PRIVATE BANKS

There is no Government stake. Equity held by private shareholders–UTI, ICICI, HDFC, IDBI, Centurion Bank.

FOREIGN BANKS

Branches of foreign banks incorporated outside India–ABN AMRO, Bank of America, Bank of Nova Scotia, ING Bank, American Express, Bank of Tokyo, Bank of Bahrain & Kuwait, Standard Chartered Grindlays.

Exhibit 3.1.

Accounts and Deposits:

- Savings Accounts
- Current Accounts
- Fixed Deposits
- Demat Accounts
- Safe Deposit Lockers

Loans:

- Personal Loans
- Home Loans
- Educational Loans
- Two-wheeler Loans
- New & Used Car Loans
- Gold Loan
- Loans Against Securities
- Loans Against Property
- Working Capital Finance
- Health Care Finance
- Construction Equipment Finance
- Overdraft loan

Cards:

- Debit Card
- Credit Card
- Pre-paid Card
- Woman's Credit Card
- Corporate Credit Card

Forex Services:

- Travellers' cheques
- Foreign currency cash
- Foreign currency draft
- Foreign currency cheque

Payment Services:

- Payment of bills
- Electronic clearance

RECENT TRENDS IN BANKING SERVICES

India's banking sector has made rapid strides in reforming and aligning itself to the new competitive business environment. Indian banking industry is the midst of an IT revolution. Technological infrastructure has become an indispensable part of the reforms process in the banking system, with the gradual development of sophisticated instruments and innovations in market practices.

IT IN BANKING

Indian banking industry, today is in the midst of an IT revolution. A combination of regulatory and competitive reasons has led to increasing importance of total banking automation in the Indian Banking Industry. Information Technology has basically been used under two different avenues in banking. One is communication and connectivity and other is business process reengineering. Information technology enables sophisticated product development, better market infrastructure, implementation of reliable techniques for control of risks and helps the financial intermediaries to reach geographically distant and diversified markets.

The bank which used the right technology to supply timely information will see productivity increase and thereby gain a competitive edge. To compete in an economy which is opening up, it is imperative for the Indian banks to observe the latest technology and modify it to suit their environment. Not only banks need to provide friendly, efficient and competitive existing services and business to the customer, they also need technology for providing newer products and newer forms of services in an increasingly dynamic and globalized environment. Information technology offers a chance for banks to build new systems that address a wide range of customer needs including many that may not be imaginable today. Following are the innovative services offered by the industry in the recent past:

Electronic Payment Services – E-cheques

Nowadays, we are hearing about e-governance, e-mail, e-commerce, e-tail, etc. In the same manner, a new technology is being developed in US for introduction of e-cheque, which will eventually replace the conventional paper cheque. India, as harbinger to the introduction of e-cheque, the Negotiable Instruments Act has already been amended to include; Truncated cheque and e-cheque instruments.

REAL TIME GROSS SETTLEMENT (RTGS)

Real Time Gross Settlement System, introduced in India since March 2004, is a system through which electronics instructions can be given by banks to transfer funds from their account to the account of another bank. The RTGS system is maintained and operated by the RBI and provides a means of efficient and faster funds transfer among banks facilitating their financial operations. As the name suggests, funds transfer between banks takes place on a 'Real Time' basis. Therefore, money can reach the beneficiary instantaneously and the beneficiary's bank has the responsibility to credit the beneficiary's account within two hours.

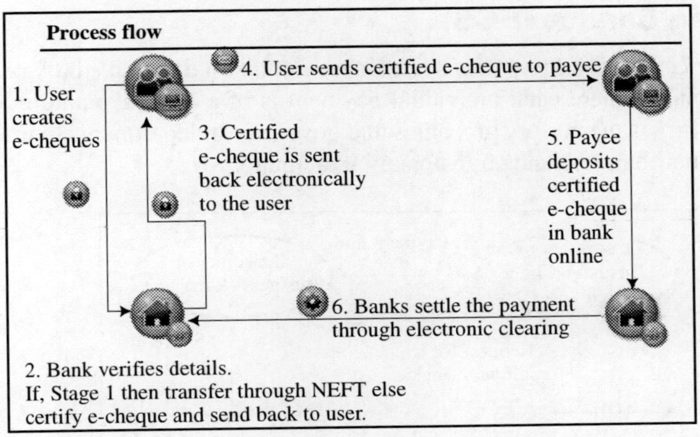

Electronic Funds Transfer (EFT)

Electronic Funds Transfer (EFT) is a system whereby anyone who wants to make payment to another person/company, etc. can approach his bank and make cash payment or give instructions/authorization to transfer funds directly from his own account to the bank account of the receiver/beneficiary. Complete details such as the receiver's name, bank account number, account type (savings or current account), bank name, city, branch name, etc. should be furnished to the bank at the time of requesting for such transfers so that the amount reaches the beneficiaries' account correctly and faster. RBI is the service provider of EFT.

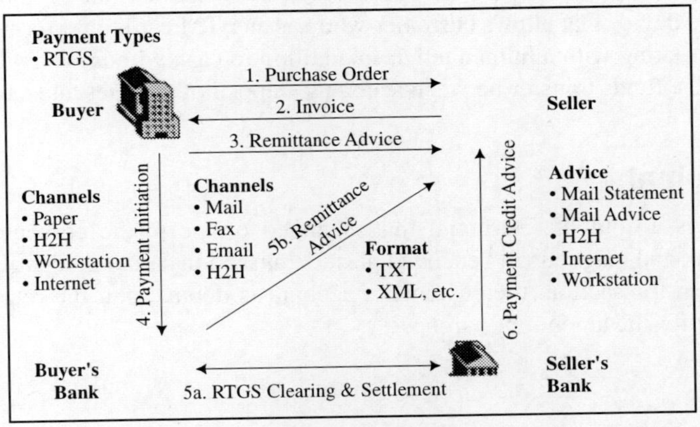

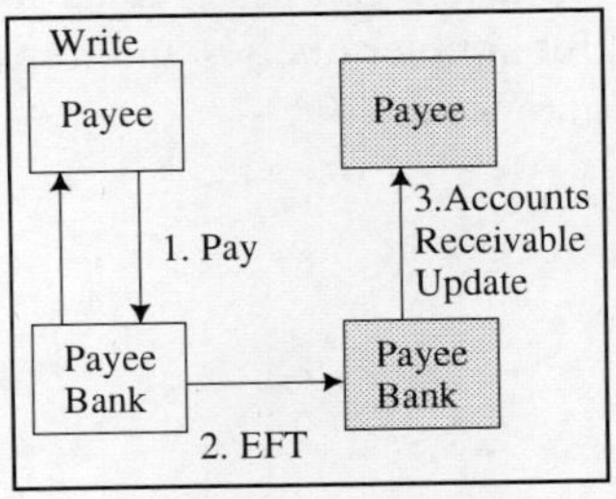

Electronic Clearing Service (ECS)

Electronic Clearing Service is a retail payment system that can be used to make bulk payments/receipts of a similar nature especially where each individual payment is of a repetitive nature and of relatively smaller amount. This facility is meant for companies and government departments to make/receive large volumes of payments rather than for funds transfers by individuals.

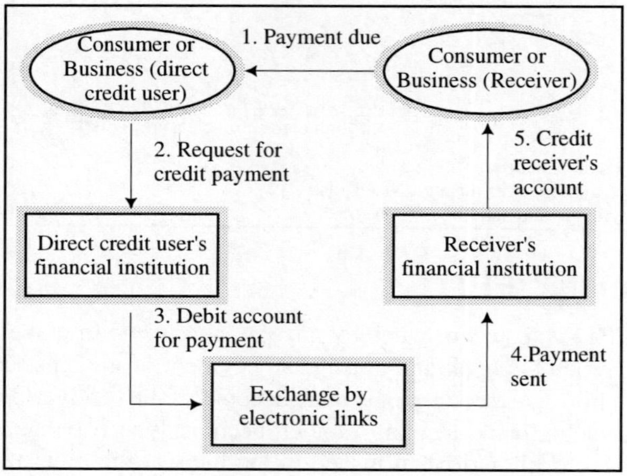

Automatic Teller Machine (ATM)

Automatic Teller Machine is the most popular device in India, which enables the customers to withdraw their money 24 × 7. It is a device that allows customer who has an ATM card to perform routine banking transactions without interacting with a human teller. In addition to cash withdrawal, ATMs can be used for payment of utility bills, funds transfer between accounts, deposit of cheques and cash into accounts, balance enquiry, etc.

Point of Sale Terminal

Point of Sale Terminal is a computer terminal that is linked online to the computerized customer information files in a bank and magnetically encoded plastic transaction card that identifies the customer to the computer. During a transaction, the customer's account is debited and the retailer's account is credited by the computer for the amount of purchase.

Tele Banking

Tele Banking facilitates the customer to do entire non-cash related banking on telephone. Under this devise Automatic Voice Recorder is used for simpler queries and transactions. For complicated queries and transactions, manned phone terminals are used.

STAR
VISA

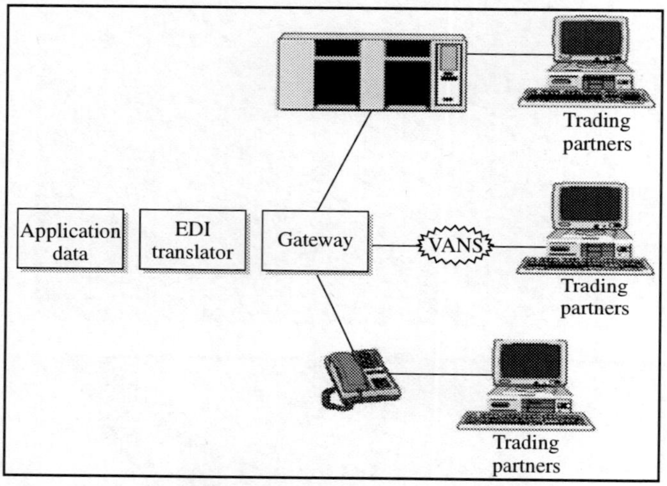

Electronic Data Interchange (EDI)

Electronic Data Interchange is the electronic exchange of business documents like purchase order, invoices, shipping notices, receiving advices, etc. in a standard, computer processed, universally accepted format between trading partners. EDI can also be used to transmit financial information and payments in electronic form.

IMPLICATIONS

The banks were quickly responded to the changes in the industry; especially the new generation banks. The continuance of the trend has re-defined and re-engineered the banking operations as whole with more customization through leveraging technology. As technology makes banking convenient, customers can access banking services and do banking transactions any time and from anywhere. The importance of physical branches is going down.

Challenges Faced by Banks, vis-à-vis, IT Implementation

It is becoming increasingly imperative for banks to assess and ascertain the benefits of technology implementation. The fruits of technology will certainly taste a lot sweeter when the returns can be measured in absolute terms but it needs precautions and the safety nets.

It has not been a smooth sailing for banks keen to jump onto the IT bandwagon. There have been impediments in the path like the obduracy once shown by trade unions who felt that IT could turn out to be a threat to secure employment. Further, the expansion of banks into remote nooks and corners of the country, where logistics continues to be a handicap, proved to be another stumbling stock. Another challenge the banks have had to face concerns the inability of banks to retain the trained and talented personnel, especially those with a good knowledge of IT.

The increasing use of technology in banks has also brought up 'security' concerns. To avoid any pitfalls or mishaps on this account, banks ought to have in place a well-documented security policy including network security and internal security. The passing of the Information Technology Act has come as a boon to the banking sector, and banks should now ensure to abide strictly by its covenants. An effort should also be made to cover e-business in the country's consumer laws.

Some are investing in it to drive the business growth, while others are having no option but to invest, to stay in business. The choice of right channel, justification of IT investment on ROI, e-governance, customer relationship management, security concerns, technological obsolescence, mergers and acquisitions, penetration of IT in rural areas, and outsourcing of IT operations are the major challenges and issues in the use of IT in banking operations. The main challenge, however, remains to motivate the customers to increasingly make use of IT while transacting with banks. For small banks, heavy investment requirement is the compressing need in addition to their capital requirements. The coming years will see even more investment in banking technology, but reaping ROI will call for more strategic thinking.

FUTURE OUTLOOK

Everyone today is convinced that the technology is going to hold the key to future of banking. The achievements in the banking today would not have make possible without IT revolution. Therefore, the key point is while changing to the current environment the banks has to understand properly the trigger for change and accordingly find out the suitable departure point for the change.

Although, the adoption of technology in banks continues at a rapid pace, the concentration is perceptibly more in the metros and urban areas. The benefit of Information Technology is yet to percolate sufficiently to the common man living in his rural hamlet. More and more programs and software in regional languages could be introduced to attract more and more people from the rural segments also.

Standards based messaging systems should be increasingly deployed in order to address cross platform transactions. The surplus manpower generated by the use of IT should be used for marketing new schemes and banks should form a 'brains trust' comprising domain experts and technology specialists.

The banking today is re-defined and re-engineered with the use of Information Technology and it is sure that the future of banking will offer more sophisticated services to the customers with the continuous product and process innovations. Thus, there is a paradigm shift from the seller's market to buyer's market in the industry and finally it affected at the banker's level to change their approach from "conventional banking to convenience banking" and "mass banking to class banking". The shift has also increased the degree of accessibility of a common man to bank for his variety of needs and requirements.

THE RESERVE BANK OF INDIA

The **Reserve Bank of India** (**RBI**, Hindi: Hkkjrh; fjt+oZ cSad) is the central banking system of India and controls the monetary policy of the rupee as well as 287.37 billion US-Dollar (2009) currency

reserves. The institution was established on 1 April 1935 during the British-Raj in accordance with the provisions of the Reserve Bank of India Act, 1934 and plays an important part in the development strategy of the government.

HISTORY

1935-1950

The central bank was founded in 1935 to respond to economic troubles after the First World War. The Reserve Bank of India was set up on the recommendations of the **Hilton Young Commission**. The commission submitted its report in the year 1926, though the bank was not set up for another nine years. The Preamble of the Reserve Bank of India describes the basic functions of the Reserve Bank as to regulate the issue of Banknotes, to keep reserves with a view to securing monetary stability in India and generally to operate the currency and credit system in the best interests of the country. The central office of the Reserve Bank was initially established in Kolkata, Bengal, but was permanently moved to Bombay (now Mumbai) in 1937. The Reserve Bank has continued to act as the central bank for Myanmar till Japanese occupation of Burma and later up to April 1947, though Burma seceded from Indian Union in 1937. After the partition, the Reserve Bank served as the central bank for Pakistan up to June 1948 when the State Bank of Pakistan commenced operations. Though originally set up as a shareholder's bank, the RBI has been fully owned by the Government of India since its nationalization in 1949.

1950-1960

Between 1950 and 1960 the Indian Government developed a centrally planned economic policy and focused on the agricultural sector. The administration nationalized commercial banks and established, based on the *Banking Companies Act*, 1949 (later called *Banking Regulation Act*) a central bank regulation as part of the RBI. Beside that the central bank was ordered to support the economic plan with loans.

1960-1969

As a result of bank crashes the Reserve Bank was requested to establish and monitor a deposit insurance system. It should restore the trust in the national bank system and was initialized on 7 December 1961. The Indian Government founded funds to promote the economy and used the slogan *Developing Banking*. The Gandhi administration and their successors restructured the national bank market and nationalized a lot of institutes. As a result the RBI had to play the central part of control and support of this public banking sector.

1969-1985

Between 1969 and 1980 the Indian Government nationalized 20 banks. The regulation of the economy and especially the financial economic was reinforced by the Gandhi administration and their successors in the 1970s and 1980s. The central bank became the central player and increased her policies for a lot of tasks like interests, reserve ratio and visible deposits. The measures aimed at a better economic development and had a huge effect on the company policy of the institutes. The banks lent money in selected sectors like agri-business and small trade companies.

The branch was forced to establish two new offices in the country for every new founded office in a town. The oil crises in 1973 resulted in increasing inflation and the RBI restricted the monetary policy to reduce the effects.

1985-1991

A lot of committees analyzed the Indian economy between 1985 and 1991. Their results had an effect on the RBI. The *Board for Industrial and Financial Reconstruction*, the *Indira Gandhi Institute of Development Research* and *Security & Exchange Board of India* investigated the national economy as a whole and the security and exchange board proposed better methods for more effective markets and the protection of investor interests. *Discount and Finance House of India* began his operations on the monetary market in April 1988, the *National Housing Bank*, founded in July 1988, was forced to invest in the property market and a new financial law improved the versatility of direct deposit by more security measures and liberalization.

1991-2000

The national economy came down in July 1991 and the Indian rupee was devalued. The currency lost 18% related to the US-Dollar and the *Narasimham Committee* advised to restructure the financial sector by a temporal reduced reserve ratio as well as the statutory liquidity ratio. New guidelines were published in 1993 to establish a private banking sector. This turning point shound reinforce the market and was often called neo-liberal. The central bank deregulated the bank interests and some sectors of the financial market like the trust and the property market. This first phase was a success and the Central Government forced a diversity liberalization to diversify the owner structures in 1998.

The National Stock Exchange of India took the trade on in June 1994 and the RBI allowed nationalized banks in July to interact with the capital market to reinforce their capital base. The central bank founded a subsidiary company – the *Bharatiya Reserve Banknote Mudran Limited* – in February 1995 to produce banknotes

Since 2000

The *Foreign Exchange Management Act* from 1999 came into force in June 2000. It should improve the foreign exchange market, international investments in India and transactions. The RBI promoted the development of the financial market in the last years, allowed online banking in 2001 and established a new payment system in 2004–2005 (National Electronic Fund Transfer). The *Security Printing & Minting Corporation of India Ltd.*, a merger of nine institutions, was founded in 2006 and produces banknotes and coins.

The national economy's growth rate came down to 5.8% in the last quarter of 2008-2009 and the central bank promotes the economic development.

Main Functions

Monetary authority

The Reserve Bank of India is the main monetary authority of the country and besides that the central bank acts as the bank of the national and state governments. It formulates, implements and monitors the monetary policy as well as it has to ensure an adequate flow of credit to productive sectors. Objectives are maintaining price stability and ensuring adequate flow of credit to productive sectors. The national economy depends on the public sector and the central bank promotes an expensive monetary policy to push the private sector since the financial market reforms of the 1990s.

The institution is also the regulator and supervisor of the financial system and prescribes broad parameters of banking operations within which the country's banking and financial system functions. Objectives are to maintain public confidence in the system, protect depositors' interest and provide cost-effective banking services to the public. The *Banking Ombudsman Scheme* has been formulated by the Reserve Bank of India (RBI) for effective redressal of complaints by bank customers. The RBI controls the monetary supply, monitors economic indicators like the gross domestic product and has to decide the design of the rupee banknotes as well as coins.

Manager of Exchange Control

The central bank manages to reach the goals of the Foreign Exchange Management Act, 1999. Objective is to facilitate external trade and payment and promote orderly development and maintenance of foreign exchange market in India.

Issuer of currency

The bank issues and exchanges or destroys currency and coins not fit for circulation. The objectives are giving the public adequate supply of currency of good quality and to provide loans to commercial banks to maintain or improve the GDP. The basic objectives of RBI are to issue banknotes, to maintain the currency and credit system of the country to utilize it in its best advantage, and to maintain the reserves. RBI maintains the economic structure of the country, so that it can achieve the objective of price stability as well as economic development, because both objectives are diverse in themselves.

Developmental role

The central bank has to perform a wide range of promotional functions to support national objectives and industries. The RBI faces a lot of inter-sectoral and local inflation-related problems. Some of these problems are results of the dominant part of the public sector.

Related functions

The RBI is also a banker to the Government and performs merchant banking function for the central and the state governments. It also acts as their banker. The National Housing Bank (NHB) was established in 1988 to promote private real-estate acquisition. The institution maintains banking accounts of all scheduled banks, too.

There is now an international consensus about the need to focus the tasks of a central bank upon central banking. RBI is far out of touch with such a principle, owing to the sprawling mandate described above. The recent financial turmoil world-over, has however, vindicated the Reserve Bank's role in maintaining financial stability in India.

Part-B: Insurance

INTRODUCTION

The Government of India (**GoI**) opened the insurance sector to private players on October 24. 2000, thus unravelling a new chapter in this field. This new policy of GoI is an outcome of India's policy of liberalization and also the result of its obligation as a signatory to the WTO to conform to its principles and guidelines relating to the reduction of barriers to trade in services. This epoch-making decision has ushered in a new era that has transgressed four decades of complete control by the public sector over the insurance sector (life insurance was nationalized in 1956 by merging 245 private insurance companies to form the Life Insurance Corporation of India (LIC), while general insurance was nationalized with the formation of General Insurance Corporation (GIC) in 1972).

This decision of the GoI has been accompanied by a set of laws and regulations governing this domain. Accordingly the Insurance Regulatory and Development Authority Act 1999 (IRDA Act) was enacted with the predominant aim of setting up an autonomous body known as the Insurance Regulatory and Development Authority (IRDA) to regulate, promote and ensure orderly growth of the insurance industry.

The influx of new players in both life and non-life sectors has made the insurance market a consumers paradise. All new players are striving to introduce innovative products. Where the old players (LIC and GIC) have a first mover advantage and have a widespread network, the new players are banking on their innovative products and superior services to surge them ahead. It is too soon to say which of the new players will succeed and which of them will perish. But the opening up of the sector is a step that will be beneficial both to the insured as well as the insurer.

The Concept of Insurance

"Insurance is a contract between two parties whereby one party called insurer undertakes in exchange for a fixed sum called premiums, to pay the other party called insured a fixed amount of money on the happening of a certain event." Insurance is a protection against financial loss arising on the happening of an unexpected event. Insurance companies collect premiums to provide for this protection. A loss is paid out of the premiums collected from the insuring public and the insurance companies act as trustees to the amount collected.

For example, in a life policy, by paying a premium to the insurer, the family of the insured person receives a fixed compensation on the death of the insured. Similarly, in a car insurance, in the event of the car meeting with an accident, the insured receives the compensation to the extent of damage.

It is a system by which the losses suffered by a few are spread over many, exposed to similar risks. Insurance is a mechanism for transferring risk and reducing risk by having a large number of individuals who share in the financial losses of the group. Risk inhibits action and is highly subjective on an individual basis. Insurance objectifies risk. People trade the possibility of financial loss for the relative certainty of the premium paid and reimbursement for loss.

Insurance frees people to take action even in the face of possible financial loss. Thus, insurance provides utility even if no loss ever occurs.

Some people believe insurance is similar to gambling or opening a savings account. Neither is true. When you place a bet, you create a risk and you have the chance of losing all or making more than your wager. Insurance companies write policies for pure not speculative risks and indemnify you when you have a covered loss. In the insurance industry, the word 'indemnify' means you cannot be put in a better position than you were before the loss.

BASIC INSURANCE TERMINOLOGIES

Insured: The person known as the policyholder, a person with insurance coverage.

Insurer: A company licensed to transact the business of insurance and issue insurance policies.

Policy: It's the written contract between an insurance company and its insured. It defines what the company agrees to cover for what period of time and describes the obligations and responsibilities of the insured.

Premium: It's the amount of money a policyholder pays for insurance protection.

Claim: It's the notice to the insurance company that under the terms of a policy, a loss may be covered.

Indemnity: Legal principle that specifies an insured should not collect more than the actual cash value of a loss but should be restored to approximately the same financial position as existed before the loss.

Agent: A licensed person or organization who sells insurance and represents the insurance company to the policyholder.

Broker: An organization or person paid by the policyholder to look for insurance on their behalf.

Deductible: It's the amount of the loss which the insured is responsible to pay before the insurance company pays the benefits.

Expiration Date: This is the date on which the policy ends.

Grace Period: A period (usually 30 or 31 days) following each insurance premium due date, other than the first due date, during which an overdue premium may be paid. All provisions of the policy remain in force throughout this period.

Limit: It's the maximum amount paid by the insurance company under the terms of a policy.

Underwriting: The process of classifying applicants for insurance by identifying characteristics such as age, gender, health, occupation and hobbies. People with similar characteristics are grouped together and are charged a premium based on the group's level of risk.

REQUIREMENTS OF AN INSURABLE RISK

(i) From the perspective of the insured:

- The risk must be high. Losses with extremely high odds and extremely low odds might best be handled in other ways.

- The loss must be unaffordable.
- The premium must be affordable or, at least, low in comparison with the possible loss.

(ii) From the perspective of the insurer:

- The loss must be fortuitous (unexpected in terms of timing and magnitude).
- The loss must non-catastrophic with neither the possibility of many losses at one time or any one loss of overwhelming magnitude.
- The losses must be personal because only people can suffer losses.
- The loss must be definite in time, place and amount. This allows for a reasonably accurate prediction of loss and thus calculation of premium.

CONCEPT OF INSURABLE INTEREST

The insured party must have an insurable interest in the person or property covered. This means that he or she must stand to suffer a loss should the peril occur. Generally, insurable interest must exist at the time that the loss occurs. Requiring insurance supports the principle of indemnity, which states that an insured should collect not more than the actual loss.

CONCEPT OF INSURANCE INDUSTRY

The important feature of insurance industry is the fact that not much capital is required to start and develop the business the equity base is always much smaller than the liabilities undertaken and the resources generated. The resources accumulation in the form of reserves investment and other assets are much more enormous than the equity base. The need for additional capital infusion in response to inflation and consequent increase in management expenses and other input is very little and non-existence. The premium income generated and proper husbanding of the resources take care of this aspect.

WHY DO PEOPLE IN INDIA TAKE INSURANCE?

People in India have been viewing insurance, especially life insurance as a form of investment. These are the common reasons why people in India take up insurance:

1. Insurance safeguards a person/his family/his business against possible losses on account of risks and perils. It provides financial compensation for the losses suffered due to the happening of any unforeseen events.
2. Tax Reliefs:
   (a) Under Section 88 of Income Tax Act, a portion of premiums paid for life insurance policies (LIC) are deducted from tax liability. Similarly, exemption is available for Health Insurance Policy premiums.
   (b) Money paid as claim including bonus under a life policy is exempted from payment of Income Tax.
3. Encourages Savings: An insurance scheme encourages thrift among individuals. It inculcates the habit of saving compulsorily, unlike other saving instruments, wherein the saved money can be easily withdrawn.
4. The beneficiaries to an insurance claim amount are protected from the claims of creditors by affecting a valid assignment.

5. Life policies are accepted as a security for a loan. They can also be surrendered for meeting unexpected emergencies.
6. Based on the concept of sharing of losses, the society will benefit as catastrophic losses are spread globally.

TYPES OF INSURANCE

Insurance has been classified into:

- Life Insurance
- General Insurance or Non-Life insurance

Life Insurance

Life insurance is a written contract between the insured and the insurer, that provides for the payment of the insured sum on the date of the maturity of the contract or on the unfortunate death of the insured, whichever occurs earlier.

The different types of life insurance are:

- Whole Life Assurance Plans
- Term Assurance Plans
- Annuities

Non-Life Insurance

There are various broad categories of non-life or general insurance as follows:

Health insurance

Just like one looks to safeguard ones wealth, these policies ensure guarding the insurer's health against any calamities that may cause long-term harm to one's life and even hamper ones earning ability for a lifetime. Some examples of this type of policy are mediclaim policy, personal accident, group accident, traffic accident, etc.

Business insurance

Risks of loss of profits/business, goods, plant and machinery is most profound in case of business. Under this head they cover the most widely used policies that cover a business from any loss of the above kind. Some of these policies are burglary insurance, shopkeepers' insurance, key-man insurance, marine insurance, public liability insurance, workmen compensation insurance, air transit insurance, fidelity guarantee insurance, etc.

Automobile insurance

Auto policy is required to be taken to cover the risks that arise to the owner, vehicle and third party. This includes the Compulsory Vehicle Policy (In India, by the Motor Vehicles Act, every car owner is required to covered against Act risks) and the Comprehensive Vehicle Policy.

Fire insurance

This policy is required to be taken to prevent any loss of profits/property from incidental fire. E.g. fire insurance and fire consequential loss policy.

Travel insurance

Every year a number of tourists dies while travelling. They lose their baggage; passports, etc. are left stranded in unfamiliar environments. Medical attention in a foreign land while very expensive is also very difficult to find in foreign land. Travel policies are designed to take care of all the problems that generally occur while travelling, whether domestic or foreign.

BRIEF HISTORY OF THE INSURANCE SECTOR IN INDIA

The insurance sector in India has come a full circle from being an open competitive market to nationalization and back to a liberalized market again. Tracing the developments in the Indian insurance sector reveals the 360 degree turn witnessed over a period of almost two centuries.

Till the end of 1999–2000, two government insurance companies, namely, Life Insurance Corporation (LIC) and General Insurance Corporation (GIC) were the monopoly insurance (both life and non-life) providers in India. In the year 2000-01, the Indian Government lifted all entry restrictions for private sector investors. Foreign investment insurance market was also allowed in the Indian market and the face of the Indian Insurance sector changed dramatically.

LIFE INSURANCE CORPORATION OF INDIA (LIC)

In 1956, 245 Indian and foreign insurers and provident societies that were prevalent in India were taken over by the central government and nationalized to form the Life Insurance Corporation of India (LIC) with a contribution of Rs. 5 crore from the Government of India. LIC was formed to spread the message of life insurance in the country and mobilize people's savings for nation-building activities. A monolith then, the corporation, enjoyed a monopoly status and became synonymous with life insurance.

Today, LIC has its central office in Mumbai and seven zonal offices at Mumbai, Kolkata, Delhi, Chennai, Hyderabad, Kanpur and Bhopal and operates through 100 divisional offices in important cities and 2,048 branch offices. LIC has 5.59 lakh active agents spread over the country. The Corporation also transacts business abroad and has offices in Fiji, Mauritius and United Kingdom. LIC is associated with joint ventures abroad in the field of insurance, namely, Ken-India Assurance Company Limited,

Nairobi; United Oriental Assurance Company Limited, Kuala Lumpur; and Life Insurance Corporation (International), E.C. Bahrain. It has also entered into an agreement with the Sun Life (UK) for marketing unit linked life insurance and pension policies in UK. LIC sold 2,32,50,078 individual policies and earned a first premium income of Rs. 14,844.05 crore during the financial year 2001-02.

Post liberalization, the company is bound to face stiff competition from the newer players in the market. However, LIC has the first mover advantage and today the common man relates life insurance with LIC and this will be the company's biggest advantage.

GENERAL INSURANCE CORPORATION OF INDIA (GIC)

The General Insurance Business in India was nationalized with effect from 1.1.1973 by the General Insurance Business (Nationalization) Act, 1972 and a Government company known as General Insurance Corporation of India was formed. 107 Indian and foreign insurers which were operating in the country prior to nationalization, were grouped into four operating companies, namely:

1. National Insurance Company Ltd.
2. Oriental Insurance Company Ltd.
3. New India Assurance Company Ltd.
4. United India Insurance Company Ltd.

The Government of India subscribed to the capital of GIC. GIC, in turn, subscribed to the capital of the above four companies. All the four companies are government companies registered under the Companies Act.

All the above four subsidiaries of GIC operate all over the country competing with one another and underwriting various classes of general insurance business except for aviation insurance of national airlines and crop insurance which is handled by the GIC and its subsidiaries have representation either directly or through branches in 18 countries and through associate/locally incorporated subsidiaries in 14 other countries. A subsidiary company of GIC India International Pvt. Ltd. is operating in Singapore and their joint venture company, Ken-India Assurance Company Ltd. in Kenya. On the whole, the foreign operations of the general insurance industry have been profitable.

GIC was converted into India's national reinsurer from December, 2000 and all the subsidiaries working under the GIC umbrella were restructured as independent insurance companies. Indian Parliament has cleared a Bill on July 30, 2002 delinking the four subsidiaries from GIC. A separate Bill has been approved by Parliament to allow brokers, cooperatives and intermediaries in the sector.

Currently insurance companies— both private and public— have to cede 20 per cent of its reinsurance with GIC. GIC is planning to increase reinsurance premium by 20 per cent which works out at Rs. 3000 crore. GIC is actively considering entry into overseas markets including West Asia, South-East Asia and SAARC region.

REASONS FOR OPENING UP OF THE SECTOR

Induce Competition: It was seen that though the waves of competition were sweeping across the economy, LIC and GIC remain overstaffed, hierarchical monolithic monopolies with little competition even between the subsidiaries. As a result, the consumers are deprived of benefits such as wider range of products, efficient service and lower price of insurance covers.

Liberalization Effort: The opening up of insurance sector was a part of the ongoing liberalization in the financial sector of India. The changing face of the financial sector and the entry of several companies in the field of life and non-life insurance segment are one of the key results of these liberalization efforts. Insurance business by way of generating premium income adds significantly to the GDP.

High Premium and Low Returns: Pointing out that the insurance industry's funds are pre-empted through government-mandated investments with low yield, the report said this affects the financial results of the insurance companies. This is why, rates of insurance premium are so high and returns on savings invested in life insurance are so low. In the absence of competition, LIC's vast marketing and services network was inadequately responsive to customer needs and there was excessive lapse of policies.

Insurance Mobilization: The entry of several private insurance companies, particularly international insurance companies, through joint ventures, will speed up the process of insurance mobilization. The competition will unleash new schemes and benefits, which will give consumers a better chance to save as well as insure. The penetration of insurance in India is extremely low and the opening up of the sector was seen as a way increasing penetration.

Flow of FDI: The policy of the government to open up the financial sector and the insurance sector is expected to bring greater FDI inflow into the country.

POTENTIAL OF THE INSURANCE SECTOR IN INDIA

Life Insurance Statistics

- Indian Population 1 billion
- GDP as on 2000 (Rs. billion) 20000
- Gross Domestic Savings as a % of GDP
- 23% Estimated Market by 2005—650 million
- Source: Indiainfoline.com and NCAER

India has an enormous middle class that can afford to buy life, health, and disability and pension plan products. The low level of penetration of life insurance in India compared to other developed nations can be judged by a comparison of per capita life premium. Despite the fact that the market is vast in India for the insurance business, the coverage is far less compared with the international standards.

Estimates show that a meagre 35–40 million, out of a population of 950 million, have come so far under the umbrella of the insurance industry. India has traditionally been a high savings oriented. Insurance sector in the Unites States is as big in size as the banking industry there. This gives us an idea of how important the sector is. Insurance sector channelizes the savings of the people to long-term investments. In India, where infrastructure is said to be of critical importance, this sector will bring the nations own money for the nation.

Life insurance sector is one of the key areas where enormous business potential exists. In India currently the life insurance premium as a percentage of GDP is 1.3% against 5.2% in the US. But in the liberalized scenario, the life insurance premiums were projected to grow at around 18% to 20% from Rs. 215 billion in 1998-99 to Rs. 592 billion in 2004-05 and to Rs. 1450 billion by 2009-10.

Corporate non-life premium was projected to grow from Rs. 84 billion in 1998-99 to Rs. 386 billion in 2009-10 and personal line non-life from Rs. 4 billion to Rs. 51 billion. The potential market is so huge that it can grow by 15 to 17 per cent per annum. Now with the entry of private insurance companies, the Indian Insurance Market may finally be able to make deeper penetration into newer segments and expand the market size manifold.

Reforms in the Sector

The eagerly awaited Insurance Regulatory and Development Authority (IRDA) Bill to open the insurance sector in India to private and foreign players, was passed by the Lok Sabha on December 2, 1999 and by the Rajya Sabha on December 7, 1999. The Bill seeks to grant statutory status to the interim Insurance Regulatory Authority and amend the 1938 Insurance Act, the 1956 Life Insurance Corporation Act and the 1972 General Insurance Business (Nationalization) Act to end the public sector monopoly. The IRDA Bill incorporates the recommendations made by the Parliamentary Standing Committee on Finance.

Salient Features of Insurance Sector Reform Bill

The bill seeks to regulate, promote and ensure orderly growth of the insurance industry and provides for solvency norms and specifies that the funds of policyholders would be retained within the country.

The minimum capital requirement for life and general insurance has been retained at Rs. 100 crore ($23.02 million) and for reinsurance firms at Rs. 200 crore ($46.04 million) as provided in the earlier IRA Bill.

- It has been stipulated that the aggregate foreign holding in an Indian insurance company shall not exceed 26 per cent of the paid up equity. Moreover, to provide a level playing field, It has been proposed that the Indian promoters would also be required to bring down their equity holding to 26 per cent after a period of 10 years from the commencement of business.
- The Bill has proposed solvency margins of Rs. 50 crores (US $11.51 million) for life and general insurance and Rs. 100 crores (US $23.02 million) for reinsurance companies.
- IRDA, in addition to other functions, would supervise the functioning of the Tariff Advisory Committee (TAC) and specify the percentage of premium income of the insurers to be set aside to finance schemes for promoting and regulating professional organizations in the insurance sectors.

REGULATORY AUTHORITY

Insurance Regulatory and Development Authority (IRDA)

IRDA is formed as an authority to protect the interests of holders of insurance policies, to regulate, promote and ensure orderly growth of the insurance industry. With the Insurance Regulatory and Development Act, the focus shifted to the following:

- The Insurance Regulatory and Development Authority (IRDA) should give priority to health insurance while issuing certificates of registration.
- Policyholders' funds will be invested in the social sector and infrastructure. The percentage may be specified by the IRDA and such regulations will apply to all insurers operating in the country;
- Insurers will be expected to undertake a certain percentage of business in the rural or social sector and provide policies to persons residing in rural areas; workers in the unorganized and informal economically back;
- In case the insurers fail to meet the social sector obligation a fine of Rs. 2.5 mn would be imposed the first time. Subsequent failures would result in cancellation of licences.

Duties, Powers and Functions of IRDA

The following are the powers and the functions of the IRDA are as follows:

(a) The IRDA issues, modifies, renews, suspends, withdraws and cancels all certificate of registration for all parties that apply.

(b) They are also responsible for the protection of the interests of the policyholders in matters concerning assigning of policy, nomination by policyholders, insurable interest, settlement of insurance claim, surrender value of policy and other terms and conditions of contracts of insurance.

(c) The IRDA specifies requisite qualifications, code of conduct and practical training for intermediary or insurance intermediaries and agents.

(d) It also specifies the code of conduct for surveyors and loss assessors.

(e) The IRDA has been given the responsibility of promoting efficiency in the conduct of insurance business.

(f) It is in charge of promoting and regulating professional organizations connected with the insurance and reinsurance business;

(g) It has been entrusted with the control of the insurance sector by calling for information from, undertaking inspection of, conducting inquires and investigations including audit of the insurers, intermediaries, insurance intermediaries and other organizations connected with the insurance business;

(h) It will also be responsible for the control and regulation of the rates, advantages, terms and conditions that may be offered by insurers.

(i) The IRDA will specify the form and manner in which books of account shall be maintained and statement of accounts shall be rendered by insurers and other insurance intermediaries.

(j) One of the most important functions is that of regulating investment of funds by insurance companies and the maintenance of margin of solvency.

(k) The other function is that of adjudication of disputes between insurers and intermediaries or insurance intermediaries.

Let us Sum Up

A bank is defined as a commercial institution licensed as a receiver of deposits and giver of loans – both short and long term. Section 5(1)(b) of the Banking Regulation Act, 1949 defines banking as, "the accepting for the purpose of lending or investment, of deposits from the public, repayable on demand or otherwise, and withdrawal by cheque, draft, order or otherwise."

Services rendered by banks: Acceptance of deposits, provision of credit, collection of cheques, demand drafts, bills of exchange, promissory notes, hundis and foreign documentary and clean bills, purchase of local and foreign currency documentary/clean bills, negotiation of bills under inland and foreign letters of credit, advising of inland and foreign letters of credit established by branches and correspondents, carrying out standing instructions for payments, issuance of performance and financial guarantees, keeping in safe custody deeds and securities, purchase and sale of securities, remittance of funds, collection of interest on securities, dividend on shares and collection of bills, credit transfers, issue of travellers' cheques and gift cheques, acting as executors and trustees, issuance of credit cards, underwriting, acting as bankers to new issues and as bankers for refunds.

Recent development in banking services: ETF, ECS, EPS, RTGS, EDI, ATM, etc.

"Insurance is a contract between two parties whereby one party called insurer undertakes in exchange for a fixed sum called premiums, to pay the other party called insured a fixed amount of money on the happening of a certain event." Insurance is a protection against financial loss arising on the happening of an unexpected event. Insurance companies collect premiums to provide for this protection. A loss is paid out of the premiums collected from the insuring public and the Insurance Companies Act as trustees to the amount collected.

For example, in a Life Policy, by paying a premium to the insurer, the family of the insured person receives a fixed compensation on the death of the insured. Similarly, in a car insurance, in the event of the car meeting with an accident, the insured receives the compensation to the extent of damage.

It is a system by which the losses suffered by a few are spread over many, exposed to similar risks. Insurance is a mechanism for transferring risk and reducing risk by having a large number of individuals who share in the financial losses of the group. Risk inhibits action and is highly subjective on an individual basis. Insurance objectifies risk. People trade the possibility of financial loss for the relative certainty of the premium paid and reimbursement for loss.

Insurance frees people to take action even in the face of possible financial loss. Thus, insurance provides utility even if no loss ever occurs.

Questions for Discussion

1. Define bank.
2. Explain the activities of any bank.
3. Discuss the concept of bank and subsidiary.
4. What are the services rendered by bank? Explain briefly.
5. What are the differences between scheduled and non-scheduled bank?
6. Explain the concept of public and private sector banks. Name few private and public sector banks.
7. Explain the recent trends in banking services.
8. How IT revolution helped grow banking industry.
9. Write short notes on:
   (i) Real-time gross settlement
   (ii) Electronic funds transfer
   (iii) Electronic clearing services
   (iv) Automatic teller machine
   (v) Point of sale terminal
   (vi) Electronic data interchange
10. Write a short note on RBI and its various functions.
11. Explain the concept of insurance.

12. Write short notes on:
    (i) Insured (ii) Insurer (iii) Policy
    (iv) Indemnity (v) Agent (vi) Underwriting
13. Why people take interest?
14. What is life insurance?
15. What are the different types of non-life insurance? Explain briefly.
16. Write short notes on: (i) LIC (ii) GIC (iii) IRDA.
17. Write short notes on: (i) Health Insurance (ii) Automobile Insurance (iii) Business Insurance.
18. Explain the reasons for growth of insurance sector.
19. Explain the salient features of insurance sector reform bill.
20. Explain the functions of IRDA.

4

Finance and Marketing Services

"I think that's more related to how much tightening will we see (of interest rates by the central banks). I think they have been a bit oversold. I think we will see financial services moving up as the market becomes reassured that we won't see further inflation." – Kate Warne

Learning Objectives

At the end of this chapter students will be able to understand

- Meaning and concepts of financial services
- Sources of revenue
- Concept financial reengineering
- Indian financial sector
- Meaning and types of marketing services
- Customer service
- Features and types
- Financial innovation
- Types of credit rating agencies and their functions
- Recent trends in the financial service sector in India
- Reasons for growth of marketing services

***Financial services** – Introduction – meaning – features – functions – types – classification of financial service industry – scope – sources of revenue – financial innovation – causes – financial engineering – merchant banking – leasing – factoring – loan syndication – venture capital – credit rating services – CRISIL – CARE – ICRA – Mutual Fund – lines of credit – Indian financial sector – the recent trends in the financial service sector in India.*

***Marketing services** – meaning – features – importance – contribution of marketing services in promoting industry and impact on growth of economy – customer service – types of marketing services.*

INTRODUCTION

Financial services refer to services provided by the finance industry. The finance industry encompasses a broad range of organizations that deal with the management of money. Among these organizations are banks, credit card companies, insurance companies, consumer finance companies, stock brokerages, investment funds and some government sponsored enterprises.

All types of activities which are of a financial nature could be brought under financial service. It means mobilizing and allocating investments, includes all activities involved in the transformation of savings into investments. It is also called as a financial intermediation; it is the process by which funds are mobilized from a large number of savers and make them available to all those who are in need of it and particularly to corporate customers. Thus, financial services sector is a key area for the Indian economy in developing industrial development.

As India is a fastest growing economy most of the financial services organizations are striving to achieve increasingly ambitious profit and growth targets against a background of heightened risk, regulation and market pressures. Customer needs and expectations are evolving in the face of increasing personal wealth, more private funding of pensions and health care and the desire for ever more accessible and personalized financial products and services. In turn, intense competition has squeezed industry margins and forced organizations to cut costs while still seeking to enhance the quality of client choice and service. The battle for talent is also heating up as companies seek to enhance innovation, customer loyalty and investment returns.

The corollary of this market evolution is increasing risk as products become more complex, organizations more diffuse and the business environment ever more uncertain. Regulation is also tightening in the wake of public and government pressure for improved governance, transparency and accountability. In this environment, the winners will be companies that can turn the challenges into opportunities to build stronger and more enduring customer relationships; sharpen process efficiency; unlock talent and creativity; use improved risk management processes to deliver more sustainable returns; and use new regulatory demands as a catalyst for strengthening the business and enhancing market confidence.

Some of the major financial services offered by the most of the financial services companies in India are:

- Capital markets (primary and secondary)
- Securities and Exchange Board of India (SEBI)
- Merchant Banking
- Hire Purchase
- Leasing
- Factoring
- Venture Capital
- Mutual Funds
- Credit Rating
- Insurance Services

Some of the innovative financial services offered by the most of the financial services companies in India are:

- Carrot and Stick Bonds
- Flip-Flop Notes
- Loyalty Coupons

- Dual Currency Bonds
- Inter-bank Participants (IBPs)
- Cyclical and Non-Cyclical Shares
- Alpha Shares
- Index-Linked Guilt Bonds
- Secured Premium Notes
- Easy Exit Bonds
- ADR and GDRs

FEATURES OF FINANCIAL SERVICES

- Intangible in nature
- Inseparable from the provider
- Customer centric
- Dynamic in nature
- Credibility of partners is very important in them
- More sophisticated
- Long-term in nature
- Need more advice
- Rapid changes
- Necessity for other sectors

FUNCTIONS OF FINANCIAL SERVICES

- Mobilization of funds
- Effective employment of funds
- Provision of need based services
- Provision of regulated services
- Enhancement of economic development

TYPES OF FINANCIAL SERVICES

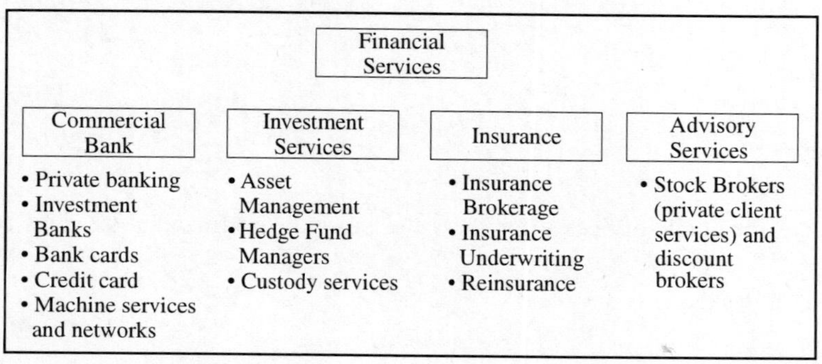

CONSTITUENTS OF FINANCIAL SERVICE SECTOR

- **Market participants**
  – Individuals, corporate entities, banks, financial institutions, mutual fund and merchant bankers.
- **Financial service providers**
  – Financial institutions, banks, non-banking financial institutions, insurance, leasing and factoring companies and mutual funds.
- **Regulatory bodies**
  – RBI, SEBI, Department of Finance, Department of Banking and Insurance of the CentralGovernment, etc.

CLASSIFICATION OF FINANCIAL SERVICES INDUSTRY

The financial intermediaries in India can be traditionally classified into two:

Capital market intermediaries: The capital market intermediaries consist of term lending institutions and investing institutions which mainly provide long-term funds.

Money market intermediaries: Money market consists of commercial banks, cooperative banks and other agencies which supply only short-term funds. Hence, the term 'financial services industry' includes all kinds of organizations which intermediate and facilitate financial transactions of both individuals and corporate customers.

The entities that provide these services are divided into the following categories:

1. Non-Banking Finance Companies (NBFCs)
2. Commercial banks
3. Investment bank

SCOPE OF FINANCIAL SERVICES

Financial services cover a wide range of activities. They can be broadly classified into two, namely:

- Traditional activities
- Modern activities.

Traditional activities: Traditionally, the financial intermediaries have been rendering a wide range of services encompassing both capital and money market activities. They can be grouped under two heads, viz., 1. Fund-based activities and 2. Non-fund-based activities (Fee-based).

Fund-based activities: The traditional services which come under fund-based activities are the following:

- Underwriting or investment in shares, debentures, bonds, etc. of new issues (primary market activities).
- Dealing in secondary market activities.
- Participating in money market instruments like commercial papers, certificate of deposits, treasury bills, discounting of bills, etc.
- Involving in equipment leasing, hire purchase, venture capital, seed capital.
- Dealing in foreign exchange market activities.

Non-fund-based activities: Financial intermediaries provide services on the basis of non-fund activities. This can be called 'fee-based' activity. Today customers, whether individual or corporate, are not satisfied with mere provisions of finance. They expect more from financial services companies. Hence, a wide variety of services, are being provided under this head.

They include:

- Managing the capital issue, i.e., management of pre-issue and post-issue activities relating to the capital issue in accordance with the SEBI guidelines and thus enabling the promoters to market their issue.
- Making arrangements for the placement of capital and debt instruments with investment institutions.
- Arrangement of funds from financial institutions for the clients' project cost or his working capital requirements.
- Assisting in the process of getting all government and other clearances.

Modern activities: Beside the above traditional services, the financial intermediaries render innumerable services in recent times. Most of them are in the nature of non-fund-based activity. In view of the importance, these activities have been in brief under the head 'new financial products and services'. However, some of the modern services provided by them are given in brief hereunder.

- Rendering project advisory services right from the preparation of the project report till the raising of funds for starting the project with necessary government approvals.
- Planning for M&A and assisting for their smooth carry out.
- Guiding corporate customers in capital restructuring.
- Acting as trustees to the debenture holders.
- Recommending suitable changes in the management structure and management style with a view to achieving better results.
- Structuring the financial collaborations/joint ventures by identifying suitable joint venture partners and preparing joint venture agreements.
- Rehabilitating and restructuring sick companies through appropriate scheme of reconstruction and facilitating the implementation of the scheme.
- Advising the clients on the questions of selecting the best source of funds taking into consideration the quantum of funds required, their cost, lending period, etc.
- Guiding the clients in the minimization of the cost of debt and in the determination of the optimum debt-equity mix.
- Undertaking services relating to the capital market, such as
  - Clearing services
  - Registration and transfers
  - Safe custody of securities
  - Collection of income on securities
- Promoting credit rating agencies for the purpose of rating companies which want to go public by the issue of debt instruments.

SOURCES OF REVENUE

There are two categories of sources of income for a financial services company, namely:

Fund-based: Fund-based income comes mainly from

- interest spread (the difference between the interest earned and interest paid),
- lease rentals
- income from investments in capital market and real estate.

Fee-based: On the other hand, fee-based income have its sources in

- merchant banking
- advisory services
- custodial services
- loan syndication, etc.

In fact, a major part of the income is earned through fund-based activities. At the same time, it involves a large share of expenditure also in the form of interest and brokerage.

CAUSES FOR FINANCIAL INNOVATION

Financial intermediaries have to perform the task of financial innovation to meet the dynamically changing needs of the economy and to help the investors cope with the increasingly volatile and uncertain marketplace. There is a dire necessity for the financial intermediaries to go for innovation due to the following reasons:

Low profitability: The profitability of the major FI, namely, the banks has been very much affected in recent times. There is a decline in the profitability of traditional banking products. So, they have been compelled to seek out new products which may fetch high returns.

Keen competition: The entry of many FIs in the financial sector has led to severe competition among them. This keen competition has paved the way for the entry of varied nature of innovative financial products so as to meet the varied requirements of the investors.

Economic liberalization: Reform of the financial sector constitutes the most important component of India's programme towards economic liberalization. The recent economic liberalization measures have opened the door to foreign competitors to enter into our domestic market. Deregulation in the form of elimination of exchange controls and interest rate ceilings have made the market more competitive. Innovation has become a must for survival.

Improved communication technology: The communication technology has become so advanced that even the world's issuers can be linked with the investors in the global financial market without any difficulty by means of offering so many options and opportunities.

Customer service: Nowadays, the customer's expectations are very great. They want newer products at lower cost or at lower credit risk to replace the existing ones. To meet this increased customer sophistication, the financial intermediaries are constantly undertaking research in order to invent a new product which may suit to the requirement of the investing public.

Global impact: Many of the providers and users of capital have changed their roles all over the world. FIs have come out of their traditional approach and they are ready to assume more credit risks.

Investor awareness: With a growing awareness amongst the investing public, there has been a distinct shift from investing the savings in physical assets like gold, silver, land, etc. to financial assets like shares, debentures, mutual funds, etc. Again, within the financial assets, they go from 'risk free' bank deposits to risky investments in shares. To meet the growing awareness of the public, innovations has become the need of the hour.

FINANCIAL ENGINEERING

The growing need for innovation has assumed immense importance in recent times. This process is being referred to as financial engineering. Financial engineering is the design, development and implementation of innovative financial instruments and process and the formulation of creative solutions to the problems in finance.

NEW FINANCIAL PRODUCTS AND SERVICES

In these days of complex finances, people expect a financial service company to play a very dynamic role not only as a provider of finance but also as a departmental store of finance. With the opening of the economy to multinationals, the free market concept has assumed much significance. As a result, the clients both corporate and individuals are exposed to the phenomena of volatility and uncertainty and hence they expect the financial services company to innovate new products and services so as to meet their varied requirements. As a result of innovations, new instruments and new products are emerging in the capital market. The capital market and the money market are getting widened and deepened.

MERCHANT BANKING

Merchant banks are financial institutions providing specialist services that generally include the acceptance of issue management, bills of exchange, corporate finance, portfolio management and other banking services.

SERVICES OF MERCHANT BANKS

A merchant banker helps in the process of issue management and his services are broadly categorized as pre-issue management and post-issue management.

The pre-issue management involves the following:

- Printing prospectus
- Pricing of issues
- Marketing the issue
- Underwriting
- Listing of securities in stock exchange

The post-issue management includes the following:

- Collection of application forms
- Screening the applications
- Deciding allotment procedure
- Mailing of letter of allotment

- Issue of share certificates
- Refund of application money to non-allotters.

A merchant banker acts as a lessoning officer at the event of mergers and acquisitions. He helps the company in managing its portfolio. A merchant banker helps their clients in offshore financing such as long-term foreign currency loans, joint ventures abroad, licensing and franchising, financing exports and imports, foreign collaboration arrangements, etc.

The services of merchant bankers also include investment advisory to (NRI) Non-Resident Indians in terms of identification of investment opportunities, selection of securities, investment management, etc. They also take care of the operational details like purchase and sale of securities, securing necessary clearance from RBI.

LEASING

The term leasing refers to a contract under which the owner of an asset allows another person or party to use the asset in return for some rent. The persons involved are lessor and lessee. Lessor is the owner of the asset and the lessee is the person getting the benefit of asset taken on lease.

Steps Involved in Leasing

A contract of lease provides a person an opportunity to use an asset, which belongs to another person. The following steps are involved in a leasing transaction:

(a) At the first instance the lessee has to take a decision regarding the required asset. Then he has to select a supplier before selecting the type of machine.

(b) The lessee then enters into a lease agreement with lessor. The lease agreement contains the terms and conditions of the lease such as, lease period, rental payments, details regarding renewal of lease period, cost of repair and maintenance, insurance and any other expenses.

(c) After the lease agreement is signed the lessor consents the manufacturer and requests him to supply the asset to lessee.

Financial lease: It is also known as capital lease or long-term lease. It is like a legal commitment to pay for the entire cost of the equipment plus interest over a specified period of time. The lessee agrees to a series of payment which in total exceeds the cost of equipment.

Operating lease: It is a rental agreement. The lessee is not committed for paying more than the original cost of equipment during contractual period. Lessor will bear the maintenance expenses and taxes of the lessor.

Types of Leasing

Sale and lease back: Under this type of lease, a firm, which has an asset, sells it to the leasing company and gets it back on lease. The asset is generally sold at its market value. The firms receive the sale price in cash and get the right to use the asset during the lease period. The firm makes periodical rental payment to the lessor. The ownership of asset rests with lessor.

Cross-border lease: This is also known as international leasing or transnational leasing. This is referred to lease transaction between the persons of two countries. The lessor and the lessee belong to two different countries.

FACTORING

It may be defined as a continuing arrangement between the financial institutions or banks and a business concern selling goods or providing services on credit, wherein the factor undertakes the task of recording, collecting, controlling and protecting the book debts and also purchasing the bills receivables of the suppliers.

Factoring involves the following functions:

(a) Purchase and collection of debts
(b) Management of sales ledger
(c) Credit investigation
(d) Provision of finance against debt
(e) Rendering consultancy services

LOAN SYNDICATION

This is also referred to as consortium financing. This work is taken up by the merchant banker and he arranges loans to the customers by accumulating money from various sources. If a single bank cannot provide a huge sum of loan, a number of banks join together and form a syndicate. It enables the members of the syndicate to share the credit risk associated with a particular loan among themselves.

VENTURE CAPITAL

It is a form of financing, designed for funding high technology, high risk and perceived high reward projects. A venture capitalist provides funds to entrepreneurs and enterprises pursuing in the new and unexplored avenues. Venture capitalist helps the promoter to actualize the project and attain commercialization.

Features of venture capital

- Venture capital is usually will be in the form of equity participation.
- The investment is made only in hi-tech projects having high growth potential.
- Venture capitalist joins the firm as a co-partner and shares the risk and reward of the enterprise.
- Once the started venture reaches the full potential and starts earning profit, the venture capitalist will withdraw his investments.
- This type of investment is generally made in small and medium scale business houses.
- Venture capital is available only for commercialization of new ideas and it is not available for the firms engaged in trading, financial services, research and development, etc.,

Credit Rating Services

Credit rating is an assessment, by an independent agency of the capacity of an issuer of debt security to service the debt and repay the principal as per the terms of issue of debt. A rating agency collects the qualitative as well as the quantitative data from a company, which has to be rated, and assesses the relative strengths and capability of company to honour its obligations contained in the debt instrument throughout the duration of the debt instrument. The rating given is based on an objective judgement of a team of experts from the rating agency involved in credit rating.

Objectives of Credit Rating

It imposes a financial discipline on the borrowers. It helps the financial intermediary in discharging the functions relating to the debt issues. It guides the investor regarding the commitment towards a particular debt instrument for better returns. It facilitates the formulation of the public guidelines on the institutional investment. It may provide adequate funds for the high rated companies at a low rate of interest. It lends greater credibility to the financial and other representatives. It encourages transparency of information and better accounting standards.

CRISIL

It was established in January 1988. It was floated by ICICI, UTI, LIC, GIC and Asian Development Bank. Its objective is to undertake the assignments of the credit rating based on the proposal made by the issuer companies for their financial products. They are debentures, fixed deposit programmes, commercial papers, short-term borrowing instruments and preference shares. CRISIL rating is necessary for the authorities and banks. The CRISIL provides not only the credit rating but also renders services to the corporate sector covering the topics like structure of the industry, degree of competition and business situations.

ICRA

It was promoted by the Industrial Corporation of India. It has come into existence in August 1991. It has headquarters at Delhi. It was an independent company limited by shares with an authorized share capital of Rs.10 crores. The main objective is to assess the credit instruments and assign a grade constant to the risk associated with such instrument. The rating is based on an objective analysis of the information provided by the client company. It helps the investors in making well-informed investing decisions. It assists the issuer company in raising funds from wider investors.

CARE

It is the third credit rating agency in India. These ratings are accepted by the SEBI, the RBI and the Government of India. The IDBI and other institutions promote it. The regulatory authorities have made rating a necessary grading for entering into the market. It is incorporated as a public limited company under the Indian Companies Act. CARE is run by Board of Directors. It consists of eminent persons with a varied experience in financial services and allied areas. The company is an autonomous body and enjoys full freedom in its operations and ratings are also accepted by the market.

MUTUAL FUND

A mutual fund is a corporation, trust or partnership that combines the assets of all its shareholders or partners into one common investment account for the purpose of providing diversification and professional management. 'A mutual fund means pooling the investments of a number of investors by way of investment in units of equal size'. The concept of mutual funds was started with unit schemes of Unit Trust of India in 1964 in India. The term mutual funds came into prominence only in 1987 when leading public sector banks like SBI, Canara bank set up their mutual funds, followed by LIC of India in 1989. From the year 1993, the mutual funds were allowed to start under private sector also. At present in India, there are 40 mutual fund companies in India.

Organization of Mutual Fund Companies in India

The organization of mutual funds involves five constituents or special bodies. They are:

(a) The sponsor/s
(b) The board or trustees
(c) The Asset Management Company (AMC)
(d) The custodian
(e) The unit holders.

A mutual fund is set up in the form of a trust, which has sponsor, trustees, asset management company and custodian. The trust is established by a sponsor or more than one sponsor who is like a promoter of a company. The trustees of the mutual fund hold its property for the benefit of the unit holders. AMC approved by SEBI manages the fund by making investments in various types of securities.

Custodian who is registered with SEBI holds the securities of various schemes of the fund in its custody. The trustees are vested with the general power of superintendence and direction over AMC. They monitor the performance and compliance of SEBI regulations by the mutual fund.

A mutual fund scheme can be classified into open-ended or closed-ended schemes depending on its maturity period. An open-ended scheme is one that is available for subscription and repurchase on a continuous basis. These schemes do not have a fixed maturity period. A closed-ended scheme has a stipulated maturity period, e.g., 5 – 7 years. The fund is open for subscription only during a specified period at the time of launch of the scheme. Investors can invest in the scheme at the time of initial public issue and thereafter they can buy or sell the units of the scheme on the stock exchanges where the units are listed.

CLASSIFICATION OF MUTUAL FUNDS

The schemes can also be classified as growth funds, income funds and balanced funds.

Growth funds: The growth funds aim to provide capital appreciation over the medium to long term. Such schemes normally invest a major part of their corpus in equities. Such funds have comparatively high risks. These schemes provide different options to the investors like dividend, capital appreciation, etc. and the investors can choose an option depending on their preferences.

Income funds: These funds aim to provide regular and steady income to investors. Such schemes generally invest in fixed income securities such as bonds, corporate debentures, government securities and money market instruments. These funds are not affected by the market fluctuations.

Balanced funds: These funds provide both growth and regular income as such schemes invest both in equities and fixed income securities. These are appropriate for investors looking for moderate growth. They generally invest 40-60% in equity and debt instruments. These funds are also affected by fluctuations in share prices in the stock market.

The other schemes are as follows:

Money market mutual funds, indexed funds, sector schemes, tax saving schemes, load funds, no load funds, etc.

Money market mutual funds: These are income funds and their aim is to provide easy liquidity, preservation of capital and moderate income. These schemes invest exclusively in safer short-term instruments such as treasury bills, certificates of deposit, commercial paper and inter-bank call money, government securities, etc.

Indexed funds: These funds invest exclusively in the government securities. Government securities have no default risk. Net asset values of these schemes also fluctuate due to change in interest rates and other economic factors as in the case of income or debt-oriented schemes.

Sector schemes: These are the funds, which invest in the securities of only those sectors or industries as specified in the offer documents. For example, Software industries, pharmaceuticals, FMCGS, etc. The returns in these funds are dependent on the performance of the respective sector. While these funds may give higher returns, they are more risky as compared to diversified funds. Investors need to keep a watch on the performance of these sectors and must exit at an appropriate time besides seeking expert advice.

Tax saving schemes: These schemes offer tax rebates to the investors under specific provisions of the income tax act of 1961, as the government offers tax incentives for investment in specified avenues. For example, equity linked saving schemes, pension schemes, etc.

Load fund: A load fund is one that charges a percentage of net asset value for entry or exit. Each time one buys or sells units in the fund, a charge will be payable. This charge is used by the mutual fund for marketing and distributing expenses.

No-load fund: This fund is one that does not charge for entry or exit. It means the investors can enter the fund at net asset value and no additional charges are payable on purchase or sale of units. The price a unit holder is charged while investing in an open-ended scheme is called sales price.

Functions of Mutual Funds

The basic function of mutual fund companies is buying and selling securities on behalf of its unit holders. It enables small investors to hold a share in a large and diversified portfolio of assets, which reduces the risks of investment. The savings so mobilized are pooled in a large, diversified and sound portfolio of equity, bonds, securities, etc.

Investors in the mutual funds are given the share in its total funds, which is evidenced by the unit certificates. Mutual funds assure professional management, which helps in earning higher rate of return. It helps the small investors who do not have adequate time and knowledge, expertise, experience and resources for directly accessing profitable avenues in capital and money markets.

Corporate advisory services: Financial intermediaries particularly banks have setup specialized branches for this. As new avenues of finance like Euro loans, GDRs, etc. are available to corporate customers, this service is of immense help to the customers.

Securitization: Securitization is a technique whereby a financial company converts its ill-liquid, non-negotiable and high value financial assets into securities of small value which are made tradable and transferable.

Derivative security: A derivative security is a security whose value depends upon the values of other basic variable backing the security. In most cases, these variables are nothing but the prices of traded securities.

Forfeiting: Forfeiting is a technique by which a forfeiter (financing agency) discounts an export bill and pays ready cash to the exporter who can concentrate on the export front without bothering about collection of export bills.

Custodial services: Under this a financial intermediary mainly provides services to clients, for a prescribed fee, like safe keeping of financial securities and collection of interest and dividends.

New products in forex markets: New products have also emerged in the forex markets of developed countries. Some of these products are yet to make full entry in Indian markets. Among them are:

(a) **Forward contract:** A forward transaction is one where the delivery of foreign currency takes place at a specified future date for a specified price. It may have a fixed or flexible maturity date.

(b) **Options:** As the very name implies, it is a contract where in the buyer of options has a right to buy or sell a fixed amount of currency against another currency at a fixed rate on a future date according to his options.

(c) **Futures:** It is a contract wherein there is an agreement to buy or sell a stated quantity of foreign currency at a future date at a price agreed to between the parties on the stated exchange.

(d) **Swaps:** A swap refers to a transaction wherein a financial intermediary buys and sells a specified foreign currency simultaneously for different maturity dates.

LINES OF CREDIT

It is an innovative funding mechanism for the import of goods and services on deferred payments terms. LOC is an arrangement of a financing institution of one country with another to support the export of goods and services to as to enable the importer to import on deferred payment terms.

CHALLENGES FACING THE FINANCIAL SERVICES SECTOR

Though financial services sector is growing very fast, it has its own set of problems and challenges. The financial sector has to face many challenges in its attempt to fulfil the ever-growing financial demands of the economy. Some of the important challenges are briefly explained hereunder:

- **Lack of qualified personnel:** The financial services sector is fully geared to the task of 'financial creativity'. However, this sector has to face many challenges. The dearth of qualified and trained personnel is an important impediment in its growth.
- **Lack of investor awareness:** The introduction of new financial products and instruments will be of no use unless the investor is aware of the advantages and uses of the new and innovative products and instruments.
- **Lack of transparency:** The whole financial system is undergoing a phenomenal change in accordance with the high time that this sector gave up their orthodox attitude of keeping accounts in a highly secret manner.
- **Lack of specialization:** In the Indian scene, each financial intermediary seems to deal in a different financial service lines without specializing in one or two areas. In other countries, financial intermediaries specialize in one or two areas only and provide expert services.
- **Lack of recent data:** Most of the intermediaries do not spend more on research. It is very vital that one should build up a proper database on the basis of which one could embark upon 'financial creativity'.
- **Lack of efficient risk management system:** With the opening of the economy to multinationals and exposure of Indian companies to international competition, much importance is given to foreign portfolio flows. It involves the utilization of multi currency transactions which exposes the client to exchange rate risk, interest rate risk and economic and political risk. The above challenges are likely to increase in number with the growing requirements of the customers. The

financial services sector should rise up to the occasion to meet these challenges by adopting new instruments and innovative means of financing so that it could play a very dynamic role in the economy.

INDIAN FINANCIAL SECTOR

India is one of the fastest growing economies in the world with a rapidly expanding financial services sector. After adjustments for purchasing power parity, India's economy is the fourth largest in the world in terms of Gross Domestic Product (GDP). An efficient securities market provides the necessary channel for flow of resources from the providers of capital to the users of capital for economic development. The overall growth of the economy and economic activity are also important factors, which determine availability of resources. In India because of the liberalization, privatization and globalization introduced by P.V. Narasimharao, the scenario has been changing in the financial services industry.

Before LPG in 1991

During the late time before the Indian economy LPG, the Indian financial services industry was dominated by the commercial banks and other financial institutions which cater to the requirements of the Indian industry. In fact, the capital market played a secondary role only. The economic liberalization has brought in a complete transformation in the Indian financial services industry.

Prior to the economic liberalization, the Indian financial service sector was characterized by so many factors which retarded the growth of the financial services sector. Some of the significant factors were:

- Excessive controls in the form of regulations of interest rates, money rates, etc.
- Too many controls over the prices of securities under the controller of the capital issues.
- Non-availability of financial instruments on a large scale as well as on different varieties.
- Absence of independent credit rating and credit research agencies.
- Lack of information about international developments in the financial sector.
- Absence of a developed government securities market and the existence of stagnant capital market without any reformation.
- Strict regulation of foreign exchange market with too many restrictions on foreign investment and foreign equity holding in Indian companies.
- Non-availability of debt and other instruments on a large scale.

After LPG in 1991

After the economic liberalization, the entire financial services sector has undergone a rapid change and now we are witnessing the emergence of new financial products and services almost everyday. The Indian financial services industry has experienced significant growth in the last few years. There has been a considerable broadening and deepening of the Indian financial markets due to various financial market reforms undertaken by the Indian regulators, the introduction of innovative financial instruments in recent years and the entry of sophisticated domestic and international financial services participants. Sectors such as banking, asset management and brokerage have been liberalized to allow private sector involvement, which has contributed to the development and modernization of the financial services sector. This is particularly evident in the non-banking financial services sector, such as brokerage, residential mortgage and insurance services, where new products and expanding delivery channels have helped these sectors to achieve high growth rates recently. Financial services accounted for approximately 14% of total GDP in fiscal 2007.

Regulatory Developments

The following are certain regulatory developments in the Indian financial sector since India's economic reforms. As part of the reforms process, the

- Capital Issues (Control) Act, 1947 was repealed in 1992 and replaced by the SEBI Act, 1992, paving the way for market-determined allocation of resources. The investor education and protection fund was established for the promotion of aware.
- Reserve Bank of India to regulate the banking and other services in India.
- Insurance regulatory and development authority for regulating and monitoring of insurance companies.
- Depository act for the settlement system on Indian stock exchanges gave rise to settlement risk due to the lapse of time before trades were settled by NSDL and CDSL.
- Different exchanges were started to trade different financial instruments.

The financial intermediaries render innumerable services in recent times. Most of them are nature of non-fund based activity. Some of the modern services are:

- Rendering project advisory services right from the preparation of the project till the raising of funds for starting the project with necessary government approval.
- Planning for mergers and acquisitions and assisting for their smooth carry out.
- Guiding corporate customers in capital restructuring.
- Managing the portfolio of large public sector corporations and undertaking risk management services like insurance, buy-back options, etc.
- Hedging of risk due to exchange rate risk, interest rate risk, economic risk, and political risk by using derivative products.
- Structuring the financial collaboration/joint ventures by identifying suitable joint venture partner and preparing joint venture agreement.
- Promoting credit rating agencies for the purpose of rating companies which want to go public by the issue of debt instruments.

Undertaking services related to capital markets such as:

- Clearing services
- Registrations and transfers
- Safe-custody of securities
- Collection of income on securities.

The recent trends in the financial services sector in India:

- The cap on foreign investments in Indian banks has been increased from 49% to 74%. Technological innovations in banking like electronic fund transfer, internet banking, cash back cards, home banking, virtual branches and video banking (where ATMs, phones can call be seen through not the staff), anywhere, anytime banking services, etc.
- In portfolio management services special services to institutional investors, to NRIs, suggesting the investors about the aversion of risk and providing the best solutions, sending updates about

latest happenings to the investors through mobile SMS and through mail alerts, reducing regulations in the services, etc.

- In mutual funds the investor is given the option to assess the risk and returns involved, and then take the investment decisions, increasing transparency, new schemes that are cater the needs of pensioners, young parents, salaried employees, investments in foreign equity markets, systematic investment plans, systematic withdrawal plans, auto debit schemes, sectoral schemes, mail alerts, etc.

In insurance services the recent trends are marriage insurance, bancassurance, work site marketing, multinational companies in life and general insurances with wide range of services in terms of the flexible policies and premiums which are convenient to all age group people, businesses, etc.

MARKETING OF SERVICES

Widespread interest in the effective management and marketing of services as well as the inconclusive debate on how distinct is the marketing of intangible services from that of the tangible products, have enriched the literature by highlighting the service characteristics as that of intangibility, immediacy, individuality, perishability, heterogeneity, ownership, inseparability of production from consumption, and being experimental.

Features

In common parlance, these characteristics are also referred as:

- Services are performed, not produced.
- Services are more people-based than technology-based.
- Services supply cannot be easily changed to meet the suddenly changed market needs.
- Service demand has greater elasticity.
- Services face unique quality control issues and a larger number of problems in customer servicing.
- Service quality is an amalgam of services.

Meaning and Types

There are the business and professional services such as advertising, marketing research, banking, insurance, and computer programming, legal and medical advice. Then there are services which are provided by professionals but consumed for reasons not of business, rather for leisure, recreation, entertainment and fulfilment of other psychological and emotional needs such as education, fine arts, travel, tourism, etc.

Faced with such a broad spectrum, we need to define the concept of service from a marketing viewpoint. Kotler offers one such definition: A service is any activity or benefit that one party can offer to another that is essentially intangible and does not result in the ownership of anything.

Its production may or may not be tied to physical product. W.J. Stanton views services as fulfilling certain wants and states that, "services are those separately identifiable, essentially intangible activities which provide want-satisfaction, and are not necessarily tied to the sale of a product or another service. To produce a service may or may not require the use of tangible goods. However, when such use is required, there is no transfer of title (permanent ownership) to these tangible goods." As in the case of a product, in the case of services also your starting point for understanding the marketing dynamics is the want satisfaction of the customers. It is important to correctly identify the particular want(s) which your service is fulfilling, since this will provide the clue for designing the most appropriate marketing strategy.

A restaurant provides satisfaction to its customers on the basis of type and quality of its food, its decor and environment and the behaviour of its staff and its location in a busy commercial-cum office complex. For instance, 'Class Touch' was started as a restaurant serving exclusive Western and Chinese cuisine with an expensive decor, a live band, beautifully liveried waiters and a high-price menu. The venture was a flop right from the start. On the advice of its marketing consultant, the restaurant changed over from serving elaborate, expensive meals to a 'fast-food' outlet providing quick, reasonably priced meals for consumption both within and outside the restaurant. Today, this restaurant is a big success. It was the correct identification of the want-satisfaction which helped the restaurant become successful. Located in a predominantly office complex, the owners realised that in lunch-break, people do not visit a restaurant for relaxation or status satisfaction. They have limited time at their disposal and want a quick clean meal at a reasonable price, with minimum frills and fancy. In this case, the restaurant was satisfying the basic hunger need, but was catering to a very specific class of customer (office-goers) with a special kind of constraint (that of time and money).

Reasons for Growth of the Service Sector

Manufacturing industries grew because they produced tangible goods which satisfied people's physiological needs of food, shelter and clothing. As the basic need was fulfilled there was demand for improved satisfaction, and this led to a proliferation of variations of the same product and a number of companies involved in its manufacture. The growth of service industries can be traced to the economic development of society and the socio-cultural changes that have accompanied it.

Sometimes, the growth of a specific service industry is the result of a combination of several reasons. Increasing affluence coupled with the desire to utilize leisure time for leisure rather than for doing odd repair jobs in the house had led to the growing tribe of plumbers and electricians. Increasing affluence combined with increasing complexity of life and increasing insecurity has led to the phenomenon of credit cards and travellers' cheques which have proved to be almost perfect substitutes for money. These credit cards provide convenience and safety. In fact, convenience is proving to be a key concept in the provision of services.

CUSTOMER SERVICE

Customer service is the provision of service to customers before, during and after a purchase. According to Jamier L. Scott. (2002), "Customer service is a series of activities designed to enhance the level of customer satisfaction – that is, the feeling that a product or service has met the customer expectation."

Its importance varies by product, industry and customer; defective or broken merchandise can be exchanged, often only with a receipt and within a specified time frame. Retail stores will often have a desk or counter devoted to dealing with returns, exchanges and complaints, or will perform related functions at the point of sale.

Customer service may be provided by a person (e.g., sales and service representative), or by automated means called self-service. Examples of self-service are Internet sites. However, in the Internet era, a challenge has been to maintain and/or enhance the personal experience while making use of the efficiencies of online commerce.

Customer service is normally an integral part of a company's customer value proposition. In their book *Rules to Break and Laws to Follow*, Don Peppers and Martha Rogers, Ph.D. write that "customers have memories. They will remember you, whether you remember them or not." Further, "customer trust can be destroyed at once by a major service problem, or it can be undermined one day at a time, with a thousand small demonstrations of incompetence."

From the point of view of an overall sales process engineering effort, customer service plays an important role in an organization's ability to generate income and revenue. From that perspective, customer service should be included as part of an overall approach to systematic improvement.

Some have argued that the quality and level of customer service has decreased in recent years, and that this can be attributed to a lack of support or understanding at the executive and middle management levels of a corporation and/or a customer service policy. To address this argument, many organizations have employed a variety of methods to improve their customer satisfaction levels, and other KPIs.

Instant Feedback

Recently, many organizations have implemented feedback loops that allow them to capture feedback at the point of experience. For example, National Express, one of the UK's leading travel companies invites passengers to send text messages whilst riding the bus. This has been shown to be useful as it allows companies to improve their customer service before the customer defects, thus making it far more likely that the customer will return next time.

A challenge working with customer service is to ensure that you have focused your attention on the right key areas, measured by the right Key Performance Indicators. There is no challenge to come up with a lot of meaningful KPIs, but the challenge is to select a few which reflects your overall strategy. In addition to reflecting your strategy it should also enable staff to limit their focus to the areas that really matter. The focus must be of those KPIs, which will deliver the most value to the overall objective, e.g., cost saving, service improving, etc. It must also be done in such a way that staffs sincerely believe that they can make a difference with the effort.

One of the most important aspects of a customer service KPI is that of what is often referred to as the "Feel Good Factor". Basically, the goal is to not only help the customer have a good experience, but to offer them an experience that exceeds their expectations. Several key points are listed as follows:

1. **Know your product** – Know what products/service you are offering back to front. In other words, be an information expert. It is okay to say "I don't know", but it should always be followed up by... 'but let me find out' or possibly 'but my friend knows!' Whatever the situation may be, make sure that you don't leave your customer with an unanswered question.
2. **Body Language/Communication** – Most of the communication that we relay to others is done through body language. If we have a negative body language when we interact with others it can show our lack of care. Two of the most important parts of positive body language are smiling, and eye contact. Make sure to look your customers in the eye. It shows that we are listening to them, not at them. And then of course smiling is just more inviting than someone who has a blank look on their face.
3. **Anticipate Guest Needs** – Nothing surprises your customer more than an employee going the extra mile to help them. Always look for ways to serve your customer more than they expect. In doing so it helps them to know that you care and it will leave them with the "Feel Good Factor" that we are searching for.

STANDARDIZATION

There are few standards on this topic. ISO and The International Customer Service Institute (TICSI) have published the following ones:

- ISO 9004:2000, on performance improvement
- ISO 10001:2007, on customer service conduct
- ISO 10002:2004, on quality management in handling customer complaints
- ISO 10003:2007, on dispute resolution
- The International Customer Service Standard (TICSS)

There is also an information technology service management standard: ISO/IEC 20000:2005. Its first part concerns specifications and its second part the code of practice.

Let us Sum Up

Financial services refer to services provided by the finance industry. The finance industry encompasses a broad range of organizations that deal with the management of money. Among these organizations are banks, credit card companies, insurance companies, consumer finance companies, stock brokerages, investment funds and some government sponsored enterprises.

Some of the major financial services offered by the most of the financial services companies in India are:

- *Capital markets (primary and secondary)*
- *Securities and Exchange Board of India (SEBI)*
- *Merchant Banking*
- *Hire Purchase*
- *Leasing*
- *Factoring*
- *Venture Capital*
- *Mutual Funds*
- *Credit Rating*
- *Insurance Services*

Some of the innovative financial services offered by the most of the financial services companies in India are:

- *Carrot and Stick Bonds*
- *Flip-Flop Notes*
- *Loyalty Coupons*
- *Dual Currency Bonds*
- *Inter-bank Participants (IBPs)*
- *Cyclical and Non-Cyclical Shares*
- *Alpha Shares*
- *Index-Linked Guilt Bonds*
- *Secured Premium Notes*
- *Easy Exit Bonds*
- *ADR and GDRs*

Widespread interest in the effective management and marketing of services as well as the inconclusive debate on how distinct is the marketing of intangible services from that of the tangible products, have enriched the literature by highlighting the service characteristics as that of intangibility, immediacy, individuality, perishability, heterogeneity, ownership, inseparability of production from consumption, and being experimental.

Features

In common parlance, these characteristics are also referred as:

- *Services are performed, not produced.*
- *Services are more people-based than technology-based.*
- *Services supply cannot be easily changed to meet the suddenly changed market needs.*
- *Service demand has greater elasticity.*
- *Services face unique quality control issues and a larger number of problems in customer servicing.*
- *Service quality is an amalgam of services.*

Questions for Discussion

1. What do you understand by financial services? Explain with example.
2. Name some of the major financial services.
3. Name few innovative financial services.
4. Explain the functions and features of financial services.
5. Discuss different types of financial services.
6. Briefly explain the constituent of financial services.
7. List out the classification of financial service industry.
8. Explain the scope of financial services.
9. Explain the reasons for financial innovation.
10. What is financial engineering? Name few financial products.
11. Write short notes on:
    (i) Merchant Banking (ii) Leasing (iii) Factoring
    (iv) Loan Syndication (v) Venture Capital
12. List out the services of Merchant Bank.
13. What are the different types of lease? Explain steps involved in leasing process.
14. Explain the functions of credit rating services.
15. Write short notes on:
    (i) CRISIL (ii) CARE (iii) ICRA
16. What do you understand by mutual fund? Explain the various classifications of mutual fund.

17. Write short notes on:
   (i) Growth funds
   (ii) Income funds
   (iii) Balanced funds
   (iv) Indexed funds
   (v) Lines of credit
18. Write briefly about Indian financial sector? Explain reasons behind the growth of Indian financial sector.

5

Health Care and Educational Services

"Health is a state of complete physical, mental and social well-being, and not merely the absence of disease or infirmity". –World Health Organization, 1948

"Education is what remains after one has forgotten what one has learned in school". –Albert Einstein

Learning Objectives

At the end of this chapter students will be able to understand

- Importance of health care industry
- Various types of health care services
- Service marketing triangle
- Understanding pharmacy, nursing and medical transcription
- Issues in education
- Contribution of health care to GDP
- PEST analysis for Indian hospital industry
- 7 Ps of marketing hospital
- Insight into Indian educations system
- Modern trends in education service.

Hospital *– Introduction – trend – health care industry and GDP in India – inputs to health care – different types of health care services – PEST analysis for Indian hospital industry – factors attracting corporate in health care – service market triangle – unique characteristics – 7 Ps of marketing hospital – pharmacy – nursing – medical transcription*

Educational services *– a brief insight into Indian education system – issues in education – modern trends in education service.*

INTRODUCTION

Health care industry in India has seen a phenomenal growth in the last decade. The market comprises health care organizations (hospitals, nursing homes, diagnostic centres, dental hospitals, clinics, ayurveda hospitals, etc.), persons (doctors, dentists, nurses, and other caregivers), and health insurance providers. Private companies play a greater role than the public sector in providing health care services as this sector is expected to be financially stronger and well managed. With the growth of the Indian middle-class segment, shift toward private health care services to obtain more value and service is expected.

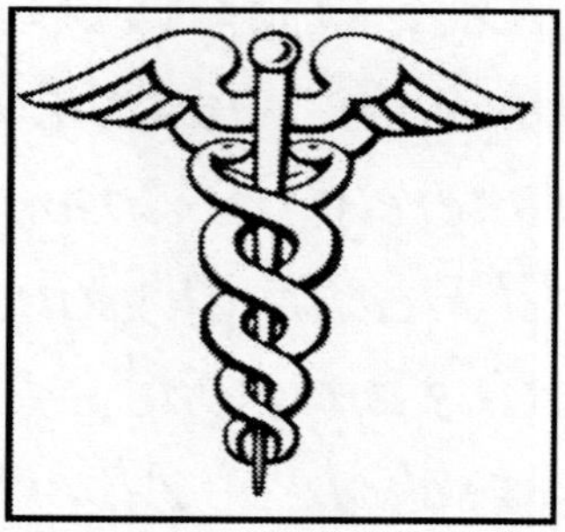

Indian health care industry is at growing stage and is thereby not subjected to strict regulations by the government. There is a general liberalization of trade and investment owing to which most devices do not need import licence. Further, no restrictions have been imposed on refurbished medical equipment. In addition, tariff rates applicable on refurbished medical equipment are same as new equipment, which ranges from 5 to 30 per cent.

Health care industry plays an important part in the economy of a country. The health care industry determines the GDP or the gross domestic product of any country. It also determines exports status, employment, capital investment, etc. Health care segment provides employment openings to many individuals directly associated with the health care sector or other associated sectors, related to the health care industry in some way or the other. Efforts are usually made to keep the dollars rolling within the country economic set up. Businesses dealing in health care add to the already existing economy by buying utility programmes, by paying taxes for property, etc.

The health care industry consists of the following:

- Dentists and doctors
- Protective care and nursing
- Pharmacies
- Allied medical, health services
- Hospitals

The present era is likely to be dominated by expansion of demands in the market, increasing prices and increasing awareness among the customers. Such changes will trigger a change in the health care industry scenario for the better. The year of 1990 witnessed a sluggish rate of growth, the health expenses per capita marked an all time low. The sluggish nature could be due to the fact that several health programmes were implemented efficiently.

HEALTH CARE INDUSTRY TREND

Health care industry trends manifest an upward growth but several areas need to be attended for enhancing health care services for the common man. Different countries like Indonesia, Russia, Mexico, Brazil, India, Turkey and China comprise approximately 1/5th of the worldwide health care sales. Health care industry trends also suggest that the medical related conditions in the developing countries which are chronic in nature, will be similar to the ones existing in the developed countries. In order to meet international standards, the existing health care industry is required to alter the mode of operation for generation of higher revenue and greater contribution to the Gross Domestic Product of the country.

Facts about the health care industry trends

- The cost related to health care was seen to rise in the 90s. Americans not possessing any health care coverage or any kind of health insurance attained the 42 million mark.
- It has been anticipated that the elderly sick people will impose considerable stress on the health care sector of US.
- The total number of different health care programmes and different health care insurance coverages are likely to increase in the coming years. There has been an escalation in the medical plans from 42.5 million in the year 2006. The health care industry trends also show that it is likely to attain 70.2 million in the year 2025.
- The health care industry trends also indicate that the expenses for preventive measures is negligible as compared to the amount spent on treating chronic diseases which accounts for 70% of the fund used for health care.
- Trends suggest that there are very less Americans (around 23%) who make an effort to prevent any lifestyle diseases by consuming the optimum level of vegetables and fruits.

Health care industry trends suggest changes in the following spheres

- The companies manufacturing medicines to provide health care plans
- More stress is to be laid on prevention than treatments
- Sufficient supply of the essential health care products should be made available to the consumers to meet the demand of the health care industry.
- Health care industry trends manifest an upward growth but several areas need to be attended for enhancing health care services for the common man.

With the invention of latest technological developments, the **world health care industry** is catching up with the other leading industries of the world. World health care industry is one of the largest industries catering to the medical needs of innumerable people around the globe. Statistics show that in the year 2004, employment provided by the health care industry accounted for 13.5 million job opportunities. Out of the 13.5 million jobs, some of the people opted for self-employment while others remained salaried workers related to the health care. It has been predicted that between 2004 through 2014, increase in the health care jobs would be by approximately 19% or as many as 3.6 million job opening would be produced. The statistics provided above reflect the health care scenario in the USA. Generally, the world health care industry comprises of the following segments:

- Hospitals
- Nursing
- Physicians
- Dentists

- Health care services at home
- Medical practitioners
- Outpatient departments
- Ambulant health care facilities
- Diagnostic laboratories and medical services
- World health care industry includes any medical institution which includes either a single medical assistant to the medical practitioner or medical practitioners attached to different hospitals and other medical establishments.

The rate of growth of the **health care industry in India** is moving ahead neck to neck with the pharmaceutical industry and the software industry of the country. Much has been said and done in the health care sector for bringing about improvement. Till date, approximately 12% of the scope offered by the health care industry in India has been tapped. The health care industry in India is reckoned to be the engine of the economy in the years to come. Health care industry in India is worth $17 billion and is anticipated to grow by 13% every year. The health care sector encompasses health care instruments, health care in the retail market, hospitals enrolled to the hospital networks, etc.

Health care industry in India and the Gross Domestic Product (GDP)

Expenses incurred by the Indian Government on health care are the highest amongst developing countries. India's expenses on health care sector comprise 5.25% of the GDP. Chances are that the health care market could experience a hike and attain a figure ranging between $53 to $73 billion in five years from now. This in turn will reflect an increase in the gross domestic product to 6.2% GDP. The health care industry in India earns revenues accounting for 5.2% of gross domestic product.

Employment opportunities are provided to as many as 4 million people in the health care segment or other related sectors catering to the health care industry in India in some way or the other. Owing to the vast differences in medical expenses in western countries and that of India, India has become one of the favourites for health care treatments. Due to the progressive nature of the health care sector in India, several foreign companies are intending to invest in the country.

Health care industry is a wide and intensive form of services which are related to well being of human beings. Health care is the social sector and it is provided at State level with the help of Central Government. Health care industry covers hospitals, health insurances, medical software, health equipments and pharmacy in it.

Right from the time of Ramayana and Mahabharata, health care was there but with time, Health care sector has changed substantially. With improvement in medical science and technology it has gone through considerable change and improved a lot.

The major inputs of health care industries are as listed below:

- Hospitals
- Medical insurance
- Medical software
- Health equipment

Health care service is the combination of tangible and intangible aspects with the intangible aspect dominating tangible aspect. Services (consultancy) offered by the doctor are completely intangible. The tangible things could be the bed, the décor, etc.

Different types of health care services available in India

- Hospitals
- Pathology Clinics
- Blood Banks
- Meditation Centres
- Emergency Services like Ambulances, etc.
- Online Medical Services
- Telemedicine
- Naturopathy
- Yoga Centres
- Fitness Centres
- Laughter Clubs
- Health Spas

In the Constitution of India, health is a state subject. Central Government's intervention to assist the state goverment is needed in the areas of control and eradication of major communicable and non-communicable diseases, policy formulation, international health, medical and para-medical education along with regulatory measures, drug control and prevention of food adulteration, besides activities concerning the containment of population growth including safe motherhood, child survival and immunization programme. The plan outlay for central sector health programme in the annual plans 1997-98 is Rs. 920.20 crore including a foreign aid component of Rs. 400 crore. A major portion of outlay is for the control and eradication of diseases like malaria, blindness being implemented under centrally sponsored schemes.

Another major component of the central sector health programme is purely central schemes through which financial assistance is given to institutions engaged in various health related activities. These institutions are responsible for contribution in the field of control of communicable and non-communicable diseases, medical education, training, research and parent-care.

PEST ANALYSIS FOR INDIAN HOSPITAL INDUSTRY

Political Factors

- Health care has been a neglected field in India.
- Special assistance to private health care sector.
- Government has to give certain concessions to private health sector.
- Gets revenue in the form of tax.

Economic Factors

- The Indian health care is the next boom in the country after the IT euphoria.
- The funds of hospitals in India is very less when compared to the other developed countries.
- The World Bank can make available funds of around Rs. 700 crore for state health systems and development projects.
- Third party payment either in the form of medical and allied insurance can boom private health care industry.

Social Factors

- Certain percentages of beds have to be kept for poor people.
- Open counselling and relief centres.
- Safe disposal of hospitals wastes.
- Spreading awareness about various diseases through campaigns and free medical checkups.

Technical Factors

- IT is transforming the way in which health services are delivered.
- The technologies today can support vast databases, network communications, quick distribution.

HOSPITAL INDUSTRY

Some Facts

- India's health care industry is currently worth Rs. 73,000 crore which is roughly 4 per cent of the GDP.
- The industry is expected to grow at the rate of 13 per cent for the next six years which amounts to an addition of Rs. 9,000 crores each year.

The national average of proportion of households in the middle and higher middle income group has increased from 14% in 1990 to 20% in 1999. The population to bed ratio in India is 1 bed per 1000, in relation to the WHO norm of 1 bed per 300. In India, there exists space for 75000 to 100000 hospital beds. Private insurance will drive the health care revenues. Considering the rising middle and higher middle income group we get a conservative estimate of 200 million insurable lives.

Over the last five years, there has been an attitudinal change amongst a section of Indians who are spending more on health care. Corporate hospitals mushroomed in the late eighties. The boom remained short-lived and out of the 22 listed hospital scrips, most are being trading below par. An increasingly fragmented market, lack of statistics, capital intensive operations and a long gestation period are all wise reasons to shy away from investing in the health care industry. Government and trust hospitals dominate the scene. Many of the trust hospitals suffer from poor management. Good corporate hospitals are still too few to amount to a critical mass.

Corporate hospitals failed a decade ago because they emerged in isolation and weren't part of a larger phenomenon. However, now, there are the insurance companies, the hospital hardware and the software companies that have come together to create the boom.

Factors Attracting Corporate in the Health Care Sector

Recognition as an Industry: In the mid 80s, the health care sector was recognized as an industry. Hence, it became possible to get long term funding from the financial institutions. The government also reduced the import duty on medical equipment and technology, thus opening up the sector.

Since the National Health Policy (the policy's main objective was 'Health for All' by the Year 2000) was approved in 1983, little has been done to update or amend the policy even as the country changes and the new health problems arise from ecological degradation. The focus has been on epidemiological profile of the medical care and not on comprehensive health care.

Socio-economic Changes: The rise of literacy rate, higher levels of income and increasing awareness through deep penetration of media channels, contributed to greater attention being paid to health. With the rise in the system of nuclear families, it became necessary for regular health check-ups and increase in health expenses for the bread-earner of the family.

Brand Development: Many family run business houses have set up charity hospitals. By lending their name to the hospital, they develop a good image in the markets which further improves the brand image of products from their other businesses.

Extension to Related Business: Some pharmaceutical companies like Wockhardt and Max India, have ventured into this sector as it is a direct extension to their line of business.

Opening of the Insurance Sector: In India, approx. 60% of the total health expenditure comes from self-paid category as against governments contribution of 25-30%. A majority of private hospitals are expensive for a normal middle-class family. The opening up of the insurance sector to private players is expected to give a shot in the arms of the health care industry.

Health insurance will make health care affordable to a large number of people. Currently, in India only 2 million people (0.2% of total population of 1 billion), are covered under mediclaim, whereas in developed nations like USA about 75% of the total population are covered under some insurance scheme. General Insurance Company (GIC) has never aggressively marketed health insurance. Moreover, GIC takes up to 6 months to process a claim and reimburses customers after they have paid for treatment out of their own pockets. This will give a great advantage to private players like Cigna which is planning to launch smart cards that can be used in hospitals, patient guidance facilities, travel insurance, etc.

The consultants, financiers and insurance agencies are to benefit from this boom. The insurers will use PPOs, that will grow into HMOs, to assume insurance risks on client's behalf. Medical equipment, medical software and hospitals will see the biggest boom.

SERVICE MARKETING TRIANGLE

- **Company:** The hospital is the company that dreams up an idea of service offering (treatment), which will satisfy the customer's (patient's) expectations (of getting cured).
- **Customer:** The patient who seeks to get cured is the customer for the hospital as he is the one who avails the service and pays for it.
- **Provider:** Doctor, the inseparable part of the hospital is the provider, as he is the one who comes in direct contact with the patient. The reputation of the hospital is directly in the hands of the doctor. A satisfied patient is a very important source of word of mouth promotion for the organization.

UNIQUE CHARACTERISTICS

The service industry has the following characteristics.

Intangibility: Intangibility means that a customer would have to visualize the service offering. Since the offering cannot be seen or felt, there would be no stock and hence one would not be able to keep a track of the sales, etc. This characteristic also makes it different to measure the benefits and utilities of the product. An individual would only be able to experience the same.

- In the product service continuum, hospitals fall in the bracket of highly intangible where the service has credence qualities.

- The services of a doctor, i.e., the consultation provided by the doctor, his diagnosis, etc. cannot be touched felt or seen. One can only visualize the same.
- They can also not measure the benefits. These can only be experienced by the customer.
- There is no ownership over the doctor or the services provided by him.

The remedial measures to overcome intangibility are:

(a) The marketer should visualize the product/service for the patient. In case of hospitals any visual of the hospital displaying the well-maintained interiors, the hi-tech equipment used for treatment would help to tangiblize the product.

(b) Association: The association of a hospital with any well-known personality would help as a good image building exercise. It would also give the customer a certain level of confidence regarding the services provided in the hospital.

Example: Hospitals like the Tata Memorial Hospital or the Hinduja Hospital are associated with corporate houses. They are owned by these corporate families. Hence, a customer is sure about the services provided in these hospitals.

(c) Physical Representation: Intangibility could also be overcome in case of hospital through physical representation in the form of:

- Colour – The Red Cross signifies the hospital.
- Uniforms – The white uniforms of the doctors and nurses in every hospitals.
- Symbols – The Red Cross is the common logo with which people identify hospitals.
- Logos of hospitals like Wockhardt.
- Buildings – In case of hospitals the external appearance of the building or the maintenance i.e., how well maintained it is?

(d) Documentation: There are a number of hospitals which have received ISO 9000 certificates, e.g., Apollo Hospital.

Perishability: A services cannot be stored. So if the service is not consumed immediately then it loses its value. For e.g., if a doctor does not reach his dispensary on time or has his clinic locked for that particular day. He loses all his patients for that day.

A situation may also arise when the doctor may be unable to attend to some of his patients due to a huge rush. In such a case, again the doctor could lose out on all his patients. Same would be the situation faced by the hospitals. In such a case the hospital too may lose all its patients for that day.

SOLUTION TO THE PROBLEM OF PERISHABILITY

(a) In such a situation the doctor can appoint an assistant who could cater to the excess patients or he could have students training under him who during their course of training could also help him with the excess patients, e.g., Rajgovind Hospital in CBD appoints interns of Medical College for night duty on a stipend.

(b) Peak time essential services: In a rush hour situation when there are too many customers to attend to only essential services should be catered to. For example, in hospitals during the late night when accident reportings are high all hands are required at the trauma centres. For example, part time volunteers for national emergencies.

Variability: It means that the quality of service provided to different people may not be the same, i.e., irrespective of the fact that the job carried out by them is the same, the service quality may differ because they may be from different backgrounds and have different aptitude, skills, attitude, etc. For example, 2 doctors, one from a municipal hospital and another from a reputed hospital may treat a person for the same problem. But their quality might differ. In such a case doctors/hospitals are the internal customers and the patients are the external customers.

Since a transaction is always two way communication, a customer's willingness, background, attitude, etc. may also effect the transaction For example, a patient may want to avail of doctor's services but may not be able to afford the services, e.g., a patient suffering from arthritis may be required to lose weight for further treatment. But the patient may not have the drive/willingness to lose weight.

Solutions

(a) The internal customers or the fresh recruiters could be given training. They could be given a chance to perform the small parts of an operation in order to gain experience. The doctors could be given training and could be updated with all the latest happenings in the medical field in regular intervals. For example, AMA prescribes for its member doctors 6 weeks training every year and 6 months training every 6 years.

(b) Training of external customers: Diabetic patients are trained to inject insulin on their own. In case of health care services, a gym instructor may teach his members to use the gym equipments on their own. Auto diagnostic equipment are used in hospital. These kinds of training programmes provided to the external customer helps to increase the quality of transaction.

Inseparability: For any service to take place it is necessary that both the service provider and the customer be present in the location at the same time. For example, an operation cannot be conducted without the doctor's presence. As a result a number of patients due to geographical distances lose out on the opportunity to get themselves treated from the very best surgeons and doctors.

Solutions

This can be overcome to a certain extent through the following:

(1) Training of internal customer: Here one experienced person can provide training to the amateurs. For example, a surgeon during an operation is surrounded by interns watching the operation. They could also carry out some small parts of the operation.

(2) Innovational service: Psychiatrists have innovated group therapy where they call in 10+ patients together to an oval conference table and encourage them to talk about themselves and their ailments.

(3) Videoconferencing: Business conferences, consultancy and the medical world. Only recently have instructions for operation through videoconferencing been initiated but mostly videoconferencing has been used in the medical world as a pedagogical tool. For example, a unique and rare brain tumour operation can be broadcast live all over the world to subscribed medical colleges.

7 PS OF MARKETING FOR HOSPITALS

(a) Product

The service product is an offering of commercial intent having features of both intangible and tangible, seeking to satisfy the new wants and demands of the consumer. Hospital industry is action oriented and there is a lot of interaction with the customers (patients). The service product of the hospitals normally has the following features:

Quality level: When we talk about marketing hospitals, it is natural that we are very particular about managing our services in the right fashion. Supportive services play an important role in improving the quality of medicare. These services which include laboratory, blood-banks, catering, radiology and laundry, in a true sense determine the quality of services made available by medical and para-medical personnel. They get a strong base for treatment since the diagnostic aspect determines a direction. To get the best result from OT, it is natural that equipment are properly sterilized. In addition, the dresses and clothes are also required to be made bacteria free. The patients are required to wear disinfected linen which should be made available. The radiology department should have hi-tech facilities keeping in view the pressure of work. Of late, we find sophisticated equipment to improve quality of service.

Accessories: This is a very good way of segmenting customers. Many hospitals provide additional services such as catering, laundry, yoga sessions, cafeterias, etc. for the customers (patients) who are willing to pay extra. Hospitals have various wards — General and Special. Certain hospitals provide services for the family members of the patients (when they are not from the same city) – accommodation and catering.

Packaging: It is the bundling of many services into the core service. Example: Apollo hospital offers a full health check-up to the patients. Similarly, other hospitals also offer package deals for health check-ups. For example, if a person has to undergo a bypass surgery, he can pay a lump sum amount during admission, say rupees 1 lakh for all procedures, tests, stay, etc., at once.

Product line: Hospitals through their services offer many choices to the patients and cover a wide range of customer needs. For example, Apollo hospital has dental department, cardiology department, etc. and within the dental department it has dental surgery, root canal, etc.

Brand name: The hospitals, to differentiate themselves, and their services from others use a brand name. The intangibility factor of the service makes it all the more important for the hospitals to do so.

(b) Place

Under hospital marketing, distribution of medicare services plays a crucial role. This focuses on the instrumentality of almost all who are found involved in making services available to the ultimate users. In case of hospitals the location of hospital plays a very important role. The kind of services a hospital is rendering is also very important for determining the location of the hospital. For example, Tata Memorial Hospital specializes in cancer treatment and is located at a centre place unlike other normal hospitals, which you can find all over other places.

It can be unambiguously accepted that the medical personnel need a fair blending of two important properties, i.e. – they should be professionally sound and should have in-depth knowledge at psychology. A particular doctor might be famous for his case handling records but he may not be made available for all the patients because of the place factor. Now in this case the service provided, that is the doctor may be a visiting doctor for different hospitals at different locations to beat the place factors.

Unlike other service industries, under hospital marketing all efforts should be for making available to the society the best possible medical aid. In a country like India, which is geographically vast and where majority of the population lives in the rural areas, place factor for the hospitals play a very crucial role. A typical small village/town may be having small dispensaries but they will not have superspeciality hospitals. For that they will have to be dependent on the hospitals in the urban areas.

(c) People

Under hospital marketing the marketing mix variable includes all the different people involved in the service providing process (internal customers of the hospitals) which includes doctors, nurses, supporting staff, etc. The earliest and the best way of having control on the quality of people will be by approving professionally sound doctors and other staff.

Hospital is a place where small activity undertaken can be a matter of life and death, so the people factor is very important. One of the major classifications of hospitals is – private and government. In the government hospital, the people factor has to be specially taken care of. In Indian government hospitals except a few almost all the hospitals and their personnel hardly find the behavioural dimensions significant. It is against this background that even if the users get the quality medical aid they are found dissatisfied with the rough and indecent behaviour of the doctors.

Under hospital marketing a right person for the right job has to be appointed and they should be adaptable and possess versatility. The patients in the hospitals are already suffering from trauma, which has to be understood by the doctors and other staff. The people of the hospital should be constantly motivated to give the best of their effort.

(d) Process

Process generally forms the different tasks that are performed by the hospital. The process factor is mainly dependent on the size of the hospital and kind of service it is offering. A typical process involved in a medium sized hospital can be as follows.

- Apart from this flow there are other allied activities like record keeping administration at services, etc. which fall under the process factor. These stages do not exist separately but are interlinked.
- The most important elements are lines of communication within the setup. The experience of the patient depends on the final interplay of all these factors.

(e) Physical Evidence

It does play an important role in health care services, as the core benefit a customer seeks is proper diagnosis and cure of the problem. For a local small time dispensary or hospital physical evidence may not be of much help. In recent days some major super speciality hospitals are using physical evidence for distinguishing itself as something unique.

Physical evidence can be in the form of smart buildings, logos, mascots, etc. A smart building infrastructure indicates that the hospital can take care of all the needs of the patient. Examples:

- Lilavati Hospital has got a smart building, which helps in developing in the minds of the people, the impression that it is the safest option among the various hospitals available to the people.
- Fortis and Apollo hospitals have a unique logo, which can be easily identified.

  Physical evidence also helps in beating the intangibility factor.

(f) Promotion

Hospitals for promotion use either advertisement or PR or both after taking into consideration the target customers, media type, budget and the sales promotion. Since a few years the prime times in T.V. are reserved for advertising social issues like family planning, use of different types of contraceptives, care for the girl child, and so on. These commercials use the common man approach for reference group appeal. In case of health care products and services use for "common man" appeal is widely prevalent.

The use of celebrities is not as effective as that of a common man. An ordinary person thinks that if it works well for people like him, it will also work equally well for others. The identification with the common man is easy and quick.

(g) Pricing

The pricing management of a social institution becomes complicated as the policy makers are expected to take social factors into considerations. The lower sections of society look forth to free and cost-free services, as they are not economically backed to support their family's health care expenses.

Naturally this jeopardizes the task of top management. It is close to impossible for even the government, especially in an overpopulated country like ours, to make available world-class services to all without charging any fee. But then, it is also not rational that we expect free services, though we have the capacity to pay, which is another problem with the middle-income class of the country.

The pricing strategy helps us to projecting our image. Not only this, if the strategies are welfare oriented, the task of satisfying the users is also simplified. But the satisfaction depends upon sophistication. And sophistication can't be possible unless we change our pricing strategies. Even the affluent sections of society expect low cost services from social institutions in general and hospitals in particular the task of innovating services in line with latest developments in the field of physical sciences is difficult.

Health care services involve the use of expensive and complex machinery, which involve huge investments. Apart from that, the cost of maintaining them and cost of running the hospital is in no terms cheap. Doctors' salaries along with the salaries of the nurses and helpers constitute a great part of the cost too. In a developing country like ours, where the level of income of the general masses is found low, it is significant that pricing decisions are liberal to the economically weaker sections of the society.

There are a number of questions that service marketers need to ask themselves as they prepare to create and implement a well – thought – out pricing strategy.

How Much to Charge?

Pricing in Govt. Hospitals

In the Indian setting where a number of persons are below the poverty line it is challenging task to formulate a pricing strategy, which is successful in serving the social interests and generating profits. It is due to this that most government hospitals are in deplorable condition. The ultimate sufferers are the society and specially the poorer sections. Since the affluent sections have an option to avail the expensive medical services made available by private hospitals. The societal marketing principles make an advocacy in favours of protecting the public interests but it is not meant that the hospitals have a uniform pricing/ free structure for all the users. The fee strategy for hospitals should be in proportion to the incomes of users, which would engineer a sound foundation for qualitative or quantitative improvements.

Discriminatory Pricing: For social institutions like govt. hospitals a discriminatory fee structure is preferred since it provides even the weaker sections of society, an opportunity to avail the quality medical services. This enables hospitals to innovate services to keep pace with the latest developments in medical sciences.

(i) ***Free service:*** Generally speaking, all categories of hospitals should adopt cost-free services to the weaker sections of the society having no source of income for paying even the nominal charges. In this context, the government hospitals should be given special grants to avoid an imbalance in their financial management.

(ii) ***Subsidized services:*** The users belonging to the low-income group should be made available subsidized services. That is, the public or hospitals make nominal charges for the services made available to them. It is more or less clear that subsidized services are a bit lower than the cost involved on treatment. Both the central and state governments would give the subsidies.

(iii) ***Cost-based services:*** This is based on the principle of no-profit, no-loss. Or say, the cost based strategy in which prices or fees are equal to the costs involved on treatment. This is basically for the middle-income group.

(iv) ***Cost plus subsidy:*** This strategy allows charging more than the costs involved on the services, but only from the better-off sections of society. The transfer of these surpluses to the account of subsidy for compensating the losses on account of providing free or subsidized services to the weaker sections and low-income group users is also necessary.

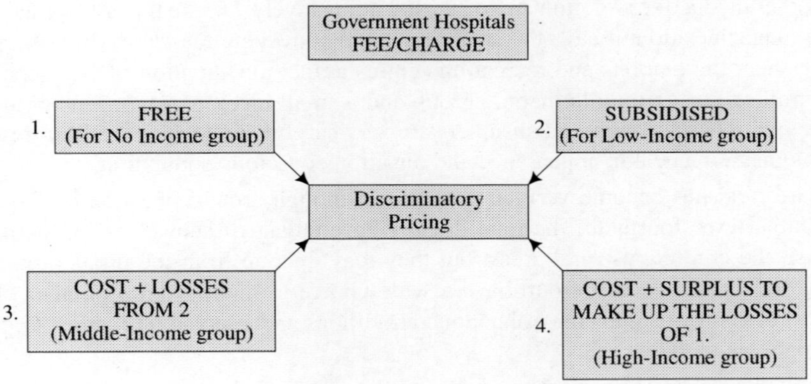

On one hand, it is judicious that no discrimination is found in respect of making available the medical aids, but on the other hand, we can't adopt uniform policy while making available to the users and their attendants other facilities like standard of room, indoor facilities and other non-medical amenities.

This is justified on the ground that all groups are not paying equal fees for availing their services. Moreover, when no income group has been availing the services without paying any fee, their expectations would not be more than the proper medical aids.

Pricing in Private Hospitals

It is difficult to offer free or subsidized services to the masses. On the other hand, the technological sophistication has raised the cost of services as the inputs used in making available the medical services are found costly due to rising inflationary pressure.

Thus, private hospitals take the following approaches to pricing:

(i) ***Cost based pricing:*** Direct price + overhead costs + profit margin.

This approach involves setting prices relative to financial costs. The hospital sets a price sufficient to recover the full costs (variable, semi-variable and fixed) of providing the service. These ads a sufficient margin to yield the described level of profit at the predicted sales volume. Hospitals generally incur high fixed costs due to expensive physical facilities. In hospital services, this method is cumbersome because the tracking and identification of costs apart from doctors fee, is difficult.

In spite of this, some hospitals in the private sector do follow this method.

(ii) ***Demand/Value based pricing:*** This involves settling a price consistent with the customer's perception of service value. That is, prices are based on what customers will pay for the services provided. Hospitals with a reputation for high quality successful treatments, etc. can and do charge a premium simply based on the sheer perception of quality health care. Those who can afford are generally willing to spend high amounts on quality care.

(iii) ***Relationship pricing:*** Hospitals may undertake relationship pricing with regard to corporate clients so as to develop and maintain long-term customer relationships. Here the hospital offers company's on treatment of its employees over a period of time.

(iv) ***Competition based pricing:*** Using other price as an anchor for the hospitals price, heterogeneity of service across and within providers makes the approach complicated.

Besides TV, other media of promotion are to be used innovatively. Unlike the urban area, in rural areas newspapers and magazines do not have the same impact in conveying messages. In villages, hoardings and wall writings near the markets and recreation centres attract the attention of villagers. This market consists of 180 million strong middle income group and a small income group. This group has a large discretionary income. These discerning consumers are very careful in choosing health care services. The last decade has witnessed a health, appearance and nutrition conscious population.

The health care field has become very competitive. Although around one-fourth of our population stays in urban India, three-fourths of the total doctors have engaged themselves in this part. Many of these doctors visit the contiguous rural areas, but they may operate from the urban area. The patients of upper middle and upper income group have a wide choice to make from a number of clinics and hospitals. Therefore, many hospitals have abandoned traditions and adopted marketing strategies to woo more and more patients to their clinics.

Word-of-mouth plays a very important role in promotion of hospitals. A person in need of a health care service does not know for sure where to search for relevant information. He consults his family members, relations and friends first. The patients who come to a hospital generally have the old patients of that hospital as referrals. Word-of-mouth plays an important role during information acquisition stage of the customers as there are no objective performance measures to judge the various alternatives available to them. Therefore, satisfied past patients of a hospital can bring more number of patients to that hospital than a number of advertisements.

In a competitive marketplace, the images of the firms will affect their competitive standing. One factor that is likely to have a significant impact on the health care scene is the growth of hospital chains such as Apollo Hospitals, Birla Health Centres, etc. Artificial heart transplants and other complex operations although are few in number and generate a small portion of the total revenue, they help in generating word-of-mouth which health care providers are actually interested. Many of these companies are spending a lot in corporate advertising for image building.

MARKETING OF HOSPITALS

Marketing in hospital was considered unethical in the eighties, when very few hospitals realized that it was necessary to incorporate marketing as an integral function in the hospital operations. But the major argument at that time lay in understanding whether this professional orientation was really required for its viability, profitability and sustainability. This argument however became favourable in the late nineties as corporate companies like Wockhardt and Max India started venturing into the hospital industry, apart from the ongoing mergers and acquisitions that were already taking place at that time. Even the TPAs started building tie-ups with corporate clients and there was already an abysmal utilisation of resources in the existing hospitals. In addition to the above, a major factor that contributed to the acceptance of marketing in hospitals was an increase in the delivery of services.

'Perception of patients' was another important consideration for hospitals, as they felt that the patients would take them as profit-oriented organization rather than service-oriented organization. Ultimately, marketing was accepted only by a few while the others discarded the concept. Hospitals who accepted marketing also carried out their functioned by concentrating around corporate clients. Lately it has been felt that many Indian hospitals have a dilemma regarding the functions of marketing. In an era where hospitals are experiencing a major shift in their clientele, they are worried more about the patients' perception of hospitals and therefore the concept of brand restructuring and brand engineering is vital.

As hospitals spend millions of rupees in technology and infrastructure, it becomes necessary, that they attract patients and generate funds. In order to do the same, the hospitals follow various marketing and brand building exercises. Some of them are listed below:

- Many hospitals have eminent personalities from the industry in their board of trustees. This indirectly leads to increase in inflow of patients, working in the companies of these Trustees. Besides the presence of eminent personalities creates a sense of confidence in the minds of people.
- Private hospitals can attract their shareholders by offering discounts. For example, a special discount of 20% on all preventive health checks is offered to all shareholders of Apollo Hospitals Limited.
- Hospitals have long-term understanding with PPOs (Preferred Provider Organizations), which further have understanding with corporate. Any case of sickness found in the employees of these corporates refer them to the PPOs, which further sends them to the hospital for check-ups and treatment.
- The success rate of crucial operations and surgeries, reflect the technological and knowledge-based edge of the hospital over the competitors. Such successes are discussed in health magazines and newspapers, which becomes a natural advantage for the hospital.
- Some hospitals by means of their past track record have created a niche market for themselves. For example, Hinduja Hospital is known for its high-quality health care at reasonable rates, whereas Lilavati Hospital is known for its five-star services.
- Hospitals hold seminars and conferences relating to specific diseases, where they invite the doctors from all round the country, for detailed discussion. This makes the hospital well known amongst the doctors, who could in future refer complicated cases to the hospital.
- Hospitals can also promote medical colleges. This helps them to generate extra resources in form of fees, using the same infrastructure.

APOLLO GROUP OF HOSPITAL

The Apollo Group of Hospitals is driven by its line of being the "architect of health care" in India, the Apollo Hospitals Group, comprising of one of the largest networks of 26 hospitals, 10 clinics and over 10,000 employees across the country, represents the changing face of health care in India contemporary and corporatized. It has been the first private company to administer health insurance in the country and Indraprastha Apollo Hospital in Delhi is the fourth largest corporate hospital in the world.

The Apollo group is India's first corporate hospital, the first to set-up hospital outside the country and the first to attract foreign investment. With 2600 beds, Apollo is one of Asia's largest health care players. The recent merger between its 3 group companies, Indian Hospitals Corporation Ltd., Deccan Hospitals Corporation Limited and Om Sindoori Hospitals Limited, will help the group raise money at a better rate and by consolidating inventory, it will save around 10% of the material cost. The group is planning to invest Rs. 2000 crore, to build around 15 new hospitals, in India, Sri Lanka, Nepal and Malaysia. Apollo claims to maintain the best of medical standards with a record of over 7.4 million treated patients, 3,15,000 preventive health checks done, 98.5 per cent success rate in 45,000 cardiac surgeries, etc. and helping the company maintain a balance between the corporate culture and rigorous medical excellence is recognition of IT as intrinsic to every process, whether it is day-to-day running of hospitals, education or telemedicine.

The application of IT in the day-to-day working of the largest hospital of the group, Indraprastha Apollo, throws light on the extent of the automation drive within the company. The management realized the fact that in order to have a modern hospital in place all the work processes had to be related to IT. Hence, the need for an end-to-end integrated solution. This led to the implementation of the Hospital Information System (HIS), which was an integral part of the hospital inception project.

The hospital today boasts of an integrated HIS, which provides for end-to-end integration of the various processes and functional areas within the hospital to make for a seamless workflow. The work processes of the hospital are primarily divided into two areas the patient (comprising inpatient and outpatient) and the non-patient all the back-end departments like housekeeping, engineering, finance, materials, purchase and HRD. The workflow process starts with the patient seeking an appointment with the doctor. HIS contains all the information relating to appointment schedules of the doctors. Depending on the availability of the doctor, the patient is given the date and time of appointment. This information is then fed into the system and the updated information is available to the doctor in real-time.

On the date of his appointment, the patient registers himself at the counter by filling up of a form, which contains all the basic information related to the patient. This data is fed into the system with a Unique Hospital Identifier (UHI) number allotted to the patient so that by the time the patient meets the doctor, he already has all the required basic information. This is followed by 15 minutes of consultation with the doctor after which the doctor gives his prescription, the data is again keyed into the system as a patient record under his UHI and is accessible for quick reference.

One of the biggest advantages of HIS is that any medically relevant information related to the patient is available at the click of a button, thereby saving precious time, which means a lot when it comes to saving a life. HIS also acts as a kind of ERP for the hospital with its automation of various back-end areas like financial, accounting and inventory, which are integrated with the patient areas wherever required.

The hospital has also developed a very effective mailing system for its employees, which is based on microsoft exchange. The company's intranet is being used to run mailing applications as well as information relating to company policies, leave information and basic information relating to the company.

Telemedicine Health Care for All

A very significant IT initiative of the Apollo Hospitals Group, and of great relevance to a developing country like India in taking health care to the masses, is the area of telemedicine. Incorporated in 1999, Apollo Telemedicine Enterprises (ATEL), the telemedicine division of the Apollo Hospitals Group, has already set up over 10 telemedicine links between the Apollo Institutions at Delhi, Hyderabad and

Chennai and distant locations across the country. It has developed competence in developing cost-effective turnkey telemedicine solutions.

Telemedicine ensures that the benefits of hi-tech medicine can go to everyone, and not just to people who live in big cities. The group has forged alliances with government organizations like the Indian Space Research Organization (ISRO) for VSAT bandwidth and Wipro for hardware, to provide telemedicine facilities to far-flung and rural areas. The division is working towards developing a strong Apollo Telemedicine Network, which allows the participant sites to collaborate with institutions in the country and abroad, and provides their clientele access to better health care in areas not adequately served by the medical community.

A patient and his doctor can interact with specialists based in the speciality centres and receive second opinion or interpretations to complex medical cases. The patient reports can be transmitted from a consulting centre to a speciality centre using the telemedicine software and the communication link, which could be ISDN or VSAT connectivity.

Other Services Offered by Apollo

- Apollo Pharmacy: Apollo pharmacy operates round the clock catering to all medicine needs.
- Café Apollo: Café Apollo is a sit down dining facility of the hospital. It offers a wide selection of snacks and a variety of meals.
- Apollo Food Plaza: There is food facility located in the atrium of the hospital serving a delightful array of delicacies.

  Timings: 8:00 a.m. – 9:00 p.m.
- Fast-food Cafe: For the convenience of ICU attendants there is a 24 hours cafe in the ICU lobby.
- Gift Shop: The gift shop carries a wide range of gifts including confectionery, cards, books, newspapers, magazines and other novelties.
- Bank Facilities: The Oriental Bank of Commerce: The Indraprastha Apollo branch of the Oriental Bank of Commerce is located at one of the gates.

  Bank Hours: Monday to Friday, 10:00 a.m. – 2:00 p.m; Saturday, 10:00 a.m. – 12:00 p.m. The bank remains closed on Sundays and National Holidays.
- The ICICI ATM Counter: The ICICI ATM counter is also located in the hospital.

Some Suggestions for Improving the Position of the Hospitals

- The general perception that large hospitals, with high bed-occupancy rate, are profitable, is misleading. Global experience shows that hospital with more than 250 beds don't do well. Many Indian hospitals are following the US health care industry, by decreasing the average length of stay of patients and increasing patient turnover. US research shows that 80% of the revenues form a patient comes in the first 72 hours post-admission. Hospitals generate a lot of revenues from general inspection, because the patient turnover is very high.
- A large per cent of revenues come from specialized services like operations and surgeries. It is because of these reasons that many corporate are planning for small 100 beds specialized hospitals, which caters to specific diseases like cardiac, cosmetic surgery, neurology, etc. Research shows that there exist a lot of space for super-specialized hospitals with 100–150 beds, which generate revenues equivalent to large 500 bed general hospital. Typically large hospitals with approximately 500 bed capacity takes about 9–10 years to break even whereas

super specialty hospitals with about 100 beds take about 6–7 years to break even. Therefore, going in for super-speciality hospitals seems to be a more viable option today.

- Hospitals could also generate revenues from medicines if they are supplying them in-house. Some hospitals make it mandatory for the patients to buy medicines from the hospital's chemist shop. A margin of 15–20 % can be charged for such medicinal supplies. Though many hospitals run by trusts do not earn this way, but new entrants or corporate for whom private health care sector is a direct extension of their line of business (e.g., Pharma companies), can generate good returns from medicine supply.
- Health plan packages can be provided by hospitals to family and corporate. For example Family Health Plan Services (FHP), a subsidiary of Apollo Hospitals does health management of employees of its clients. With a wide network of hospitals and health care providers countrywide, and a tie-up with General Insurance Corporation of India, FHP offers a range of services to employees and dependants, such as preventive health care, corporate counselling, welfare programmes, claims administration, patient-care coordination, and so on. So FHP's health care packages, optimize the benefits while keeping the cost under control.
- Apart from preventive health care, stress management programmes could be provided. For example, 'Effective Stress Management Programme' offered by Wockhardt Hospital. This programme provides a medical perspective of stress and is conducted by a medical professional. The programme includes a series of one-to-one sessions, with a clinical psychologist highlighting the factors responsible for inducing stress, and the methodologies, which can be adopted to cope with this phenomenon practically.
- Hospitals can become integrated health care systems, i.e., when medicines, food services, laundry and linen, etc. will become "purchased" services. These third-party operations will increase the profit margins.
- Mergers could be used for synergy of skills, i.e., to help the merged organizations benefit from one another's individual strengths by applying them across the board. It also helps them to make joint investments in branding or information technology and also to react effectively to the changed market forces.

Alternatively hospitals can go in for Group Purchases, as in USA. The buying power of large GPOs in USA like Premier, VHA/UHC and AmeriNet gives them the clout to exert price pressure on suppliers, particularly for products in lower demand. And as GPOs have consolidated, manufacturers have offered bigger discounts to hang on to their contracts. So there exists a lot of supply management opportunity, which will affect spending productivity.

HOSPITAL EXTENSION SERVICES

Pharmacy

Pharmacy is the health profession that links the health sciences with the chemical sciences and it is charged with ensuring the safe and effective use of pharmaceutical drugs. The scope of pharmacy practice includes more traditional roles such as compounding and dispensing medications, and it also includes more modern services related to health care, including clinical services, reviewing medications for safety and efficacy, and providing drug information. Pharmacists, therefore, are the experts on drug therapy and are the primary health professionals who optimize medication use to provide patients with positive health outcomes.

An establishment in which pharmacy (in the first sense) is practiced is called a pharmacy, chemist's or drug store. These stores commonly sell not only medicines, but also miscellaneous items such as candy (sweets), cosmetics, and magazines, as well as light refreshments or groceries.

The word *pharmacy* is derived from its root word pharma which was a term used since the 1400–1600s. In addition to pharma responsibilities, the pharma offered general medical advice and a range of services that are now performed solely by other specialist practitioners, such as surgery and midwifery. The pharma (as it was referred to) often operated through a retail shop which, in addition to ingredients for medicines, sold tobacco and patent medicines. The pharmas also used many other herbs not listed.

In its investigation of herbal and chemical ingredients, the work of the pharma may be regarded as a precursor of the modern sciences of chemistry and pharmacology, prior to the formulation of the scientific method.

Disciplines

The field of pharmacy can generally be divided into three primary disciplines:

- Pharmaceutics
- Medicinal chemistry and pharmacognosy
- Pharmacy practice

The boundaries between these disciplines and with other sciences, such as biochemistry, are not always clear-cut; and often, collaborative teams from various disciplines research together.

Pharmacology is sometimes considered a fourth discipline of pharmacy. Although pharmacology is essential to the study of pharmacy, it is not specific to pharmacy. Therefore, it is usually considered to be a field of the broader sciences.

Other specializations in pharmacy practice recognized by the Board of Pharmaceutical Specialties include: cardiovascular, infectious disease, oncology, pharmacotherapy, nuclear, nutrition, and psychiatry. The Commission for Certification in Geriatric Pharmacy certifies pharmacists in geriatric pharmacy practice. The American Board of Applied Toxicology certifies pharmacists and other medical professionals in applied toxicology.

Pharmacists

Pharmacists are highly trained and skilled health care professionals who perform various roles to ensure optimal health outcomes for their patients. Many pharmacists are also small-business owners, owning the pharmacy in which they practice.

Pharmacists are represented internationally by the International Pharmaceutical Federation (FIP). They are represented at the national level by professional organizations such as the Dutch Pharmacists Association, Royal Pharmaceutical Society of Great Britain (RPSGB), the Pharmacy Guild of Australia (PGA), the Pakistan Pharmacists Society (PPS) and the American Pharmacists Association (APhA). *See also: List of pharmacy associations.*

In some cases, the representative body is also the registering body, which is responsible for the ethics of the profession. Since the shipman inquiry, there has been a move in the UK to separate the two roles.

TYPES OF PHARMACY PRACTICE AREAS

Pharmacists practice in a variety of areas including retail, hospitals, clinics, nursing homes, drug industry, and regulatory agencies. Pharmacists can specialize in various areas of practice including but not limited to: haematology/oncology, infectious diseases, ambulatory care, nutrition support, drug information, critical care, pediatrics, etc.

Community Pharmacy

Pharmacy (commonly the **chemist** in Australia, New Zealand and the UK; or **drugstore** in North America; **retail pharmacy** in industry terminology; or Apothecary, historically) is the place where most pharmacists practice the profession of pharmacy. It is the community pharmacy where the dichotomy of the profession exists—health professionals who are also retailers.

Community pharmacies usually consist of a retail storefront with a dispensary where medications are stored and dispensed. The dispensary is subject to pharmacy legislation; with requirements for storage conditions, compulsory texts, equipment, etc., specified in legislation. Where it was once the case that pharmacists stayed within the dispensary compounding/dispensing medications; there has been an increasing trend towards the use of trained pharmacy technicians while the pharmacist spends more time communicating with patients.

All pharmacies are required to have a pharmacist on-duty at all times when open. In many jurisdictions, it is also a requirement that the owner of a pharmacy must be a registered pharmacist (R.Ph.). This latter requirement has been revoked in many jurisdictions, such that many retailers (including supermarkets and mass merchandisers) now include a pharmacy as a department of their store.

Likewise, many pharmacies are now rather grocery store-like in their design. In addition to medicines and prescriptions, many now sell a diverse arrangement of additional items such as cosmetics, shampoo, office supplies, confections, snack foods, durable medical equipment, greeting cards, and provide photo processing services.

Hospital Pharmacy

Pharmacies within hospitals differ considerably from community pharmacies. Some pharmacists in hospital pharmacies may have more complex clinical medication management issues whereas pharmacists in community pharmacies often have more complex business and customer relations issues.

Because of the complexity of medications including specific indications, effectiveness of treatment regimens, safety of medications (i.e., drug interactions) and patient compliance issues (in the hospital and at home) many pharmacists practicing in hospitals gain more education and training after pharmacy school through a pharmacy practice residency and sometimes followed by another residency in a specific area. Those pharmacists are often referred to as clinical pharmacists and they often specialize in various disciplines of pharmacy. For example, there are pharmacists who specialize in hematology/oncology, HIV/AIDS, infectious disease, critical care, emergency medicine, toxicology, nuclear pharmacy, pain management, psychiatry, anti-coagulation clinics, herbal medicine, neurology/epilepsy management, pediatrics, neonatal pharmacists and more.

Hospital pharmacies can usually be found within the premises of the hospital. Hospital pharmacies usually stock a larger range of medications, including more specialized medications, than would be feasible in the community setting. Most hospital medications are unit-dose, or a single dose of medicine.

Clinical Pharmacy

Clinical pharmacists provide direct patient care services that optimize the use of medication and promote health, wellness, and disease prevention. Clinical pharmacists care for patients in all health care settings but the clinical pharmacy movement initially began inside hospitals and clinics. Clinical pharmacists often collaborate with physicians and other health care professionals to improve pharmaceutical care.

Clinical pharmacists are now an integral part of the interdisciplinary approach to patient care. They work collaboratively with physicians, nurses and other health care personnel in various medical and surgical areas. They often participate in patient care rounds and drug product selection. In most hospitals in the United States, potentially dangerous drugs that require close monitoring are dosed and managed by clinical pharmacists.

Compounding Pharmacy

Compounding is the practice of preparing drugs in new forms. For example, if a drug manufacturer only provides a drug as a tablet, a compounding pharmacist might make a medicated lollipop that contains the drug. Patients who have difficulty in swallowing the tablet may prefer to suck the medicated lollipop instead.

Another form of compounding is by mixing different strengths, (g, mg, mcg) of capsules or tablets to yield the desire therapy indicated by the doctor. This form of compounding is found at community or hospital pharmacies or in-home administration therapy.

Compounding pharmacies specialize in compounding, although many also dispense the same non-compounded drugs that patients can obtain from community pharmacies.

Consultant Pharmacy

Consultant pharmacy practice focuses more on medication regimen review (i.e., "cognitive services") than on actual dispensing of drugs. Consultant pharmacists most typically work in nursing homes, but are increasingly branching into other institutions and non-institutional settings. Traditionally consultant pharmacists were usually independent business owners, though in the United States many now work for several large pharmacy management companies (primarily Omnicare, Kindred Health care, etc). This trend may be gradually reversing as consultant pharmacists begin to work directly with patients, primarily because many elderly people are now taking numerous medications but continue to live outside of institutional settings. Some community pharmacies employ consultant pharmacists and/or provide consulting services.

The main principle of consultant pharmacy is pharmaceutical care developed by Hepler and Strand in 1990.

Internet Pharmacy

Since about the year 2000, a growing number of Internet pharmacies have been established worldwide. Many of these pharmacies are similar to community pharmacies, and in fact, many of them are actually operated by brick-and-mortar community pharmacies that serve consumers online and those that walk in their door. The primary difference is the method by which the medications are requested and received. Some customers consider this to be more convenient and private method rather than traveling to a community drugstore where another customer might overhear about the drugs that they take. Internet pharmacies (also known as Online Pharmacies) are also recommended to some patients by their physicians if they are homebound.

While most internet pharmacies sell prescription drugs and require a valid prescription, some internet pharmacies sell prescription drugs without requiring a prescription. Many customers order drugs from such pharmacies to avoid the 'inconvenience' of visiting a doctor or to obtain medications which their doctors were unwilling to prescribe. However, this practice has been criticized as potentially dangerous, especially by those who feel that only doctors can reliably assess contraindications, risk/benefit ratios, and an individual's overall suitability for use of a medication. There also have been reports of such pharmacies dispensing substandard products.

Of particular concern with internet pharmacies is the ease with which people, youth in particular, can obtain controlled substances (e.g., Vicodin, generically known as hydrocodone) via the internet without a prescription issued by a doctor/practitioner who has an established doctor-patient relationship. There are many instances where a practitioner issues a prescription, brokered by an Internet server, for a controlled substance to a 'patient' s/he has never met. In the United States, in order for a prescription for a controlled substance to be valid, it must be issued for a legitimate medical purpose by a licensed practitioner acting in the course of legitimate doctor-patient relationship. The filling pharmacy has a corresponding responsibility to ensure that the prescription is valid. Often, individual state laws outline what defines a valid patient-doctor relationship.

Veterinary Pharmacy

Veterinary pharmacies, sometimes called *animal pharmacies*, may fall in the category of hospital pharmacy, retail pharmacy or mail-order pharmacy. Veterinary pharmacies stock different varieties and different strengths of medications to fulfil the pharmaceutical needs of animals. Because the needs of animals, as well as the regulations on veterinary medicine, are often very different from those related to people, veterinary pharmacy is often kept separate from regular pharmacies.

Nuclear Pharmacy

Nuclear pharmacy focuses on preparing radioactive materials for diagnostic tests and for treating certain diseases. Nuclear pharmacists undergo additional training specific to handling radioactive materials, and unlike in community and hospital pharmacies, nuclear pharmacists typically do not interact directly with patients.

Military Pharmacy

Military pharmacy is an entirely different working environment due to the fact that technicians perform most duties that in a civilian sector would be illegal. State laws of technician patient counselling and medication checking by a pharmacist do not apply.

PHARMACY INFORMATICS

Pharmacy informatics is the combination of pharmacy practice science and applied information science. Pharmacy informaticists work in many practice areas of pharmacy, however, they may also work in information technology departments or for health care information technology vendor companies. As a practice area and specialist domain, pharmacy informatics is growing quickly to meet the needs of major national and international patient information projects and health system interoperability goals. Pharmacists are well trained to participate in medication management system development, deployment and optimization.

ISSUES IN PHARMACY

Separation of Prescribing from Dispensing

In most jurisdictions (such as the United States), pharmacists are regulated separately from physicians. These jurisdictions also usually specify that *only* pharmacists may supply scheduled pharmaceuticals to the public, and that pharmacists cannot form business partnerships with physicians or give them 'kickback' payments. However, the American Medical Association (AMA) Code of Ethics provides that physicians may dispense drugs within their office practices as long as there is no patient exploitation and patients have the right to a written prescription that can be filled elsewhere. Seven to 10 per cent of American physicians practices reportedly dispense drugs on their own.

In some rural areas in the United Kingdom, there are dispensing doctors who are allowed to both prescribe and dispense prescription only medicines to their patients from within their practices. The law requires that the GP practice be located in a designated rural area and that there is also a specified, minimum distance (currently 1.6 kilometres) between a patient's home and the nearest retail pharmacy.

In other jurisdictions (particularly in Asian countries such as China, Malaysia, and Singapore), doctors are allowed to dispense drugs themselves and the practice of pharmacy is sometimes integrated with that of the physician, particularly in traditional Chinese medicine.

In Canada it is common for a medical clinic and a pharmacy to be located together and for the ownership in both enterprises to be common, but licensed separately.

The reason for the majority rule is the high risk of a conflict of interest and/or the avoidance of absolute powers. Otherwise, the physician has a financial self-interest in "diagnosing" as many conditions as possible, and in exaggerating their seriousness, because he or she can then sell more medications to the patient. Such self-interest directly conflicts with the patient's interest in obtaining cost-effective medication and avoiding the unnecessary use of medication that may have side effects. This system reflects much similarity to the checks and balances system of the US and many other governments.

A campaign for separation has begun in many countries and has already been successful (like in Korea). As many of the remaining nations move towards separation, resistance and lobbying from dispensing doctors who have pecuniary interests may prove a major stumbling block (e.g., in Malaysia).

NURSING

Nursing is a health care profession focused on the care of individuals, families, and communities so they may attain, maintain, or recover optimal health and quality of life from birth to death.

Nurses work in a large variety of specialties where they work independently and as part of a team to assess, plan, implement and evaluate care.

History of nursing

Florence Nightingale, *"Lady with the Lamp"*, pioneer of modern nursing.

Nursing comes in various forms in every culture, although the definition of the term and the practice of nursing has being known as a wet nurse and the latter being known as a *dry nurse*. In the 15th century, this developed into the idea of looking after or advising another, not necessarily meaning a woman looking after a child. Nursing has continued to develop in this latter sense, although the idea of nourishing in the broadest sense refers in modern nursing to promoting quality of life.

Nursing was viewed during the 17th century as a very low job in the social hierarchy. They had a reputation for being drunk and obnoxious, a view amplified by the doctors of the time to make themselves seem more important and able. It was not until Florence Nightingale, a well educated woman from a middle-class family, became a nurse and improved it drastically that people began to accept nursing as a respectable profession. Other aspects also helped in the acceptance of nursing. In 1853, Theodore

Fliedner set up a hospital where the nurses he employed had to be of good nature. Many people were impressed with this facility and because of it the British Institute of Nursing Sisters was set up.

Prior to the foundation of modern nursing, nuns and the military often provided nursing-like services. The religious and military roots of modern nursing remain in evidence today in many countries, for example in the United Kingdom, senior female nurses are known as "sisters". It was during time of war that a significant development in nursing history arose when English nurse Florence Nightingale, working to improve conditions of soldiers in the Crimean War, laid the foundation stone of professional nursing with the principles summarized in the book *Notes on Nursing*.

Nurses have experienced difficulty with the hierarchy in medicine that has resulted in an impression that nurses primary purpose is to follow the direction of medics. This tendency is certainly not observed in Nightingale's *Notes on Nursing*, where the doctors are mentioned relatively infrequently and often in critical tones, particularly relating to bedside manner.

The modern era has seen the development of nursing degrees and nursing has numerous journals to broaden the knowledge base of the profession. Nurses are often in key management roles within health services and hold research posts at universities.

Nursing as a Profession

The authority for the practice of nursing is based upon a social contract that delineates professional rights and responsibilities as well as mechanisms for public accountability. In almost all countries, nursing practice is defined and governed by law, and entrance to the profession is regulated at national or state level.

The aim of the nursing community worldwide is for its professionals to ensure quality care for all, while maintaining their credentials, code of ethics, standards, and competencies, and continuing their education. There are a number of educational paths to becoming a professional nurse, which vary greatly worldwide, but all involve extensive study of nursing theory and practice and training in clinical skills.

Nurses care for individuals who are healthy and ill, of all ages and cultural backgrounds, and who have physical, emotional, psychological, intellectual, social, and spiritual needs. The profession combines physical science, social science, nursing theory, and technology in caring for those individuals.

Nursing Practice

Nursing practice is primarily the caring relationship between the nurse and the person in their care. In providing nursing care, nurses are implementing the nursing care plan, which is based on a nursing assessment.

Although nursing practice varies both through its various specialities and countries, these nursing organizations offer the following definitions:

Nursing encompasses autonomous and collaborative care of individuals of all ages, families, groups and communities, sick or well and in all settings. Nursing includes the promotion of health, prevention of illness, and the care of ill, disabled and dying people. Advocacy, promotion of a safe environment, research, participation in shaping health policy and in patient and health systems management, and education are also key nursing roles.

Nursing Theory and Process

In general terms, the nursing process is the method used to assess and diagnose needs, plan and implement interventions, and evaluate the outcomes of the care provided. Like other disciplines, the profession has developed different theories derived from sometimes diverse philosophical beliefs and paradigms or worldviews to help nurses direct their activities to accomplish specific goals.

MEDICAL TRANSCRIPTION

Medical transcription, also known as **MT**, is an allied health profession, which deals in the process of transcription, or converting voice-recorded reports as dictated by physicians and/or other health care professionals, into text format.

History

Evolution of transcription dates back to the 1960s. The method was designed to assist in the manufacturing process. The first transcription that was developed in this process was MRP, which is the acronym for Manufacturing Resource Planning, in 1975. This was followed by another advanced version namely MRP2. But none of them yielded the benefit of medical transcription.

However, transcription equipment has changed from manual typewriters to electric typewriters to word processors to computers and from plastic disks and magnetic belts to cassettes and endless loops and digital recordings. Today, speech recognition (SR), also known as continuous speech recognition (CSR), is increasingly being used, with medical transcriptionists and or 'editors' providing supplemental editorial services, although there are occasional instances where SR fully replaces the MT. Natural-language processing takes 'automatic' transcription a step further, providing an interpretive function that speech recognition alone does not provide (although MTs do).

In the past, these medical reports consisted of very abbreviated handwritten notes that were added in the patient's file for interpretation by the primary physician responsible for the treatment. Ultimately, this mess of handwritten notes and typed reports were consolidated into a single patient file and physically stored along with thousands of other patient records in a wall of filing cabinets in the medical records department. Whenever the need arose to review the records of a specific patient, the patient's file would be retrieved from the filing cabinet and delivered to the requesting physician. To enhance this manual process, many medical record documents were produced in duplicate or triplicate by means of carbon copy.

In recent years, medical records have changed considerably. Although many physicians and hospitals still maintain paper records, there is a drive for electronic records. Filing cabinets are giving way to desktop computers connected to powerful servers, where patient records are processed and archived digitally. This digital format allows for immediate remote access by any physician who is authorized to review the patient information. Reports are stored electronically and printed selectively as the need arises. Many MTs now utilize personal computers with electronic references and use the Internet not only for web resources but also as a working platform. Technology has gotten so sophisticated that MT services and MT departments work closely with programmers and information systems (IS) staff to stream in voice and accomplish seamless data transfers through network interfaces. In fact, many health care providers today are enjoying the benefits of handheld PCs or personal data assistants (PDAs) and are now utilizing software on them for dictation.

Overview

Pertinent, up-to-date, confidential patient information is converted to a written text document by a medical transcriptionist (MT). This text may be printed and placed in the patient's record and/or retained only in its electronic format. Medical transcription can be performed by MTs who are employees in a hospital or who work at home as telecommuting employees for the hospital; by MTs working as telecommuting employees or independent contractors for an outsourced service that performs the work offsite under contract to a hospital, clinic, physician group or other health care provider; or by MTs working directly for the providers of service (doctors or their group practices) either onsite or telecommuting as employees or contractors. Hospital facilities often prefer electronic storage of medical records due to the sheer volume of hospital patients and the accompanying paperwork. The electronic storage in their database gives immediate access to subsequent departments or providers regarding the patient's care to date, notation of previous or present medications, notification of allergies, and establishes a history on the patient to facilitate health care delivery regardless of geographical distance or location.

The term transcript or 'report' as it is more commonly called, is used as the name of the document (electronic or physical hard copy) which results from the medical transcription process, normally in reference to the health care professional's specific encounter with a patient on a specific date of service. This report is referred to by many as a 'medical record'. Each specific transcribed record or report, with its own specific date of service, is then merged and becomes part of the larger patient record commonly known as the patient's medical history. This record is often called the patient's chart in a hospital setting.

Medical transcription encompasses the MT, performing document typing and formatting functions according to an established criteria or format, transcribing the spoken word of the patient's care information into a written, easily readable form. MT requires correct spelling of all terms and words, (occasionally) correcting medical terminology or dictation errors. MTs also edit the transcribed documents, print or return the completed documents in a timely fashion. All transcription reports must comply with medico-legal concerns, policies and procedures, and laws under patient confidentiality.

In transcribing directly for a doctor or a group of physicians, there are specific formats and report types used, dependent on that doctor's speciality of practice, although history and physical exams or consults are mainly utilized. In most of the off-hospital sites, independent medical practices perform consultations as a second opinion, pre-surgical exams, and as IMEs (Independent Medical Examinations) for liability insurance or disability claims. Some private practice family doctors choose not to utilize a medical transcriptionist, preferring to keep their patient's records in a handwritten format, although this is not true of all family practitioners.

Currently, a growing number of medical providers send their dictation by digital voice files, utilizing a method of transcription called speech or voice recognition. Speech recognition is still a nascent technology that loses much in translation. For dictators to utilize the software, they must first train the program to recognize their spoken words. Dictation is read into the database and the program continuously "learns" the spoken words and phrases.

Poor speech habits and other problems such as heavy foreign accents and mumbling complicate the process for both the MT and the recognition software. An MT can 'flag' such a report as unintelligible, but the recognition software will transcribe the unintelligible word(s) from the existing database of 'learned' language. The result is often a 'word salad' or missing text. Thresholds can be set to reject a bad report and return it for standard dictation, but these settings are arbitrary. Below a set percentage rate, the word salad passes for actual dictation. The MT simultaneously listens, reads and 'edits' the correct version. Every word must be confirmed in this process. The downside of the technology is when the time spent in this process cancels out the benefits. The quality of recognition can range from excellent to poor, with whole words and sentences missing from the report. Not infrequently, negative contractions and the word 'not' is dropped all together. Voice recognition is similar to the voice prompts one hears on dialling '411', when information provides the wrong number and charges for the '411' call. These flaws trigger concerns that the present technology could have adverse effects on patient care. Control over quality can also be reduced when providers choose a server-based program from a vendor Application Service Provider (ASP).

Downward adjustments in MT pay rates for voice recognition are controversial. Understandably, a client will seek optimum savings to offset any net costs. Yet vendors that overstate the gains in productivity do harm to MTs paid by the line. Despite the new editing skills required of MTs, significant reductions in compensation for voice recognition have been reported. Reputable industry sources put the field average for increased productivity in the range of 30%–50%; yet this is still dependent on several other factors involved in the methodology. Metrics supplied by vendors that can be 'used' in compensation decisions should be scientifically supported.

Another unresolved issue is high-maintenance headers that replace simple interfaces to become the 'platform' of choice. Pay rates should reflect this lost-opportunity cost for the MT.

Operationally, speech recognition technology (SRT) is an interdependent, collaborative effort. It is a mistake to treat it as compatible with the same organizational paradigm as standard dictation, a largely "stand-alone" system. The new software supplants an MT's former ability to realize immediate time-savings from programming tools such as macros and other word/format expanders. Requests for client/vendor format corrections delay those savings. If remote MTs cancel each other out with disparate style choices, they and the recognition engine may be trapped in a seesaw battle over control. Voice recognition managers should take care to ensure that the impositions on MT autonomy are not so onerous as to outweigh its benefits.

Medical transcription is still the primary mechanism for a physician to clearly communicate with other health care providers who access the patient record, to advise them on the state of the patient's health and past/current treatment, and to assure continuity of care. More recently, following Federal and State Disability Act changes, a written report (IME) became a requirement for documentation of a medical bill or an application for Workers' Compensation (or continuation thereof) insurance benefits based on requirements of Federal and State agencies.

As a Profession

An individual who performs medical transcription is known as a *medical transcriptionist* or an *MT.* The equipment the MT uses is called a *medical transcriber.* The individual who performs medical transcription should always be called a "medical transcriptionist". A medical transcriptionist is the person responsible for converting the patient's medical records into typewritten format rather than handwritten, the latter more prone to misinterpretation by other health care providers. The term *transcriber* describes the electronic equipment used in performing medical transcription, e.g., a cassette player with foot controls operated by the MT for report playback and transcription. In the late 1990s, medical transcriptionists were also given the title of Medical Language Specialist or Health Information Management (HIM) paraprofessional.

There are no "formal" educational requirements to be a medical transcriptionist. Education and training can be obtained through traditional schooling, certificate or diploma programs, distance learning, and/or on-the-job training offered in some hospitals, although there are countries currently employing transcriptionists that require 18 months to 2 years of specialized MT training. Working in medical transcription leads to a mastery in medical terminology and editing, MT ability to listen and type simultaneously, utilization of playback controls on the transcriber (machine), and use of foot pedal to play and adjust dictations — all while maintaining a steady rhythm of execution.

While medical transcription does not mandate registration or certification, individual MTs may seek out registration/certification for personal or professional reasons. Obtaining a certificate from a medical transcription training program does not entitle an MT to use the title of Certified Medical Transcriptionist (CMT). The CMT credential is earned by passing a certification examination conducted solely by the Association for Health care Documentation Integrity (AHDI), formerly the American Association for Medical Transcription (AAMT), as the credentialling designation they created. AHDI also offers the credential of Registered Medical Transcriptionist (RMT). According to AHDI, the RMT is an entry-level credential while the CMT is an advanced level. AHDI maintains a list of approved medical transcription schools.

There is a great degree of internal debate about which training program best prepares a MT for industry work. Yet, whether one has learned medical transcription from an online course, community college, high school night course, or on-the-job training in a doctor's office or hospital, a knowledgeable MT is highly valued. In lieu of these AHDI certification credentials, MTs who can consistently and accurately transcribe multiple document work-types and return reports within a reasonable turnaround-time (TAT) are sought after. TATs set by the service provider or agreed to by the transcriptionist should be reasonable but consistent with the need to return the document to the patient's record in a timely manner.

Curricular requirement experience that is directly related to the duties and responsibilities specified, and dependent on the employer (working directly for a physician or in hospital facility).

- Knowledge of medical terminology.
- Above-average spelling, grammar, communication and memory skills.
- Ability to sort, checks, count, and verify numbers with accuracy.
- Skill in the use and operation of basic office equipment/computer; eye/hand/foot coordination.
- Ability to follow verbal and written instructions.
- Records maintenance skills or ability.
- Good to above-average typing skills.

Basic MT Knowledge, Skills and Abilities

- Knowledge of basic to advanced medical terminology is essential.
- Knowledge of anatomy and physiology.
- Knowledge of disease processes.
- Knowledge of medical style and grammar.
- Average verbal communication skills.
- Above-average memory skills.
- Ability to sort, check, count, and verify numbers with accuracy.
- Demonstrated skill in the use and operation of basic office equipment/computer.
- Ability to follow verbal and written instructions.
- Records maintenance skills or ability.
- Above-average typing skills.
- Knowledge and experience transcribing (from training or real report work) in the basic four work types.
- Knowledge of and proper application of grammar.

- Knowledge of and use of correct punctuation and capitalization rules.
- Demonstrated MT proficiencies in multiple report types and multiple specialities.

Duties and Responsibilities

- Accurately transcribes the patient-identifying information such as name and Medical Record or Social Security Number.
- Transcribes accurately, utilizing correct punctuation, grammar and spelling, and edits for inconsistencies.
- Maintains/consults references for medical procedures and terminology.
- Keeps a transcription log.
- Foreign MTs may sort, copy, prepare, assemble, and file records and charts (though in the United States (US) the filing of charts and records are most often assigned to Medical Records Techs in Hospitals or Secretaries in Doctor offices).
- Distributes transcribed reports and collects dictation tapes.
- Follows up on physicians' missing and/or late dictation, returns printed or electronic report in a timely fashion (in US Hospital, MT Supervisor performs).
- Performs quality assurance check.
- May maintain disk and disk backup system (in US Hospital, MT Supervisor performs).
- May order supplies and report equipment operational problems (in US, this task is most often done by Unit Secretaries, Office Secretaries, or Tech Support personnel).
- May collect, tabulate, and generate reports on statistical data, as appropriate (in US, generally performed by MT Supervisor).
- May have ample of time

The Medical Transcription Process

When the patient visits a doctor, the doctor spends time with the patient discussing his medical problems, including past history and/or problems. The doctor performs a physical examination and may request various laboratory or diagnostic studies; will make a diagnosis or differential diagnoses, then decides on a plan of treatment for the patient, which is discussed and explained to the patient, with instructions provided. After the patient leaves the office, the doctor uses a voice-recording device to record the information about the patient encounter. This information may be recorded into a hand-held cassette recorder or into a regular telephone, dialed into a central server located in the hospital or transcription service office, which will 'hold' the report for the transcriptionist. This report is then accessed by a medical transcriptionist, it clearly received as a voice file or cassette recording, who then listens to the dictation and transcribes it into the required format for the medical record, and of which this medical record is considered a legal document. The next time the patient visits the doctor, the doctor will call for the medical record or the patient's entire chart, which will contain all reports from previous encounters. The doctor can on occasion refill the patient's medications after seeing only the medical record, although doctors prefer to not refill prescriptions without seeing the patient to establish if anything has changed.

It is very important to have a properly formatted, edited, and reviewed medical transcription document. If a medical transcriptionist accidentally typed a wrong medication or the wrong diagnosis, the patient could be at risk if the doctor (or his designee) did not review the document for accuracy. Both the doctor and the medical transcriptionist play an important role to make sure the transcribed dictation is correct and accurate. The doctor should speak slowly and concisely, especially when dictating medications or details of diseases and conditions, and the medical transcriptionist must possess hearing acuity, medical knowledge, and good reading comprehension in addition to checking references when in doubt.

However, some doctors do not review their transcribed reports for accuracy, and the computer attaches an electronic signature with the disclaimer that a report is "dictated but not read". This electronic signature is readily acceptable in a legal sense. The transcriptionist is bound to transcribe verbatim (exactly what is said) and make no changes, but has the option to flag any report inconsistencies. On some occasions, the doctors do not speak clearly, or voice files are garbled. Some doctors are, unfortunately, time-challenged and need to dictate their reports quickly (as in ER reports). In addition, there are many regional or national accents and (mis)pronunciations of words the MT must contend with. It is imperative and a large part of the job of the transcriptionist to look up the correct spelling of complex medical terms, medications, obvious dosage or dictation errors, and when in doubt should "flag" a report. A "flag" on a report requires the dictator (or his designee) to fill in a blank on a finished report, which has been returned to him, before it is considered complete. Transcriptionists are never, ever permitted to guess, or 'just put in anything' in a report transcription. Furthermore, medicine is constantly changing. New equipment, new medical devices, and new medications come on the market on a daily basis, and the Medical Transcriptionist needs to be creative and to tenaciously research (quickly) to find these new words. An MT needs to have access to, or keep on memory, an up-to-date library to quickly facilitate the insertion of a correctly spelled device.

EDUCATION SERVICES

Introduction

Education is knowledge or skill obtained or developed by the learning process. Mostly development of knowledge is education. Education is learning the skill to survive. The purpose of education is, it develops to understand the circumstances, builds brainpower to improve systems to raise, increases the living standard, and it improve the society and culture. Most important concern in our modern social life is how to earn and live comfortable and safe life, so education is an important one in the life.

Education in its broadest sense is any act or experience that has a formative effect on the mind, character, or physical ability of an individual.

Education is the process by which society deliberately transmits its accumulated knowledge, skills and values from one generation to another through institutions.

Education and Economy

The next thing is economy. Education plays an important role in economy. Education is mainly to improve the financial and the economic status of a person. The countries economy is mainly depend on the education. If a country provides better education automatically that country economic status improves. Because of education only some countries are rich and some countries are still poor because of bad education.

Education System in India

Education is one of the most powerful things in the growth of Indian economy. The higher levels of literacy will give the greater economic output, higher employment levels, better health, better social structures, and higher marks along a number of other development indicators. Educating girls and women has been shown to result in rapid improvements in family planning, nutrition, health, and income and is seen as one of the best tools for promoting social and economic development.

Today, Indian education covers one of the largest higher and secondary education systems in the world. This has been made possible by a large number of schools, colleges and universities that are offering various courses. Moreover, the distance learning courses and online degrees are also helping in the democratization of the Indian education system.

There are lot of universities and colleges, schools made transmission of knowledge in the technological sectors. The Indian Institute of Technology and various Engineering Colleges are playing the important role in the technical areas. Thus today, India is known as the talent-pool of the world, where intelligent, educated people are very easy to find, and this fact has definitely given a boost to India education.

Indian educational system consists of six stages they are Nursery, Primary, Secondary, Higher Secondary, Graduation and Postgraduation.

Nursery

In this there are two stages are there Lower Kinder Garden and Upper Kinder Garden. In this the children have to spend two years. This is the starting stage of the education.

Primary

In this stage, we have to spend five years. Here we will study class 1 to class 5. The start at the age of 6 and the finish at the age of 11. Here they will learn about the basic subjects like English, Regional Language, Mathematics, Science, General Knowledge and History.

Secondary

In this stage also they have to spend five years. Here we will study class 6 to class 10. The start at the age of 11 and the finish at the age of 15. Here they will learn about the basic subjects like English, Regional Language, Mathematics, Science and History.

Higher secondary

After finishing the secondary education they have to study higher secondary for two years. Here they enter at the age of 16 and finish it at 17. Here they will study the class 11 and class 12.

Graduation

After finishing the higher secondary education they will enter into the Graduation. Here only they enter in to the particular field. In Indian education system the Professional course is 4 years, medical 5 years, diploma course 3 years and art and science 3 years.

Postgraduation

Here the time period is 2 years to 3 years.

All levels of education in India, from primary to higher education, are overseen by the Ministry of Human Resource Development (Department of Higher Education and Department of School Education and Literacy)

Need for Marketing Educational Services

Need to "market" their services have not really been felt by the educational sector. This is because there is always Demand > Supply. But in the recent years, there is a shift in trends. Large number of institutions for specialized fields has been set up in the recent years for fields like management and computer education. This has lead to increase in competition. This makes them come face to face with questions like

- product differentiation
- product extension
- diversification
- and service integration

Education as a Service

Services are those separately identifiable, essentially intangible activities, which provide want satisfaction and are not necessarily tied to the sale of product another service. Education as a service can be said to be providing an intangible benefit (increment in knowledge, aptitude, professional expertise, skill) produced with the help of a set of tangible (infrastructure), and intangible (faculty expertise and learning) aids. A consumer may have tangible physical evidence to show for the service exchange transaction. But the actual benefit accrued is purely intangible in nature. Education is a service which is geared primarily to the consumer market.

Characteristics

Intangibility: Education is an intangible dominant service–impossible to touch, see or feel and because of this standardization is very difficult. Lack of standardization opens up marketing opportunity of differentiated need based course packages. Education as a service cannot be patented.

Perishability: Production and consumption are simultaneous activities in education. *No inventories* can be made up. Example: A lecture scheduled cannot be stored. (Nowadays with technologic lecture can be stored and listened afterwards)

Inseparability: It is impossible to separate a service from the provider. There is a need for the service provider to be present when the service is to be performed and consumed. This limits the scale of operations—the number of providers available would define the number of simultaneous performances possible.

Other characteristics

- High fixed cost, low variable cost
- Specialized and need based
- Competition
- Customer limitations
- Lack of ownership
- Heterogeneity

MARKETING MIX

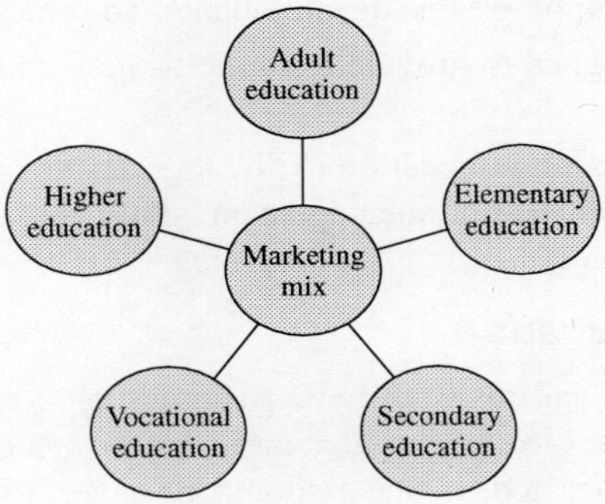

Issues in Indian Education System

(*Source:* http://nationaldebate.nic.in/edu/approach.htm)

Primary education

At the primary level, prevention of dropouts must become a matter of top priority. From this point of view, designing a detailed and in-depth study of the causes of dropout should become the very first step of a long-term planning in this direction. Immediate action should include extending necessary facilities and providing right incentives to the young learners as well as to the teaching fraternity.

If there is one singular factor, which is of utmost importance in primary education, it is the imparting of education in the mother tongue or the regional language. There must be a firm resolve to implement this without any delay.

Besides, other measures in this direction should include:

- Making the content of education relevant to the needs of day-to-day life. (The curriculum should be indigenous and within the comprehension of both the teacher and the taught)
- Effecting suitable changes in the timetable and academic calendar in accordance with the lifestyles and occupations of the concerned people.
  - Undertaking a mass awakening programme to drive home the importance of literacy and education.
  - Making learning an enjoyable and a productive activity.
  - In addition following issues should guide our immediate attention towards the primary education.
  - Emphasis on imparting of sanskaras.
  - Equipping the schools with the basic infrastructural facilities.
  - An appropriate training to the teacher– not only in respect of reading, writing, arithmetic and core subjects but also on vital issues concerning culture.

Secondary education

The vocational stream must be strengthened. Following ideas may be seriously considered for inclusion in this respect:

- Bridging the gap between the world of knowledge and world of work.
- Inculcating the value of respect for manual work and dignity of labour.

- Connecting the course content and pedagogy with local and regional needs so as to develop an appropriate indigenous technology for 'development' and social change.
- Curriculum must be redesigned to provide for a multi-track path to future vocation instead of a uni-track path.
- Development of skills like communication skills, logical skills, comprehension skills, creative skills, information technology, and management skills must get priority over mere book learning.

Universities and higher education

Universities as centres of learning and research have an important role in expanding the horizons of knowledge and providing intellectual leadership to society. Unfortunately, many of them have become mere examination-conducting bodies today. Steps should be taken to restore the universities to the original role expected of them. A few concrete suggestions for serious debate and consideration are listed below:

- Gradual dispensing with the **system of affiliation**.
- Giving a fair trial to the concept of **autonomous colleges**. Efforts should be made to see that the experiment succeeds.
- **Applied and meaningful research** that directly addresses to the questions relevant to community's needs.
- **Infrastructural facilities** Though we have a large system of higher education with around 240 universities and 9000 colleges, nearly 40% of the colleges are reported to be non-viable. We should not fail to note that the number of students entering into the doorways of colleges and universities is only 6% of the relevant age group. With a large number of them receiving substandard education in ill-equipped colleges, we cannot expect to produce man power capable of meeting the challenges in different fields. Immediate steps need to be taken to improve the conditions of the colleges.
- Feasibility of community system of higher education combining formal and non-formal systems and providing for horizontal and vertical mobility within the academic framework must be examined.
- The new technological revolution particularly in the field of information technology has made a tremendous impact on the field of education at all levels. While it has opened up a world of new opportunities for our young men and women, it has posed serious problems to the system as well. It has brought about a total paradigm shift with regard to the role of the teacher, the method of the pedagogy and the character of the educational institutions. How to adapt the new technology to our needs and conditions without allowing it to damage our values and identity is also a matter which deserves serious consideration.
- One of the negative impacts of the invasion of new technology is the relegation of the basic sciences and humanities to the background. Both of them have great significance from the point of view of original research in different spheres of knowledge a well as from the point of view of quality of social and cultural life. Care should be taken to protect and promote these disciplines in a meaningful way.
- Higher education is of crucial importance for the developmental process. Strengthening the system is the need of the hour. Government has a major role to play in supporting and strengthening the system of higher education. The argument that higher education is getting a greater share

at the cost of primary education has little justification. Each has its own importance. Primary education must get all the due attention; but neglecting higher education would be disastrous.

Commercialization of education

Private agencies do have an important role in the field of education. However, leaving the field open the market forces in the name of privatization is a self-defeating proposition. Commercialization will not only denude education of all the noble values and ideals associated with it, it will also lead to widening the gap of social disparity. Therefore, commercialization of education needs to be curbed in the larger interest of education.

Financing of education

Expenditure on education is an investment for the future. Educational targets cannot be achieved unless sufficient funds are made available. Determined and time-bound efforts will have to be made to move towards reaching the target of 6% of the GDP on education. While the non-government efforts can play a supporting role in this behalf, the major responsibility inevitably rests with the government.

Examination system

Examination system should be thoroughly revised to make it a comprehensive system of evaluating the abilities and achievements of the students. It should cease to be a fault-finding and mechanical exercise.

Teacher-training

This needs to be seriously considered for reformation. It is important that the teacher is equipped and motivated for the central role that he/she is expected to play in a meaningful educational system.

Let us Sum Up

With the invention of latest technological developments, the world health care industry is catching up with the other leading industries of the world. World health care industry is one of the largest industries catering to the medical needs of innumerable people around the globe. The rate of growth of the health care industry in India is moving ahead neck to neck with the pharmaceutical industry and the software industry of the country. Much has been said and done in the health care sector for bringing about improvement. Till date, approximately 12% of the scope offered by the health care industry in India has been tapped. The health care industry in India is reckoned to be the engine of the economy in the years to come. Health care industry in India is worth $17 billion and is anticipated to grow by 13% every year. The health care sector encompasses health care instruments, health care in the retail market, hospitals enrolled to the hospital networks, etc.

Employment opportunities are provided to as many as 4 million people in the health care segment or other related sectors catering to the health care industry in India in some way or the other. Owing to the vast differences in medical expenses in western countries and that of India, India has become one of the favourites for health care treatments. Due to the progressive nature of the health care sector in India, several foreign companies are intending to invest in the country.

Health care industry is a wide and intensive form of services which are related to well being of human beings. Health care is the social sector and it is provided at State level with the help of Central Government. Health care industry covers hospitals, health insurances, medical software, health equipment and pharmacy in it.

Pharmacy is the health profession that links the health sciences with the chemical sciences and it is charged with ensuring the safe and effective use of pharmaceutical drugs. The scope of pharmacy practice includes more traditional roles such as compounding and dispensing medications, and it also includes more modern services related to health care, including clinical services, reviewing medications for safety and efficacy, and providing drug information. Pharmacists, therefore, are the experts on drug therapy and are the primary health professionals who optimize medication use to provide patients with positive health outcomes.

Nursing is a health care profession focused on the care of individuals, families, and communities so they may attain, maintain, or recover optimal health and quality of life from birth to death.

Nurses work in a large variety of specialties where they work independently and as part of a team to assess, plan, implement and evaluate care.

Medical transcription, also known as MT, is an allied health profession, which deals in the process of transcription, or converting voice-recorded reports as dictated by physicians and/or other health care professionals, into text format.

Questions for Discussion

1. What do you understand by health care?
2. Explain the recent trends in health care industry.
3. Name the different segments in health care industry.
4. What are the major inputs to health care industry?
5. Name the different types of health care services available in India.
6. Do a PEST analysis for Indian hospital industry.
7. Explain the different factors attracting corporate in health care.
8. Briefly discuss the concept of service market triangle.
9. Explain the characteristics of health care industry.
10. Explain the concept of 7 Ps in hospital marketing.
11. Write short notes on: (i) pharmacy (ii) nursing (iii) medical transcription.
12. Write briefly about Indian education system.
13. Explain the characteristics of education marketing.
14. Explain various issues in Indian education system.

References

Service Marketing: Valarie A Zeithmal, Mary Jo Bitner & Ajay Pandit -TMH, 4/e, 2004.

Service Marketing: Christopher Lovelock, Pearson Education, 5/e, 2004.

Service Marketing: Rajendra Nargundkar- TMH, 1/e, 2004.

Service Marketing: Ravi Shankar, Excel Books, 2006.

Service Marketing Text & Cases: Harsh V Varma, Pearson Education, 1/e, 2008.

Service Marketing: S M Jha, HPH, 2007.

Service Marketing & Management: Audrey Gilmore, Sage Publication, 1/e, 2003.

Service Marketing: People, Technology, Strategy: Christopher Lovelock & Jochen Wirtz, PHI, 2008.

Service Marketing: Roland T. Rust, Anthony J. Zahorik, Timothy L. Keiningham, HarperCollins College Publishers, 1996.

Index

T